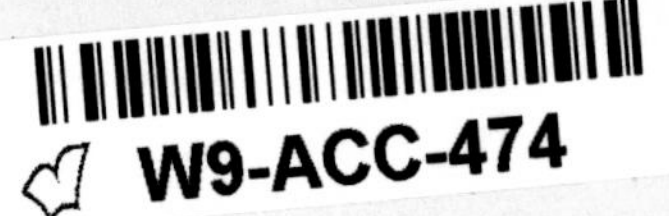

frenzy

BOOKS BY THIS AUTHOR

Comes a Horseman

Germ

Deadfall

Deadlock

Dreamhouse Kings Series

1 *House of Dark Shadows*

2 *Watcher in the Woods*

3 *Gatekeepers*

4 *Timescape*

5 *Whirlwind*

6 *Frenzy*

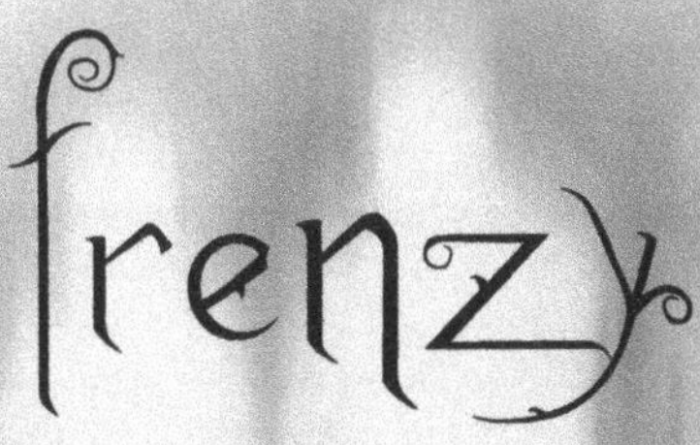

Frenzy

BOOK SIX OF
DREAMHOUSE KINGS

ROBERT LIPARULO

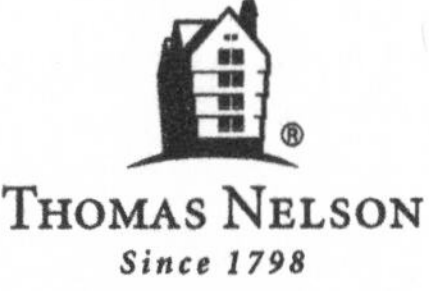

THOMAS NELSON
Since 1798

NASHVILLE DALLAS MEXICO CITY RIO DE JANEIRO

Published in Nashville, Tennessee, by Thomas Nelson. Thomas Nelson is a registered trademark of Thomas Nelson, Inc.

Thomas Nelson, Inc., titles may be purchased in bulk for educational, business, fund-raising, or sales promotional use. For information, please e-mail SpecialMarkets@ThomasNelson.com.

ISBN 978-1-59554-894-8 (trade paper)

Library of Congress Cataloging-in-Publication Data

Liparulo, Robert.
Frenzy / Robert Liparulo.
p. cm. — (Dreamhouse Kings ; bk. 6)
Summary: When Xander travels through the portals in the King's strange house to visit Uncle Jesse as a boy, he learns that David has died and determines to do whatever it takes, and visit as many worlds as necessary, to change the future.
ISBN 978-1-59554-816-0 (hardcover)
[1. Supernatural—Fiction. 2. Dwellings—Fiction. 3. Family life—California—Fiction. 4. California—Fiction. 5. Horror stories.] I. Title.
PZ7.L6636Fre 2010
[Fic]—dc22

2010002287

Printed in the United States of America

10 11 12 13 14 QG 5 4 3 2 1

To Jodi . . .

My love and inspiration

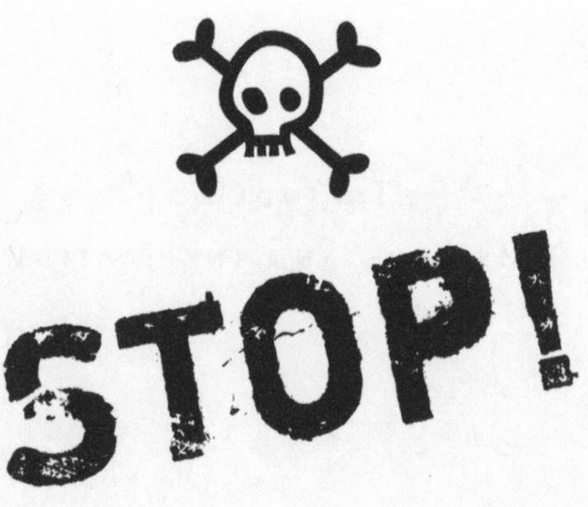

READ *HOUSE OF DARK SHADOWS*,
***WATCHER IN THE WOODS*,**
***GATEKEEPERS*, *TIMESCAPE*,**
AND *WHIRLWIND*
BEFORE CONTINUING!

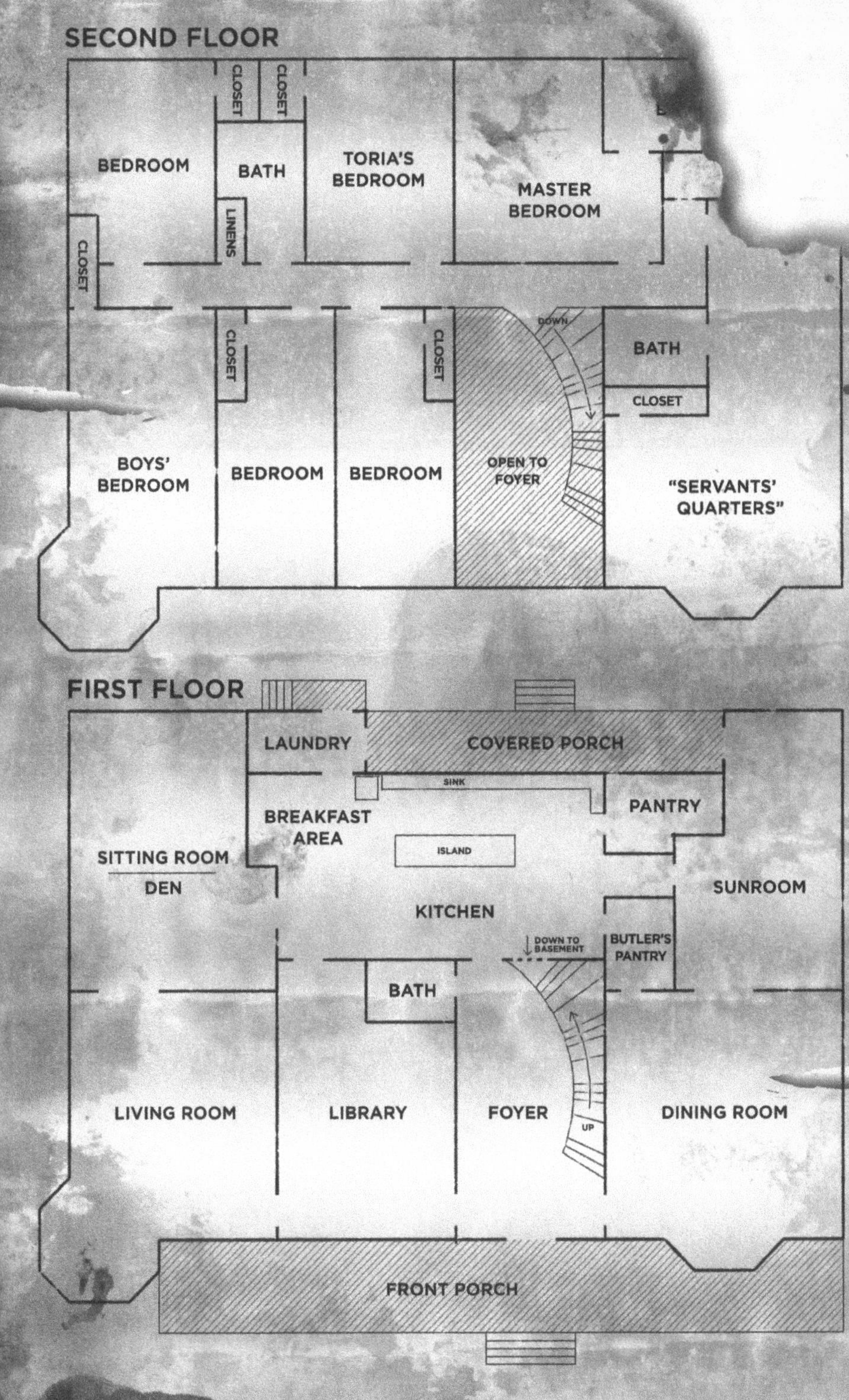

SECOND FLOOR
CLOSET
CLOSET
BEDROOM
BATH
TORIA'S BEDROOM
MASTER BEDROOM
LINENS
CLOSET
DOWN
CLOSET
CLOSET
BATH
CLOSET
BOYS' BEDROOM
BEDROOM
BEDROOM
OPEN TO FOYER
"SERVANTS' QUARTERS"
FIRST FLOOR
LAUNDRY
COVERED PORCH
SINK
PANTRY
BREAKFAST AREA
ISLAND
SITTING ROOM
DEN
SUNROOM
KITCHEN
DOWN TO BASEMENT
BUTLER'S PANTRY
BATH
LIVING ROOM
LIBRARY
FOYER
UP
DINING ROOM
FRONT PORCH

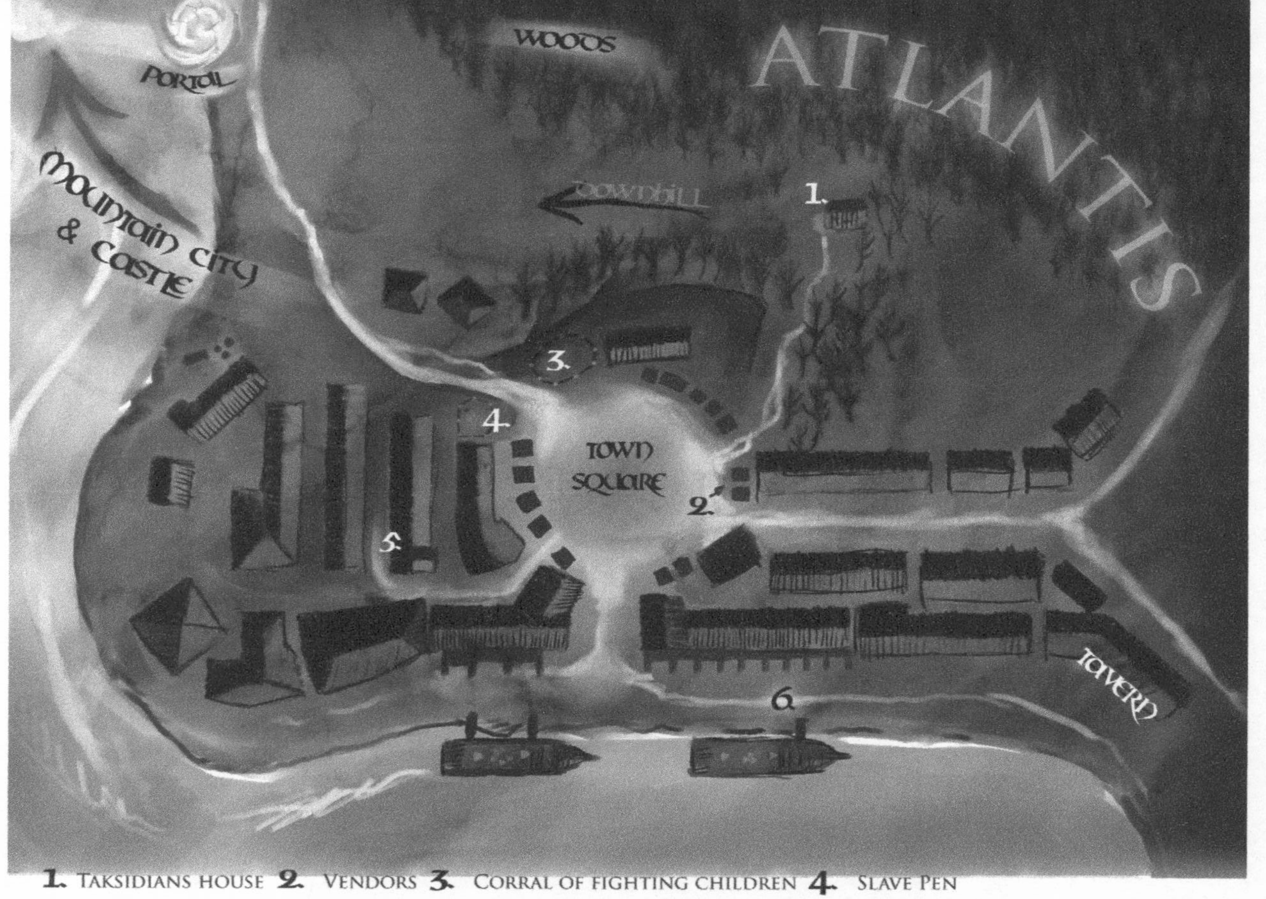

Map by Justin S. Buus

"We are not here on earth to change
our destiny, but to fulfill it."

—GUY FINLEY

"What good is the present
if we can't change the future?"

—EDWARD KING

Prologue

SOMETIME IN THE NEAR FUTURE . . .

Xander flew out of the portal as though shot from a cannon. His legs kicked, his arms spun. His feet hit the ground, tangled together, and he went down. He tumbled over pine needles, a small bush. His shoulder struck a tree trunk. Clawing at the bark, he scrambled to stand.

Cold wetness struck his face, contrasting with the warmth of his tears, of the blood already on his cheeks.

Holding the tree, he turned his eyes skyward. Beyond the branches and needles, ash-colored clouds churned as though stirred by angry fingers. Rain burst from them, spattering fat drops across the woods. For the briefest moment he thought, *Of course, of course the heavens would be crying too!*

Then he pushed off the tree and began running. His sneakers slipped and slid over the wet ground cover. They sailed out from under him, and he fell, soaking his hip and leg with mud. He rose and ran, feeling he was heading the right direction, but not certain. He crested a small hill and descended the other side.

He stopped to get his bearings. He blinked rain out of his eyes, only to have it replaced by tears. He pushed a palm into each socket, shook his head, and tried to get ahold of himself. To his right, he recognized a short cliff of earth, tree roots protruding like veins. He knew where he was.

He stumbled forward, raised his face again, and screamed: rage, pain, grief . . . it all roared out of him. He dropped his head and sobbed.

No, no, no . . .

This isn't happening. It isn't!

Then he saw the underside of his forearms, and knew it was happening . . . it had happened. The blood was still there. It glistened darker than movie blood, thicker. It coated his arms as though someone had slathered paint over them with wide brushstrokes.

Oh, God, he prayed, *let it be paint! Let there have been some mistake and make it not blood, anything but blood!*

But he knew better.

Raindrops plopped on his forearms, cleaning away the red

in small starbursts and long streaks. Suddenly, he didn't want it to be gone, washed away. There was a finality to it that he couldn't stand. He crossed his arms over his chest, protecting them from the rain.

He ducked his head and plowed into the bushes. Branches scratched at his face, his arms; they snagged his clothes. He yanked himself free and tumbled out on the other side, landing in the long grass of a meadow. He pushed himself up and saw the log where he and David had first found Young Jesse—the boy who would become their great-great uncle—sitting there, carving a piece of wood.

He ran across the meadow to another clump of tall bushes and pushed through. The rain slowed and stopped. Water dripped frm the trees like ghosts of a once-mighty army. He kept going, mounted a hill, and looked down a shallow slope to where the house stood.

Barely a house, really. Only the framework had been completed, two-by-fours forming the shape of the house in which Xander and his family had been living for barely eight days.

How could so much have changed in eight days?

He spotted Jesse then, standing under a dripping roof on the railless porch—at least that much of the house was finished. He was talking to a man. Had to be his father. He looked rugged: scruffy stubble over a square jaw and hollow cheeks, short-cropped hair, and muscles pushing against a dirty white T-shirt.

The man noticed Xander and scowled. He reached back to a workbench, grabbed a hammer, and stepped forward.

Jesse, seeing Xander now as well, slapped his hand against his father's chest. A big grin broke out on the boy's face and he yelled, "Xander!" He turned to his father. "That's Xander, one of the boys I told you about," he said. "Your great-great grandson."

The man's scowl softened. Then he noticed Xander's condition, and his features became worried and puzzled.

Jesse hopped off the porch and ran toward Xander. "You're back!" he said. "You said you would be, but—"

He stopped, eyed Xander up and down. He took in the blood, Xander's deep frown, his wet, red eyes. "What . . . what . . . ?" He looked past Xander. "Where's David?"

Xander fell to his knees. He covered his face and smelled the blood on his hands. He looked up at Jesse. "Dae's . . . *dead.* Jesse, Taksidian *killed* him!"

••••••••

Jesse's image clouded away as tears filled Xander's eyes. He cried, big wailing sobs. Now that he'd said it, nothing could hold back the torrent of his emotions.

Someone dropped down beside him, put strong arms around him.

It was Jesse's father, hugging him. He didn't say a word, just embraced him, as if knowing it was the only thing he could do. Xander reached to the arm that was crossing his chest and gripped it.

Jesse said, "Are you . . . are you sure?" His voice was high, like a six-year-old kid's, and he was trembling. Tears poured down his cheeks.

Xander nodded. "I saw it. He . . . stabbed him. Taks . . . he ran away. Keal . . . our friend . . . he's a nurse . . . he checked . . . there was no . . . no . . ." He couldn't say it: *no pulse, no heartbeat,* because that said too much: *no life . . . no David.* It was too late.

He pushed Jesse's father away so he could look at him. "Don't build it," Xander said. "Don't build the house." He looked past Jesse to the towering framework. "Burn it! You have to!"

Jesse's father shook his head. "That won't help, son."

"But if there's no house, then we wouldn't move in. Taksidian wouldn't try to take it. David and Taksidian would never meet, and Taksidian won't *kill him!*"

"You're here," Jesse's dad said. "If we don't build it, *someone* will. You being here now proves it. We can't change that. I'm sorry."

"But . . . but . . ." Xander looked from the man to Jesse and back again. He dropped his head.

Jesse's father touched his face. "You're hurt," he said. "That's a bad gash on your chin."

Xander slapped away his hand. "It's not me!" he yelled.

"David . . . it's David. There has to be something we can do!" he said, then whispered, pleadingly: "Something." He looked at Jesse, and his anguish turned to anger. "Why didn't you warn us?" he yelled. "You see me here now, telling you what happened. You're fourteen. You come to the house to help when you're in your nineties! You must have known. You never warned us! Why?"

Jesse's lips quivered. "I . . ." He squeezed his eyes, pushing out fat drops. "I don't know!" He rushed to Xander and knelt in front of him. He grabbed Xander's shoulders. "I will! I promise, I will!"

"You don't," Xander said. "You didn't." A fact. Simple as that.

Xander stared into Jesse's eyes. They were so blue, like the old man Jesse's. For a moment he felt it was *him*—Old Man Jesse, not fourteen-year-old Jesse—making the promise. Xander wanted to punch him, punch him and never stop punching him.

"I wouldn't forget this," Jesse said. "I wouldn't, not ever."

"Maybe," Xander said, "maybe . . ." He turned to Jesse's dad. "I need to write it down, what happened. I need paper, paper and a pen."

"Son, it's too late."

"I need a pen and paper!" Xander yelled. *"Please."*

Jesse's dad rose, looked toward the house, back to Xander.

"Please," Xander said. "I have to try. Something. Anything."

Jesse's dad trudged off toward the house, head low.

"What are you thinking?" Jesse said. He sniffed.

"Keep my letter," Xander pleaded. "Read it every day. Maybe you won't forget now. Maybe you *will* warn us."

"I will. I promise." Jesse's eyes dropped to Xander's arms. He pushed his fingers into the blood, then looked at his red fingertips. His face scrunched up in pain and sorrow.

Jesse's dad sloshed back through the mud with a scrap of paper and a pencil. Xander leaned back to sit on his heels. He spread the paper over his thigh and scribbled a word. His hands were shaking so badly, even he couldn't read it. He groaned, tried again. Then he drew a picture. He looked at it and knew it was pointless. David was dead. Jesse never warned them. He crumpled the paper in his fist.

He leaned forward, wanting nothing more than to disappear, to be gone from this pain and this day.

David. David.

His brother's face filled his mind: floppy long hair, dimples, Dad's hazel eyes—more green than brown. Those eyes always seemed to sparkle . . . until they didn't. He had held David in his arms, yelling for help. So much blood. David had watched Xander's face. He hadn't seemed scared, he'd seemed almost at peace. Then his breathing had failed, and those eyes stopped sparkling; they had focused on something far away and stayed that way.

Xander's forehead landed in the mud between Jesse's knees.

He felt the boy's hands on his back, comforting. But nothing could comfort him now. He let out a long howl. The tears came again, the wrenching sobs, and he knew they would never stop . . .

CHAPTER

one

Atlantis, 9552 BC

David had gotten himself into a real mess this time.

He and Xander had followed Phemus, the big man who had kidnapped their mom, from their house to this awful place. Taksidian and Phemus captured them in a town square, and while soldiers were chaining them to a line of children heading to war, David broke away. He darted into a workshop of some kind, heard the soldiers looking for him in an alley. But when he turned from the door, a group of tough Atlantian kids waited for him. They had come through a door on the opposite side of the workshop. Knowing what was coming, David had spun to the door behind him.

Now the six boys rushed up behind David, intending—he was sure—to kill him.

Their screams chilled his heart, but he moved: he grabbed the length of wood that barred the door and yanked it from its brackets.

His attackers' shadows fell over him.

He hollered—an animal-sounding gush of effort and frustration—and spun, swinging the wood like a baseball bat and striking the lead attacker in the head. The energy of the impact vibrated into David's arms, and the boy collapsed in front of him. The others braked, reeling back as David swung again, missing two of them by inches.

A kid kicked at the fallen boy, saying, "Theseus?"

Theseus groaned, and the others turned snarling faces toward David. Six of them—five now that one was down. All of them were armed with weapons: a club, a chain, a hammer. Every one bore signs of the rough life he had led, from a black eye and bruised ribs to fresh, bleeding gashes and missing teeth.

"Go!" David yelled, shaking the length of wood toward the door behind the boys, at the far side of the room. It was open, and sunlight streamed in, turning the attackers into shadowy figures. The place was as big as a barn, with planks of wood stacked taller than David. The only open area was between the two doors, where he and the boys now faced off. "Go!" David repeated.

Instead, a boy dived in, whipping a chain in front of him. David swung the wood. It struck the boy's hand, and the chain went flying. The boy screamed and wheeled away, clutching his hand.

Before David could reverse his swing, a kid of about ten lunged in with a jagged piece of metal. David twisted away, and the weapon tore into his tunic-like shirt. The boy tried to pull away, but David turned to swing, and the boy got the metal tangled in the shirt. The boy's eyes squeezed shut as the wood sailed toward his head.

David slowed it down in midswing. He didn't want to kill the kid, even if these punks wanted to kill *him.* There was no hate in his heart—only panic and an intense desire to get away. Still, the impact made a sickening *thunk!* and the boy released his weapon, freed his hand, and stumbled back. He tumbled over the boy already on the floor—Theseus—and landed beside him.

Immediately another boy leaped, a hammer raised over his head. David jabbed, making contact with the boy's stomach. The kid buckled and fell sideways.

David felt a fist slam into his own stomach, and the air inside him burst out of his mouth. He bent over, trying to pull oxygen back into his lungs. The kid who'd punched him did it again, this time on the side of his face. David spun, and someone shoved him hard. He crashed into the door. On the other side of it, he knew, soldiers were pacing the alley, looking for him. Someone kicked him in the small of the back, and he yelled.

Turn! he told himself. *Fight! If you don't, you're dead!*

But he was desperately in need of air that wouldn't come . . . his back pulsated with pain . . . and the bony punch to his face had him seeing stars. The expression was true, he registered in some corner of his brain; dark starbursts flashed in front of his eyes as he tried to regain his senses.

He knew what was coming: a club cracking into his skull or a piece of metal slicing into skin, muscle, guts.

No!

He pushed off the door and started to turn. Hands grabbed him. They seized his arms, his shirt; one gripped his hair. They pulled, trying to get him into the center of the room, where all of them could pounce from every angle. He kicked the door, kicked it again, making it rattle and thump.

The boys roughly turned him around and hoisted him up, and he saw Theseus was on his hands and knees, shouting angry commands.

"Ton arpakste! Ton kratiste! Thelo to proto htypima!"

Theseus rubbed his head and ear where David had clobbered him. As he rose, he picked up the club he had dropped. He squared himself in front of David, a wicked smile on his face.

David thrashed, kicked, pulled. A boy twisted his left arm—the broken one—and David screamed in pain. His knees gave out, and blackness flooded his vision, but he didn't pass out.

Theseus stared at the arm. He pointed the club at it and said, *"Labi ayto ekso!"*

The boy holding it pulled it straight. The kid on the other side tugged on his right arm, forcing him to form the letter T with his body.

"No!" David said. "Please, no . . ."

But Theseus just glared at David as he hefted the club up over his head with both hands.

CHAPTER

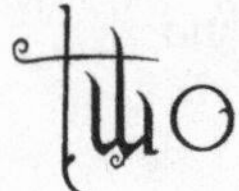

"David!"

Xander's scream left his mouth and was swept away by the pandemonium of the town square: men fighting, soldiers barking out commands, corralled slaves shrieking for no apparent reason. He strained against his chains to get a glimpse of the place he'd last seen David, running between two vendors' stalls.

He yelled his brother's name again.

Ahhhgg . . .

He knew he shouldn't be calling for him. He wanted David

to *run*, to get home, even if he, Xander, couldn't. But he couldn't help himself. He was so worried, his stomach was cramping. It had been five minutes, and the guards chasing David had not returned. What would they do to him if they caught him? He didn't want to think about it.

Heaven knew this awful society had no regard for human life, especially the lives of kids. The chain gang of perhaps fifty children, to which he was tethered, was proof of that. Taksidian had said they would be put aboard a ship, where they would work until reaching Greece. Then they would be sent into battle ahead of the soldiers to confuse their enemy and force them to use their arrows. It was evil, pure and simple.

He pulled against the chains and yelled again: "Dav—"

The sting of a whip flared in his shoulder before the *crack!* reached his ears. He hissed in a breath, dropped his shoulder, and fell to his knees. He craned around to see the man who'd been following the chain gang pull the whip back for another strike.

"Stop!" Xander yelled. He lowered his head, and the whip slapped against his back. His T-shirt did nothing to temper its bite, and he yelled out. Gritting his teeth, he rose and tried to turn to his attacker. The chains binding his wrists stopped him. Xander felt tears in his eyes and blinked them away, then lifted his hand to wipe at them, but the chains prevented even that.

The whip-man spat out some words and gestured for Xander to face forward.

Xander turned. Rage tightened every muscle in his body. He wanted to rip away the chains, lash the man behind him with them, and run to find David.

Another man near them barked out a word. Chains rattled at the head of the line of bound children, then the boy in front of Xander began shuffling his feet. The chains drew taut and yanked at Xander. He stumbled forward, turning to look for his brother.

Run, David, he thought. *Hide.*

They were taking them to the ship. It was going to leave—without David! Yes! It was better that he stayed here, as horrible as Atlantis was. Once they set sail, there would be no escaping, except into the ocean depths or the arrows of Atlantis's enemies. Here they knew there was at least one portal home, the one through which they'd followed Phemus from their house in Pinedale, California, to ancient Atlantis. Here David at least had a chance.

A familiar voice sprang up on Xander's left. Taksidian—still standing in the square next to that human weapon, Phemus—was calling to the man leading the chain gang, waving to get his attention. He spoke in the native Atlantian tongue, and the chain gang stopped.

Taksidian sauntered over to Xander. "Can't leave without your brother," he said. "I'm sure he'll return shortly."

Xander focused on keeping hold of his anger, as though it were a dog trying to break its leash. But he couldn't: He lunged for Taksidian, snapping to a stop at the end of his short chains. "Wait all you want," he said through clenched teeth. "David got away. He's gone. Live with it."

Taksidian smiled. He brushed strands of kinky black hair off his face and rolled his head on his neck, as though the boredom of sending the King boys to their death, had made his muscles stiff. He leveled his cold green eyes at Xander. "You still don't get it, do you?" he said. "I won, I always do. You, your family—you were just a speed bump on the highway to my destiny."

He took a deep breath of the foul air that filled the square, as though it were as fresh as a sea breeze. "You were just a little annoyance that life threw at me to make things . . . *interesting*. I was getting lazy. Not hard to do with that house." He held up his hand, pretending to lift something heavy. "Like having the power of God in my hand."

Xander stretched toward him. He said, "I'll tell you what you have in your hand, and it's not the power of God!" He spat, and a glob of sudsy spit landed in Taksidian's palm.

The man flinched. He blinked, then calmly reached out and wiped his hand on Xander's hair.

Xander jerked away, but, chained, there was nothing he could do. He growled and shook, frustrated and helpless. He snapped his face back toward Taksidian, who had stepped back and was frowning at his palm.

"You don't even know," Xander said. "Whatever you're

doing—using our house to go back in time and tinker with history—it's not making something wonderful, for you or anyone else. We've *seen* it: the future. It's all destroyed. Everything!"

"You see?" Taksidian said, wiping his hand on his black overcoat. "I win."

CHAPTER

three

"Don't," David said. *"Please!"*

But Theseus—who must have known what David meant, even if he couldn't understand the words—only squinted at his target: David's left arm. The club rose higher as the boy sucked in a breath to give the swing all he had.

David tugged at his arm, but the other boy held his wrist like it was the last piece of bread in a hungry world.

He closed his eyes.

The sound was deafening—a crashing *boom!*—and for a moment David thought his brain was screaming. Then he realized the noise was the door behind him bursting open. He looked and saw Theseus still holding the club over his head and staring wide-eyed over David's shoulder. The other boys released their hold on him. He pulled his arms close to his body and instinctively crouched. He turned and saw a soldier standing in the doorway. The door itself rocked on one hinge. Then it broke free and crashed to the floor.

The soldier strode in, followed by two more.

They heard me! David thought. *They heard my kicks against the door!*

The lead soldier said something sharp and harsh.

Two kids behind Theseus dropped their weapons and ran for the other door, away from the soldiers. The one who had held David's left arm jumped at the soldier, his fists flying. The soldier slammed his own fist into the boy's forehead, and the kid stumbled backward and went down, whimpering. He rolled over, got his feet under him, and ran out the door.

The boy on David's right backed away into the dark shadows of the room. A soldier ran to him and grabbed his arm, hard enough to make him squeal. The soldier pulled him to another boy on the floor—the kid David had clobbered. The soldier hooked a hand in that boy's armpit and hoisted him up.

That left Theseus: he was backing toward the far door, the club wavering over his head.

The lead soldier stepped around David. He held his hand

out to Theseus, apparently for the club, and spoke. *"To moy doste se, agori!"*

Theseus shouted back and made like he was going to swing. The soldier drew closer.

The last soldier, standing in the doorway behind David, watched intently. His hand was on the hilt of a sword, sheathed on a belt.

David slowly lowered his hands to the floor and began crawling away. Xander's belt dangled from his neck to the floor, like a rottweiler's collar on a Chihuahua. He had used it as a sling until his arm had slipped out sometime between being grabbed by Phemus and his escape from the chain gang.

He headed for the stacks of wood on the other side of the open area from where the soldier held the two boys. He moved out of the light coming through the doors and felt a twinge of hope. He reached the first stack and started around it. A hand clamped down on the back of his neck.

"Ow . . . ow . . ." he said, as the hand squeezed tighter. Reaching back to hold the muscular wrist at the back of his head, David got to his feet. The soldier turned him and marched him toward the rear entrance.

Theseus was still backing toward the other exit, the lead soldier matching his movements step for step. Then the kid threw the club and shot out the door. The soldier ducked and took off after him.

David jabbed his elbow into the ribs of the man holding

him. It was like striking a brick wall. He kicked the man's legs. The guy continued moving him toward the door. Lashing back, David got his hand on the hilt of the sword. The soldier gripped his wrist, twisted it painfully until David let go, then yanked his arm over his head.

Squeezed by the neck, arm craned up high, David stumbled into the alley.

CHAPTER

four

Xander glared at Taksidian. "You win?" he said. "How does the destruction of the world mean you win?"

Taksidian shrugged. "What do I care? By the time all that happens, I'll have had my fun."

Xander shook his head. If Taksidian thought he made sense, Xander wasn't getting it. "But," he said, "the *whole world*?"

Taksidian's eyes narrowed. He appeared as perplexed by Xander's logic as Xander was by his. "Why not?" he said.

"What do I care about other people? Nobody cares about anyone else, not really." He shrugged. "You're simply too young to have learned that yet."

"No," Xander said. "People don't think that way."

"Then they should," Taksidian said. "If *you* did, you wouldn't be here, chained, whipped, heading for a battle you won't survive. Besides, tinkering with time—making incredible, big things happen—is fun."

"Fun?"

"Like a Rubik's cube." He moved his hands as if twisting the puzzle this way and that. "You know, one of those cubes with the little, different-colored squares . . ."

"I know what a Rubik's cube is," Xander said. "But how can you say causing the end of the world is like that?"

"Think about it. It's challenging, tinkering with history: a little change in the year 1912, another in 1482. Suddenly everything's falling into place, and I get to cause something that affects billions of people. If that's not rewarding, I don't know what is."

"So . . . what?" Xander said. "You destroy the world because you *can*? How can you be so . . . so . . ." He wasn't finding the right word. *Heartless, cruel, evil* . . . none of them seemed strong enough to describe Taksidian.

The man waved a hand at him, as if Xander were talking gibberish. He looked away, toward two men in the center of the square who were pounding on each other with their fists.

"I don't care about any of that, whether mankind skips into the future happy and healthy . . ." He glanced at Xander. "Or doesn't. What you saw in the future is merely a byproduct of my work, not my work itself."

"A byproduct? Like an *accident*?"

"One I don't feel compelled to prevent, especially if it means giving up what I have."

"What you have?" What Xander meant was, *Nothing one person had could possibly be worth all of life on the planet.*

But Taksidian misunderstood, obviously thinking Xander wanted to know what he had, for the man raised his eyebrows and said, "You don't know who I am, do you?"

Xander didn't answer. He remembered what he'd said to David just last night: *What if he's like . . . I don't know, a demon?*

Taksidian laughed. "You mean you start a fight and don't even find out who your enemy is?"

"We didn't start anything," Xander said. "And what more do we need to know, besides you want our house and you'll do anything to get it?"

"Well," Taksidian said, "I make it a point to know who *my* enemies are."

Xander knew it was true. The man had been stalking the King family since they'd moved to Pinedale. And the truth was, they *had* wanted to find out more about him. But between defending themselves from his attacks, looking for Mom, and trying to figure out how the portals worked, when did they have time? They had met the man only last Sunday—*five days ago!*

"If you *had* learned about me," Taksidian continued, "you might have saved yourself the trouble of trying to beat me. I'm a powerful man, Xander. I own corporations that employ tens of thousands of people . . . all of it thanks to that house."

"What are you talking about?" Xander said. "What corporations?"

"If a war needs it, I supply it." He smiled at Xander's puzzled expression. "Armed conflict requires weapons, consultants, transportation, food, oil . . . so many things. My companies provide them all. And I make a hundred times more money from wars than I do from peace."

"War," Xander said. He recalled a map he'd seen in Taksidian's house. It had plotted wars all over the world—and all through history. And it dawned on him: "You're using the house to *cause* wars. You're . . . you're . . . setting up wars in the past that somehow lead to wars now, in the present time!"

Taksidian nodded. "You'd be surprised how a war in the eighteenth century can lead to hostilities in the twenty-first. Humankind is a warring species. It doesn't need *my* help . . . much. Just a nudge here, an assassination there."

Xander closed his eyes. He couldn't begin to imagine the deaths, the grief and sorrow this one man had caused. *Why?* he thought, and didn't realize he had spoken the question out loud until Taksidian answered.

"Because it makes me a . . . *king,*" Taksidian said.

Xander looked to see the man smiling.

"A real king," Taksidian said. "Not in name." He said *name* as though it were a dirty word, and scanned Xander as though he were equally dirty.

"You're no king," Xander said.

"A king takes what he wants," Taksidian said. "Like I'm taking your house, as easily as . . ." He reached out, and Xander flinched. Taksidian grabbed the tassel hanging from Xander's belt loop and ripped it off.

Xander's chest tightened. It was one of the items he'd taken from the antechamber. The present—*his* present, the time in which he belonged—wanted the items back. It pulled at them, leading whoever had them—or followed them—to the portal home. Without the tassel, they might not be able to find their way back. Then he remembered: He had another antechamber item in his pocket, a rock.

A lot of good it'll do, he thought. The shackles around his wrists felt as heavy as bowling balls.

Taksidian dangled the tassel in front of Xander's face. He said, "As easily as I took this." He pushed it into his coat pocket. "So you see, I am a king, even of the house you think is yours." He lifted his face to the sun, closing his eyes and brushing the hair off his face. "It's a grand life, Xander: servants, limousines, breakfast in Paris, dinner in Tokyo."

"If you're so rich and powerful," Xander said, "what are

you doing hanging around Pinedale? Your life doesn't seem all that glam to me."

Taksidian shook his head. "I go there only when I need to use the house—to make sure my business is not only good, but great."

"More war, more business, more money," Xander said, disgusted. He'd seen enough movies to know how it went: The rich always wanted more money, the powerful more power. There was no such thing as *enough*.

"And of course, despite the people I control," Taksidian said, "it's a task only I can do. Good thing I enjoy it. Except when people like your family get in my way, start meddling in my work. I can't allow that. Where I come from, we served our king, who had everything. Nothing for us, only for him. Then I stumbled through a portal . . . into the house. I saw right away that in the twentieth century, I could have everything the ancient world of my birth denied me. Everything. Before, I killed for the king. Now, I kill for *myself*."

Xander felt dizzy. He said, "It's . . . not *right*."

Taksidian laughed again, but this time it was loud and booming. Such laughter in this horrible place must have been rare: faces turned to gawk.

"Sweet, innocent Xander," Taksidian said. "Too bad you won't live long enough to learn how naïve you are." He looked beyond Xander and smiled. "You . . . or your brother."

Xander spun, and his heart sank as he saw David come

stumbling into the square. He held his head at an odd angle, and his face showed that he was in pain. The soldier behind him had one hand on David's neck and the other on his wrist, raising it high into the air.

CHAPTER

five

SOMEWHERE ON THE EUROPEAN CONTINENT,
C. 29300 BC

Keal stood in a dark cave and cursed himself for being so stupid. He never should have gone through the portal after David and Xander. As foolish as it had been for the boys to follow Phemus, it was doubly foolish for *him* to plunge in without knowing what awaited him on the other side.

But no, he knew that wasn't true. He cared for those boys, and nothing could have stopped him from trying to help them.

Still . . . this wasn't good.

He stood close to the wall of the cave. He waved a tight bundle of burning straw, which he had managed to light with a flint from the antechamber. It illuminated a painting on the wall: a crude image of warriors fighting a bear-like beast. Unlike the cave paintings he'd seen in books, this one was bright. It looked new.

Great. He looked at the spear he'd found in the cave, nothing more than an antler tine tied to a stick, and brought his eyes back to the painting. He was sure now, he was in some prehistoric time. Which meant the beast he'd heard breathing in the cave was . . . he touched the painted bear-thing on the wall. It dwarfed the figures of the men. *Great,* he thought again.

He moved backward through the cave, the spear in one hand, the torch in the other. He waved the makeshift torch back and forth, hoping to catch a glimpse of whatever was stalking him. Its breathing was slow and deep, with just the hint of a guttural stutter—a growl—like a big empty barrel rolling along a gravel road.

He looked over his shoulder into the blackness of the cave behind him. "David!" he yelled. "Xander!"

The thing in the cave didn't just hint at a growl now; it let loose with a roaring ear-splitting bellow that rumbled past Keal as though the cave itself was the beast's throat.

Stumbling back, he yelled, "Boys! You there?"

Keal shook his head. He was Jesse's *nurse,* for crying out loud!

But since bringing the boys' great-great-uncle to the Kings' house, he'd seen nearly as much life-threatening action as he had as an Army Ranger. It was almost as if the house *thrived* on stress, fear, and action.

After dropping the boys off at school that morning, he had started working on the walls at the bottom of the third-floor stairs. Then the big guy, Phemus, came through a portal. They'd fought in the third-floor hallway, and Keal had been knocked out. When he woke, David was there, telling him he and Xander were *following* Phemus back through the portal. *Ugh!*

But David and Xander—he found himself having trouble breathing at the very thought of the boys—were in danger again.

Keal had crawled to the portal they'd gone through, grabbed the remaining items in the antechamber—the torch, flint, and a leather pouch of stone marbles—and gone over. Now, here was he was in the cave with no sign of the boys.

The beast in the darkness in front of him wasn't so much breathing as it was huffing . . . and snorting. Another sound reached Keal now: clicking, like claws on the rock surface of the cave floor. It was coming closer.

Keal turned and walked fast in the other direction. More of the same, just a circular tunnel carved through rock. It bent one way, then the other, opened up a bit, then shrank a little, like a stone giant's intestines. He stopped, and heard the clicking claws right behind him. He swung around: nothing. But the blackness huffed and snorted just beyond the reach of his light.

Running wasn't going to work. He was sure the beast following him would eventually catch him. Maybe it would wait until Keal tripped or walked into a dead end. That would be worse than facing it now.

He tightened his grip on the spear, got it pointed straight out, and held the torch up.

If this thing turns out to be a rabbit or a mangy mutt, he thought, *I'm going to laugh until I pass out.*

He stepped toward the beast.

The shadows stirred. Something shimmered. As he took a step, the thing moved closer and came fully into the light. Keal stared into the beady eyes of the biggest, ugliest bear he had ever seen. It had a long snout, a domed head level with Keal's, and a hunched back. Its brownish-golden coat rippled like water. It opened a mouthful of thick, sharp fangs and roared, rising up on two legs until its head and shoulders pressed against the ceiling of the cave. Furry arms the size of tree trunks reached out for Keal, each ending in a cluster of knifelike claws.

Keal yelled, turned, and ran.

CHAPTER

Friday, 12:19 p.m.

Los Angeles, California

Dad pulled the rental car into the drive-through of In-N-Out Burger.

"Can't we call them?" Toria said. "Xander and David?"

Dad shook his head. "Keal should have picked up new phones this morning, but I don't know the numbers. And we can't call our old phone in case Taksidian is listening in."

They'd discovered yesterday that he'd bugged their phones. "What do you want?"

Toria looked out the window at the menu. "Double cheeseburger, fries, chocolate malt."

He turned a doubtful eye on her. "You're *nine*, Toria. Where are you going to put all that?"

She smiled. "I'll eat it all, I promise." David and Xander were going to be so mad when they found out what she had for lunch. In Pinedale, there was nothing like the In-N-Out. Just the dumpy diner.

Dad placed their order, then she said, "Xander and David are going to freak out. We know where Phemus came from: Atlantis!" She turned to her teddy bear, strapped in beside her on the backseat. "Good job, Wuzzy," she told it.

They had just left the UCLA office of Dad's friend Mike Peterson. The ancient languages expert had listened to the words Phemus had said the night he kidnapped Mom, words that had been captured on Wuzzy's voice recorder. Using a computer program, Mr. Peterson told them where Phemus had come from and what he'd said: *Have you come to play?*

But then Mr. Peterson had added: "Considering the violent 'games' the Atlantians engaged in to prepare their young people for war, Atlantis is the last place you want to go to 'play.'"

Toria didn't want to think about what that meant.

Dad pulled up to the window and paid.

Toria stared out at the bustling streets, more people on

the sidewalks than you'd see driving all the way through Pinedale, and everything almost glowing in sunshine that seemed brighter, more golden than it was six hundred miles north. All of it brought back memories of their life here, and that got her thinking of Mom. She felt sadness coming on: a tightening in her stomach, an ache in her heart, pressure behind her eyes, like the tears were always there, waiting to come out. She didn't want that, to feel sad thinking about Mom. She'd believed Dad and Xander and David when they said they would get her back. They were really trying too. She thought about Mom coming home, her smile, how she'd sweep Toria up in her arms and hug her like she was never going to let go.

Dad pulled a bag into the car, and the air filled with the smell of burgers and fries.

"Oh," Toria said, patting her stomach, "I think I gained five pounds just from the smell!" It was something Mom always said.

Dad smiled back at her.

"I'm glad we came here, Daddy. To see Mr. Peterson, I mean."

"I think it was a good trip," he said. He took their drinks from the girl at the window and handed one to Toria.

"It makes me feel like I'm helping," she said. "You know, to find Mom. The boys are always going over to those other worlds and everything. I don't get to do anything."

Dad reached back and grabbed her knee. "You found Nana," he said.

"I think she found us." She and David were just trying to find a way out of the Civil War world when Nana, dressed in the bloody smock of a nurse, ran up to them. Toria would never forget Dad's face when he saw his mother for the first time in thirty years.

He said, "But she couldn't have found you if you weren't there, right?"

Toria smiled.

Dad pulled out of the drive, his hand digging in the bag on the passenger seat. "Well, I hope the boys are enjoying school."

"You're kidding!"

He shrugged. "It's the only chance they get to rest these days."

She laughed. "Wait'll they hear what we found out! They're not going to believe it. Atlantis!"

CHAPTER

Seven

The Atlantian soldier marched David across the square. People pointed and laughed. Playing to the crowd, the soldier jerked him one way, then the other, making him wobble and shake like a puppet.

David closed his eyes, trying to ignore the pain in his arm, shoulder, and neck. His back hurt where one of the boys had kicked him, but it was nothing next to the pulses of agony in his raised, broken arm and the intense ache under the fingers squeezing his neck. The soldier waggled him back and forth again. If the guy was trying to humiliate him—well, who cared about a stupid thing like that at a time like this?

He heard footsteps run up. Hands grabbed him. His feet left the ground as the men carried him the rest of the distance to the chain gang.

"David?" Xander said.

He looked to see his brother only a few feet away, chained at the end of the line of kids.

"You all right?"

They dropped him back onto his feet and knocked him into place behind Xander.

"Those kids," David said. "The ones we saw fighting earlier. They caught me. I think they wanted to kill me." His chest felt hollow, pounded empty by defeat. His knees gave out, but one of the soldiers held him up. The other one stooped to pick up a chain from the cobblestoned ground.

The soldiers forced his hands in front of him and clamped three-inch-wide iron shackles over his wrists, then threaded the chain through hoops on the cuffs. The first soldier tugged it toward Xander and clamped the last link to the chain between the boys with a big, clunky padlock. He reversed a step, and the soldier behind David shoved him into Xander's back. The two men walked away, laughing.

David leaned his face into his brother and hitched in a breath, trying not to cry.

Xander spoke over his shoulder: "Be strong, Dae," he said.

David almost laughed. *Strong and courageous!* It was easy to say when you didn't have to be. What was finding the courage to check out a noise in your house . . . to run for a portal with people chasing you . . . to face some unknown threat . . . what was any of that compared to this—next to knowing you were going into battle for the sole purpose of being killed?

The whip cracked behind him. He felt the wind of it on his neck. The chain jerked. Xander fell onto his knees, was pulled a yard before he found his feet again.

David stumbled and leaned his shoulder into Xander. He struggled to stand and caught a glimpse of Taksidian: The man nodded and said, "Have fun, boys." He was watching them shuffle toward the ship. Then he turned and patted Phemus on the chest the way you would pat a dog and say, *Let's go, big fella.* The men walked away, heading toward the house where David and Xander had entered Atlantis.

David wished he had a superpower, one that could blast out bursts of energy with just a look. He'd send those two crashing into the vendors' stalls. The chains snapped tight, and the shackles cut into his wrists. He shuffled along as the ship loomed larger with each step.

"Xander," he said. "What are we going to do?" But his brother didn't respond. He simply trudged forward, shoulders stooped, head bowed.

Then Xander swam out of focus as tears filled David's eyes.

CHAPTER

eight

The bear snorted and huffed right behind Keal, who was running as fast as he could. Its claws clicked and scraped on the stone. Every time Keal zagged around a bend, he could hear the beast slam into the wall of the cave, correct itself, and roar after him.

Stop, turn, let it run into the spear, Keal thought. But he was pretty sure the thing would not stop so easily. It would crash into him, all teeth and claws. The thought of hitting a dead end made him want to give the maneuver a try anyway, but he pushed the thought away. *Only as a last resort,* he told himself.

The torch acted like really dim headlights, illuminating only a few feet ahead of him. Too late, it showed him a sharp bend in the tunnel. He slammed into it and fell. Using the momentum, he rolled away. The light caught the bear ramming its shoulder into the wall. Its neck stretched out and its mouth snapped at Keal's legs; its arm levered its claw-blades at his feet. Keal kicked away, rolled, and propelled himself up like a sprinter pushing off the blocks.

He made the next turn more gracefully and saw daylight radiating at the end of the tunnel like the gates of heaven.

The bear hit a wall, grunted, came barreling after him.

Squinting against the growing light, Keal pictured himself leaping out of the cave, scrambling for a tree or boulder or anything that would get him away from the beast. Then he could jab the spear down at it. *Out and up,* he thought. *Out and up.*

Fifteen feet to the cave opening . . . ten . . . five . . .

Leap! he thought.

But it didn't quite work out that way. He tripped, hit the ground, and slid out of the cave. His head sailed out over a ledge just outside the cave, and he stopped. He looked down at jagged rocks forty feet below. He flipped onto his back, preparing to kick at the bear, but it wasn't there.

He heard it panting in the blackness of the cave. Still back in the tunnel, it slowly stepped into the light. *As if it knows I'm stuck,* he thought.

He saw that the ledge he was on ran only a few feet to one side of the cave before ending in a drop-off. He looked the other way and smiled. The ledge turned into a wide path that sloped down. He scrambled up and stooped to pick up the spear and still-burning torch, which he didn't remember dropping. He'd need them eventually to lead him to a portal home—he hoped. He edged away from the cave opening, watching the bear watching him. He spun to sprint down the path, and stopped. The path kept widening until it was as broad as a football field where it met a grassy, tree-studded meadow. A dozen lean-tos, covered in animal skins, were aligned along the bank of a river. People mingled around them.

But what made him stop were the men coming up the path. Four of them, animal pelts cinched around their waists, spears and bows in their hands. They pointed at him and began running.

Keal headed for them, glancing over his shoulder at the cave. An arrow flew past him and bounced off the rock around the opening. He ducked and returned his attention to the men. Another arrow hit the ground beside him and skimmed away.

"Hey!" he yelled. "Wait!"

One of the men cocked his spear over his shoulder and threw it.

Keal jumped away, and the spear pierced his footprint. He

hurried back to the cave and looked in. The bear hadn't moved, its head barely in the light. Keal realized the thing knew it wasn't safe out there. He slipped around the edge into the cave. Another arrow clattered against the opposite wall and bounced along the floor, stopping at the bear's claws. It rose onto its hind legs, snarling.

Keal ran toward it and jabbed the spear at its chest. A big paw slapped it away, but Keal held on tight. He stepped closer and jabbed again, making firm contact. The bear roared and did what Keal expected: it charged, swinging claws like scythes.

Keal stumbled away, just out of its reach. He stepped from the cave and hooked left, onto the stubby ledge that ended in a drop-off. The bear followed, trying to pull Keal into its embrace. Then its roar turned into an angry bellow, and it turned its back to Keal. Two arrows protruded from its shoulders. It lumbered toward the men who had shot it, allowing Keal to dart back into the cave.

He ran, then turned to check for the bear. It stood in the sunlight, swinging its paws. An arrow struck its arm, and the beast went for the men, disappearing from the front of the cave. Animal roars and human yells drifted in to Keal.

He held up the burning straw and ran deeper into the cave.

CHAPTER

nine

David kept his eyes on the chain linking him to Xander and the rest of the child prisoners. It would droop or snap tight depending on how well he matched his brother's steps.

"Xander," he said. "Please . . . just say something." Xander's silence was worse than anything, worse even than crying or screaming. It was the sound of giving up. Dad had once told him, *Where there's life, there's hope.* And they weren't dead, not yet.

So there was hope. The hope of escape. The hope of surviving this hopeless situation. *"Xander!"*

Xander glanced over his shoulder. "Quiet, Dae," he whispered. "Don't give them any reason to use that whip on us."

Anger flared inside David. This wasn't right, treating people this way. That the victims were children made the evil even worse.

"What do I care?" he said, raising his voice. "We're prisoners, Xander . . . *slaves.* We're going to die on some battlefield because Taksidian said so, because we moved into the wrong house!"

Xander twisted to throw a shocked expression at David. The blue of his irises appeared darker, as though the terror and desperation inside him were seeping into them. "What are you doing?" he said. He glanced around. "Be quiet!"

"Why?" David practically yelled. "What are they going to do, chain us up? Kill us?"

The chains jerked Xander forward, then David. Xander said, "They can make you wish you were dead. That whip hurts."

David tilted his head toward the sky and screamed long and hard: "Aaaaahhhhhggggg!"

The whip bit into his side. It felt like a bullet shattering his ribs. He buckled over, fell, and bumped over the cobblestones on his stomach as the chain gang pulled him along. His chin cracked against the road. Bits of garbage and dirt scraped his arms, sprayed his face. He slid through a puddle of liquid so foul smelling, his lungs clamped shut. He gagged and coughed.

"David!" Xander said, trying to see him, manage the chains, and walk at the same time.

David could tell Xander had shifted to a bow-legged walk to keep his heels from kicking David's face. Xander tried to stop, leaning back to yank on the chains. But there were too many kids in the line, all trudging forward like sled dogs. He stumbled forward and almost fell himself.

David grabbed Xander's waistband, tugged himself up, got walking again. He blinked, pushing tears out of his eyes. The gross stuff he'd slid through soaked his tunic, and every breath made him want to puke. He whispered, "Don't say it."

"What?"

"Don't say *I told you so.*"

The line turned left out of the square and onto a street that ran beside a wide river. It bent out of sight behind him, and David realized it was the same river he and Xander had seen from Taksidian's hillside home. It separated this awful place of boisterous men, child slaves, and peddlers of weapons and slaughtered animals from a beautiful mountain city. He looked back across the square. Over vendor stalls, buildings, and a rocky hill, he could see the golden castle that perched atop the mountain. It glittered in the sun. Flags spaced along its ramparts fluttered, while a waterfall flowed from beneath the castle and dropped to the avenue below, sparkling as though diamonds churned beneath its surface.

Taksidian had said it was there Mom was taken after being kidnapped from their house. But she'd escaped. David prayed she'd found a way out of Atlantis, away from this culture obsessed by violence and war.

I'm sorry, Mom, he thought. *We tried to find you, we really did.* He could hardly stand the thought that he would never see her again. Somehow that seemed even worse than heading into battle against his will.

The water was on the chain gang's right side. On the left side, buildings lined the street as far as David could see. The nearest were open garage-sized stalls filled with crates. Farther up appeared to be a series of taverns. Laughter, shouts, and weird music like cats stuck in a box wafted out at them. To their right was the ship, a big *Pirates-of-the-Caribbean*-type thing. As they shuffled past, David watched the sailors on board: moving crates, coiling ropes, checking their swords and spears, bows and arrows, helmets and body armor. But he wasn't seeing them, not really. He was thinking, letting his mind examine every possible way of escape—the way he might have studied the size, speed, and movements of an opposing soccer team back in Pasadena, when winning a game was the only thing he had to worry about.

He bumped into Xander and realized the line had stopped. Chains rattled as the kids shuffled into a tight group. The front guard stomped up a gangplank leading up to the rear of the ship. He hopped onto the ship's deck, looked around, and disappeared through a door. David could hear his footsteps descending stairs.

That's where they'll keep us, he thought. *Down in some dark, smelly hold.*

He didn't know how long the voyage to Greece would take, but he'd bet it would be weeks. Didn't these old sailing ships take forever to get anywhere? Weeks down there, smashed in with three dozen other kids, maybe a bunch of adult slaves and sailors. If they were lucky, some of them would see the light of day now and then, when they were ordered to swab the decks or something.

He wondered if his stomach would get used to the lurching ocean movements. Last year, his sixth-grade class had gone out on a tugboat from Los Angeles Harbor. Half of them had barfed their lunches over the railing. David hadn't, but he'd felt like it. Probably these Atlantians wouldn't even feed them, so before long they'd have nothing to puke up.

The guard reappeared and yelled down to the man with the whip, obviously ticked about something. The whip-man returned his own angry words. He grunted in disgust and pushed past the children to the gangplank. Halfway up he turned back, pointed at the kids, and shook the whip at them. The kids gasped and yelped in fear. Most of them ducked their heads. Satisfied, the whip-man boarded the ship and disappeared into the hold with his partner.

"They're probably mad that they've given us too much room," Xander said. "Like a broom closet."

The shackles were heavy on David's wrists. They were wide and thick contraptions, rusty and showing hammer marks from being pounded into shape. The left one ground into his cast, the right one was a little looser. He wiggled his hand, tried to slip it through, but it was too tight.

If only . . .

Then he remembered.

"Xander," he whispered. When his brother turned a miserable expression toward him, David smiled and said, "I have an idea!"

CHAPTER

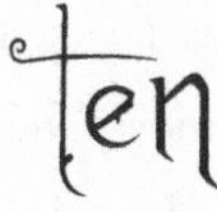

The cluster of Atlantian children shifted nervously on the dock beside the ship that was to take them to war. Their chains rattled, the sound of lost hope. Bound to them, but standing apart, the King brothers whispered to each other.

"Look," David said, swiveling his butt toward Xander and hitching up his tunic to expose his jeans.

His brother scowled at him. "Yeah, that tunic totally makes

your butt look fat. I think you've been hit on the head too many times."

"My pocket!" David said. "I can't reach."

Xander squinted. "What is that?"

"Shampoo. I was going to squirt it in Phemus's eyes when we were hiding in the tub. Then you took off after him, and I stuck it in my pocket. I forgot."

"I don't think these guys care if your hair's clean, David." He shook his head.

"Just get it, will you? *Can* you?"

Xander shifted around as far as the chains would let him, and stretched his arms. "Almost," he said. Then: "Got it." He showed David. It was oval-shaped and not "family sized"—both features that had allowed it to fit in his pocket in the first place. But now it was also bent and crushed. Yellowish shampoo oozed from the top and coated the bottle.

"Oh, no," David said. "Is there any left?"

Xander shook it. "Feels like it."

David held up his shackles. "Squirt some on my wrist."

Xander smiled. "I get it, yeah." They stretched toward each other, and Xander snapped his head back, a pinched look on his face. "Holy cow, man. You stink."

David glanced down at the wet stain that covered his shirt from neck to belly button. "Tell me about it," he said. "Come on . . ." He rattled his shackles.

Xander squeezed a glob out onto the back of David's right

hand. David smeared the slippery goop around and worked it under the edge of the shackle. Holding the brace with his left hand, he rotated his hand and tried to tug it through.

"Is it working?" Xander said.

"Give me a minute." David felt the bones in his hand compressing and sliding under the rough metal. His hand popped out of the shackle. He grinned at Xander and looked around to see if anyone was watching. He let the cuff hang by the chain looped through the other shackle and grabbed the bottle. The left one proved more difficult: the soldier had squeezed the cuff into his cast. But the shampoo made even that slick enough to get his hand out.

"Get mine," Xander said—as if David wouldn't.

David squirted the shampoo on Xander's hand, and his brother started working on it. Watching for the guards, David said, "Hurry."

"These are kid-sized shackles," Xander observed, grunting at the effort. "Bet they're all the same size. That's why it was so easy for you. I'm bigger."

"It's not working?" David said, panicked.

"No," Xander said. "Just go, save yourself." But his hand was already out, and he was smiling.

"Come on," David said, irritated at the lump in his throat Xander's joke had given him. "Get the other one."

When he was free, Xander said, "Let's go."

David grabbed his arm. "Wait," he said. "Give me the

shampoo." When Xander handed him the bottle, David turned back to the chained kids. He stepped up to a boy about his age. Scratches and bruises showed through his ripped rags. The boy's head hung low, partially hiding a face that seemed molded in a plastic mask of sadness. David lifted the boy's shackles and began rubbing shampoo over his wrists and hands.

Xander appeared at his side. "Good idea," he said. "The more kids they have to catch, the less likely they'll catch *us*."

"I just want to help as many people as we can," David said. He forced a hand free. The kid's eyelids fluttered, and he seemed to come more fully aware with each blink. David thought he saw the beginnings of a smile.

"Give me some," Xander said.

David squirted shampoo into Xander's cupped hand. He freed the boy's other arm and gave him a shove. "Go," he said. The boy shuffled toward the taverns, moving slowly, as though invisible chains still bound him. David pushed him again, and the boy picked up his pace.

David turned to another prisoner, a teenager who nodded and bounced with excitement. When he was free, David grabbed his arm to keep him from running. He held up the shampoo and gestured toward the remaining chain gang. The teen didn't understand until David pulled him to another boy and pointed at the shackles. Then he nodded, and David gave him a palm full of shampoo.

Xander was working quickly, moving from boy to boy,

slapping shampoo on their hands. David followed, helping the ones who needed it.

A shout came from the ship. The whip-man was running toward the gangplank. He turned to yell into the hold—calling for help, David thought.

"Run!" Xander yelled. He pushed at the freed kids who were helping others or milling around, looking lost and unsure.

Three kids were still chained. David ran to them and squirted freedom onto their wrists. Xander grabbed his shirt and pulled him away. "Time to go," he said.

They ran toward the corner, which was a good soccer field away.

"Wait, wait," Xander said. He was looking back. The kids were running along the dock toward the taverns. Some jumped off the dock into the water. The whip-man ran away from Xander and David, moving toward one kid, then changing course to go after another. He had shoved the handle of his whip into his belt at the small of his back. It played out behind him like a rat's tail.

Or a demon's, David thought.

Xander pulled him into one of the covered holding areas. They slipped behind a crate and watched as the other guard came out of the hold, then two soldiers. The men saw the scattering kids, clambered down the gangplank, and scrambled after them.

"They would have spotted us before we got to the corner,"

Xander said. "Look." He pointed at a half dozen sailors who were leaning over the ship's railing to observe the commotion.

Xander pulled the silver rock from his pocket and let it rest in his palm. "No pull," he said.

"Didn't it come from the antechamber?" David said. "We've been here long enough. It should be showing us where the portal home is by now."

"I don't know. Maybe it's not working because we followed Phemus and didn't end up where the antechamber *thought* we would."

David remembered going through the portal, seeing a dark cave, then getting yanked away from it. At the time, he'd thought portals had never felt like that before, violent and somehow unsure. They'd wound up not in a cave, but in Taksidian's Atlantian home.

The silver rock rolled over in Xander's palm.

"Did you do that?" David said.

"No, but that's not much. I don't feel anything pulling, nothing to follow."

"We'll have to give it some time," David said. The items from the antechamber seemed to become more anxious about returning to it as time passed, like a horse wanting to get back to its stable.

"I'm not waiting," Xander said. "Let's get back to Taksidian's house. We know it has a portal."

"I saw him and Phemus heading for it," David said.

"Good. If they open the door, we can slip through before it closes." The door covering the portal was a heavy stone slab.

"I don't want to be anywhere near those guys," David said.

"You want to stay *here*?" Xander shot a glance at the ship.

"No, but—"

"Okay," Xander said. "I think we just have to get away from the guards and soldiers who know we're supposed to be chained up. No one cared about us until Taksidian told them to get us. Get around the corner and we're home free."

David wasn't so sure, but he nodded.

"Come on." He shot out of the holding area and ran for the corner. David stayed so close he could have been his brother's shadow.

CHAPTER eleven

Taksidian climbed the path toward his house, thinking about the boys and how he should have taken from each of them a finger or an ear . . . something to help rebuild the sculpture Xander had broken. These kids were particularly troublesome and trophies from them would have been especially satisfying.

No matter, he thought. Maybe I'll just take two from the others, the little girl and Dad.

He reached the terrace outside his front door and waited

for Phemus to catch up. Phemus—he had heard the Kings use that name to describe his Atlantian slave. Previously, Taksidian had called the brute simply, "Slave." Phemus was more colorful, and Taksidian decided to use it.

He leaned against a stone railing. On the other side a grassy hill sloped far down to a river. Beyond that lay the Atlantis of legends. It was a mountain around which a city had been built, slowly rising to the golden castle on top. Massive bridges made of rare stone; agricultural wonders; peace among those fortunate enough to live there, to be part of one of the royal families—all of it a millennium ahead of its time.

What history—or at least poets and songwriters—forgot to mention was the incredible war machine required to make such advancements. And war machines were never pretty: cogs made of conquered enemies-turned-slaves, powered by a ruthlessness that had no regard for anyone and greased by blood.

Taksidian shook his head. In one way Atlantis was indeed the perfect society, in that it represented man's nature: greedy, violent, unapologetic. He had witnessed hundreds of cultures, societies, and times. In every one of them, these traits ruled. Those who embraced them instead of fighting them became the kings of their time. Taksidian embraced them, so he *deserved* the luxury and power he was amassing.

He realized others disagreed, but they were wrong.

Phemus finally reached the terrace, his massive shoulders

rising and falling from the exertion of moving his bulk up the hill. The man had been captured by the Atlantians as a child. He'd fought many battles, some for Atlantis, many for Taksidian. The dumb brute was a massive attack dog: vicious and obedient to his master.

Taksidian slapped the man's arm, and told him in Phemus's language, "Good . . . come." He walked to the other side of the terrace and stopped at a sundial. The *gnomon*—a pencil-like shaft—rose from the center of an intricately carved dial face. Its shadow pointed at a symbol, showing that it was about three in the afternoon.

He selected a black marble from a stone cup and dropped it in a dimple above the symbol that represented seven o'clock. "I have to get back to Pinedale before Time comes for me," he said, eyeing Phemus. He pointed at the marble. "Go to the house when the shadow strikes this marble. If an opportunity presents itself . . ." He smiled. "Do some damage."

Phemus nodded.

"We're almost finished ridding ourselves of this current enemy," Taksidian said. "Rest now." He opened the door to the house and entered.

Phemus followed, trudged to the bed, and sat.

Taksidian thought Phemus's "resting mode" was like a vacuum cleaner waiting to be used. *The man would have no life at all without me.*

He caught sight of an empty peg on the wall and sighed.

"That kid took my tunic. I tell you, those boys were a thorn in my side to the end. Get me another one."

Phemus nodded.

Taksidian approached the heavy door that blocked the portal to the other house. It was counterbalanced, which allowed it to open with a light touch in just the right place. He opened it now. Beyond the doorway, black shadows swirled through slightly less-black shades, like different types of oil mixing together. A cool breeze touched his skin, and he paused.

Normally, the Atlantian portal led directly to the house—thanks to the items from there he had stolen and affixed to this portal's doorframe. Time, as it always did, tried to pull the items through the portal so it could deposit them where they belonged: in the Pinedale house—which opened a tunnel from Atlantis into one of the antechambers (always a different one).

But, like a closet, the antechambers were normally breezeless and without temperature variations. The cool breeze told him the portal wanted to take him on a brief detour before delivering him to the house. The only time it did *that* was when he possessed a specific antechamber item. Then the item itself directed the portal to take him to the time and place it represented . . . then to the house.

Not that he minded the detours. Usually, they showed him boring scenes of woods or streets. But sometimes they treated him to history's most entertaining action sequences: hordes of screaming families snatched up by the tsunami that devastated

Alexandria in the year 350; the nuclear age's equivalent at Hiroshima; the slaughter of General Custer's Seventh Cavalry by Crazy Horse's and Sitting Bull's warriors.

Those detours he expected, because of an antechamber item he had brought with him; this one puzzled him.

He scanned the items around the portal, thinking maybe the boys had messed with them. A plank of wood, a scrap of wallpaper, a doorknob, a nail, a shingle. They all seemed in order.

He patted his pockets and pulled out the braided-leather tassel he'd taken from Xander. It trembled in his hand, anxious to zip through the portal.

Ahh, he thought. An antechamber item. He felt pleasure lighten his mood as he realized those little pests wouldn't be using it: they weren't going home. He returned it to his pocket and stepped through.

CHAPTER

twelve

Keal was deep inside the cave now. The sounds of the bear-human fight had faded away long ago. He swung the torch back and forth to make sure he wasn't missing something, like a sign from one of the boys or another passage. So far he'd found nothing other than more cave drawings. He wished he could see farther in front of him. Moving through the cave in the small circle of light felt like scuba diving in murky water:

You never knew what might show itself—and be too near for you to do anything about it.

As he'd been doing for the last five minutes, he called out to the kids: "David! Xander!" His voice bounced against the stone and scurried away like a small animal afraid of the light.

They can't be here, he thought. The way the walls of the cave hurled his voice far ahead of him, they would have heard him by now, he was sure of it. They would have called back, and he would have heard *something,* even if it was the faintest vibration of air. But he'd heard nothing.

Where could they have gone? He was sure he had gone into the same antechamber David had disappeared into. He had kept his eyes on it, and the door was still open when he had arrived. Unless following Phemus had somehow altered the way the portals worked. Maybe David and Xander had *never* been in the cave. Maybe Phemus had pulled them somewhere else completely.

The torch's flame flickered and fluttered, as though in a brisk wind. All he saw was blackness. He listened: silence. The whole time, there had been a faint breeze blowing through the cave from the entrance. But whatever moved the flame now was stronger. The flame flickered, bending like fingers back toward the front of the cave. He turned around to head in the direction of the pointing fire.

Then he felt it, first in the torch, then the spear. They were vibrating . . . *pulling*. The portal! He began running, retracing his steps through the cave.

It was either the portal home, or perhaps the portal that David and Xander had gone into. Either way, he would find out. The items' pull grew stronger, and he entered a cavern. He remembered passing through it. It was like a big, domed room. In the center, his light had reached up only as far as the tips of stalactites—rock formations hanging like icicles from the ceiling.

Now he could see *all* of the stalactites, as well as the tallest part of the ceiling. A shimmering rectangle hovered higher than his head, throwing out a rainbow of sparkling light. The flames whipped toward it, then disappeared, as though the portal had sucked up the fire itself. He released the torch. It flew into the rippling rectangle and disappeared. The spear quivered violently. It slipped through his hand and vanished, presumably joining the torch on the other side.

But how was *he* going to go through? It was too high to leap into. He looked around at the cavern's stalagmites—like stalactites, but rising from the ground. They appeared too fragile and were definitely too pointed for him to climb and jump from. He spotted a broken one, similar in shape and size to a tree stump. If he leaped from it, his hands would reach the portal—but was that enough? Would the portal pull the rest of his body through?

Something appeared in the portal, startling him. A black

shape. Hazy at first, it took on the form of a man. The figure was just standing there, legs slightly apart, hands at its sides. It appeared to be wearing a cape, which fluttered and whipped around in the portal's currents. Then Keal realized: not a cape, but a black overcoat. At the head, long black hair snapped one way then another.

Taksidian.

Keal waited for him to fall through. When he didn't—he seemed to simply hover there—Keal lost his patience. He planted his foot on the broken stalagmite, leaped, and grabbed the man's ankles.

CHAPTER

thirteen

David and Xander ran around the corner onto a short roadway that rose from the docks and ended at the square. They hit the square and beelined it for the path that would take them to Taksidian's house. If Xander were right, no one would give them a second thought.

Stomping right behind Xander, David glanced around and mentally kicked himself. He remembered the other day, when Phemus had attacked them in their house and chased them into the clearing. Everything Xander said their enemy couldn't do, he did. David had told Xander, "Anything else you think he *can't* do, so I have a heads-up about what he's *going* to do?"

It was a lesson his brother apparently hadn't learned, for now the two of them seemed to be the *only* things the Atlantians noticed. The brawlers at the center of the square, the vendors, the pedestrians—they were all glaring at them. Several pointed. Others shouted. A few started toward them. David saw the kids who had tried to kill him. They were back in the corral on the opposite side of the square, pushing and taunting each other into another fight. They heard the shouts, spotted him, and clambered through the fence rails to come after him.

"Xander!" David yelled.

"I see them! Keep running!"

"But—" David said. More people dropped what they were doing to move in.

"We can make it to the path before they reach us!" Xander said.

That means we can't, David thought, but he didn't see anywhere else to run. At least they were heading for a portal. He picked up speed, pulled up beside Xander, and passed him. His speed encouraged his brother to push harder, and he stayed with him. At first, all he saw ahead of him was a wall of vines and leaves. As he drew closer, the path's opening became a vertical band of shadow among the foliage.

Xander was right: they were going to beat the Atlantians to it. Still, their shouts, combined with the increasingly loud slapping of their feet, sounded to David like a rising, clattering movie soundtrack—one that signaled the coming of something terrible. It scared the tar out of him, and he was certain he would trip or miss the path and entangle himself in the vines or simply choke and freeze in place.

But then he was there, swinging onto the path. He grabbed the gate on his right to stop himself. Xander crashed into him, and was working the latch before David even remembered there *was* a latch. The gate swung open, and they stumbled through it. Xander slammed it closed.

David turned to run up the path to the house, but Xander grabbed him. "Give me my belt!" he said. "Hurry!"

"What?" David said. "Why?" He slipped the belt over his head and handed it over.

Xander unbuckled it, looped it through the bars of the gate, and tied it in a knot. He made another knot, then a third. David watched his brother's muscles bulge as he pulled each one tight.

The first of the Atlantians stomped up to the gate: the two men who had fought in the center of the square. They were big and strong and bloody. They sputtered out sharp words David didn't understand and thrust their arms through the bars. Xander backed away.

"Let's go!" David said.

"Hold on a sec," Xander said, leaning over to rest his palms on his knees. He was panting hard.

The men rattled the gate. They hadn't spotted the belt yet. A crowd was piling up behind them, wailing—David was sure—for the boys' heads on a stick.

"Xander!" He couldn't believe it, Xander standing right there, not four feet from a mob trying to get him. He had a feeling his brother loved it. It was his way of telling them, *Ha! Thought you had me, didn't you? Ha!*

"Can't," Xander said. "Got a stitch in my side."

"You'll have more than that if those guys get through. Come on!"

Xander looked at the crowd, then swiveled his face to David. He was smiling.

"What?" David screamed.

"You know what I thought of when you ran past me back there?"

"Tell me later," David said. He took a couple of steps, then stopped because Xander hadn't moved.

"That joke," Xander said. "You know, the two guys running from a lion. One of them says, 'What are we doing? We can't outrun a lion!' The other says, 'I don't have to. I just have to outrun *you!*'"

Despite his fear, David smiled . . . a little. He said, "Well, that's going to come true if you don't get moving. Look!" The bulky fighter had found the belt and was working on the first knot. The crowd behind him was shoving him into the gate, making his task more difficult.

Thank you, God, David thought.

Xander rose, took a deep breath and—*finally!*—started up the path toward David. They ran again, around the bend, ascending toward Taksidian's house.

"What about Taksidian and Phemus?" David said.

"You said," Xander said, pushing out words between breaths, "they headed up here awhile ago. They're probably gone. Back to the house."

"And if they aren't?"

"I don't know, Dae! But what choice do we have?"

The house was directly in front of them, up the last steep incline. They reached the terrace and stopped.

"I don't think those people are on the path yet," David whispered. "I can still hear the gate rattling." And their voices, which had melded into a single rumbling roar, seemed far away. But that might have only been the foliage absorbing their cries.

Xander hitched his head toward the front door and put his finger over his lips. He unlatched the door and pushed it open. Through the threshold, David could see the portal. His heart skipped a beat: the heavy stone door was closed over it. Xander stepped in and moved toward it. He turned to wave David in.

They were halfway to the portal door when something in the room creaked. David turned to see Phemus rising up from the bed.

CHAPTER

fourteen

FRIDAY, 1:25 P.M.
PINEDALE, CALIFORNIA

Keal felt himself pulled up and into the portal. He had the sensation of tumbling through space, but still he gripped Taksidian's boots as though they were a lifeline, because they probably were. Light flashed into his eyes with the force of an explosion. He landed gut-down on a hard surface and squinted at the antechamber around him.

Taksidian was scrambling along the floor toward the hallway door, pistoning his legs, trying to shake free of Keal.

The portal door slammed into Keal's thigh. It pushed him sideways as it tried to close. He remembered David telling him how the door had cut a metal bat in half. It would have no problem slicing through his legs. But he couldn't move forward with Taksidian kicking like this, and he couldn't get his leg up under himself enough to let the door swing past.

The door shoved him farther, pinching his legs into the doorjamb. Even so, there was no way he was going to let Taksidian go. Not until he knew where the boys were.

He rolled onto his back, using all the strength in his arms to force Taksidian to roll with him. He threw his legs up high, using their momentum and the leverage of Taksidian's ankles to lift his backside, then his hips and torso. As his body sailed over his head, he tucked his head in to complete the somersault. The door slammed closed.

He released his grip on Taksidian and sat down hard on the man's stomach. He heard him *oomph!* Keal was facing his foe's feet. Before he could decide on his next move, pain flared in his sides, and he screamed. He grabbed Taksidian's hands and pulled the man's claws from his flesh. Keal spun off him, rose, and stumbled back into a corner of the room. He rubbed his fingers over his sides, feeling warm wetness, stabbing pain. He looked at his hands, covered in blood.

Taksidian lay on his back, glaring up at him. He snapped

his head to one side, clearing the hair from his face. He smiled.

Holding his sides, gritting his teeth, Keal groaned. He said, "Where are they, David and Xander?"

Ignoring his question, Taksidian said, "Now that was one wild ride. Where did *you* come from?" He laughed and propped himself up on his elbows. "I mean, one second I'm coming through a portal, and the next I got you clinging to me like a remora."

Keal gaped at him.

"You know," Taksidian continued, "one of those sucker fish that attach themselves to sharks—"

"Where are the boys?" Keal repeated, almost growling out the words. "It's not a coincidence they went into that cave, and that's where I found you. Where are they?"

Taksidian looked at his bloody nails. He said, "They're *gone,* my friend. Eleven thousand years gone."

Gone. The word hit Keal like an arrow.

"Not dead," Taksidian said, "but as good as."

Not dead. That's what he wanted to hear. "Take me to them. Now."

Taksidian sat up and Keal crouched, ready to dive into him. Taksidian held up his palm to stop him. He placed a hand on the bench, lifted himself, and slid onto it. He said, "Take you to them? I don't think so."

Keal's eyes flicked to an item on the floor near his feet: the spear, which had sailed through the portal ahead of him. He stooped for it. From the corner of his eyes he saw Taksidian come off the bench. Keal lifted the spear and swung it around, stopping Taksidian in his tracks. The sharp antler at the tip of the spear hovered an inch from the man's chest.

Keal noticed a dagger in Taksidian's hand. Where . . . how . . . ? The guy was *fast.*

As if to prove it, Taksidian's arm swung around in a blur, knocking the spear aside. And he moved in.

CHAPTER

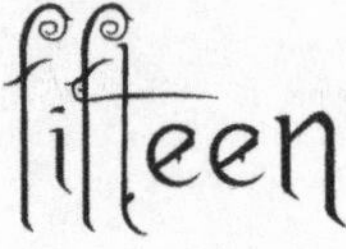

Phemus raised his hands and started across the floor toward them.

David lunged for the portal as Xander went for the house's exit, and they slammed into each other.

"Xan—" David said, but his brother already had hold of him and was shoving-lifting-carrying him out the door.

"Move!" Xander said. "We don't have time to move that stone in front of the portal."

Entangled with each other, they stumbled onto the terrace. David's broken arm smacked down, and he screamed.

The sound of the mob reached them, loud and close. They looked down to the path and saw the first of them—the brawlers—barreling toward them. David glanced back to see Phemus filling the doorway, stepping out.

Xander pulled David up. He tossed him over the stone railing that separated the terrace from a steep grassy hill. David swiveled in midair to avoid landing on his injured arm. He face-planted into the turf. His legs flipped over, and he was tumbling. He caught a quick glimpse of Xander diving over the railing, Phemus's huge hands reaching for his feet. David went end over end, seeing nothing but sky . . . grass . . . sky . . . grass . . . He stuck his arm out, which pivoted his body, and he rolled. The view didn't change . . . sky . . . grass . . . sky . . . grass . . . but the journey was easier on his body.

Xander tumbled behind him. Farther up the hill, Phemus trudged down, holding his arms out for balance, waddling back and forth, trying to control his descent. And behind *him*, the first of the Atlantians were leaping over the railing.

David tried to slow himself down to see where he was heading. The grassy hill ended at a narrow footpath. Lining its far edge were small boulders, embedded in the ground between the path and a wide river. As he rolled, he only saw brief flashes of it, but he knew what was on the other side of the river: the beautiful land of sparkling streams, structures that seemed more like artwork than architecture, and bushes trimmed to look like animals. Watching over all of it was the golden castle at the top of a mountain. The difference between that side of the river and this one could not have been greater if they were from different universes. Heaven and hell.

Rolling, rolling, he thought of the happy families he'd seen on the other side. But they were on that side and he was on this side. *Of course* he was running—rolling—for his life while they picnicked. *Of course* screams of hate filled his ears while music filled theirs.

He hit the path, skidded, flipped, and landed on the boulders. He blinked at the water five feet below him. His reflection blinked back, a boy with wild hair and wilder eyes. Xander slammed into a boulder beside him, cracking his head hard.

"Oooh," Xander said, slapping his hand on the back of his skull.

David scrambled up. Phemus was halfway down, the mob closing the gap behind him. David gave Xander a hand up and looked both directions along the path. Going left would take them back to the village and the square. The other way was unknown; the path continued along the river and disappeared around a bend, where dense woods sprang up. "Which way?" he said.

Xander pulled the metallic stone from his pocket and held it up. It seemed to hop out of his hand. It struck the ground, bounced and spun like a top, and rolled away along the path toward the wood.

Xander pointed at it. "Run!"

David took off. Even at full speed, he was falling farther and farther behind the stone. It rolled, popped up, came down, continued rolling, faster than before.

Like the square, the path was just plain *gross.* At first, David tried to dodge around the dead fish, animal bones, and chicken heads. But as the stone picked up speed, he stomped over all of it.

The stone popped up, and in midair it jerked to the left. It bounced off a boulder and vanished over the edge. It plunked into the water, spreading ripples like rings of heated air from an atomic bomb.

David slid to a stop. "Xander!" he yelled, watching the ripples fade. He spun as his brother caught up to him. Phemus and at least twenty Atlantians had reached the path and were booking toward them.

Xander stared at the spot where the stone had disappeared.

"It's gone," David said. "It just popped up and fell into the river."

"No," Xander said. "It didn't *fall.* It was *pulled.*"

The surface still rippled, but not from the stone. It was a portal.

"Go," Xander said.

David didn't have to be told twice. He jumped and watched

the portal grow large between his kicking feet. He plunged into the water. It was cold, knocking the air out of him. And salty, stinging his eyes. His stomach lurched and his head spun. He closed his eyes and waited for it to be over.

CHAPTER

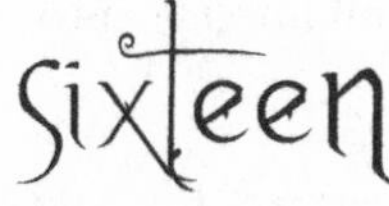

FRIDAY, 1:27 P.M.

Taksidian moved quickly, stepping toward Keal as soon as the spear was away from his chest. The man snapped the dagger up, but Keal knew better. It was an old hand-to-hand combat trick: pretend to do the expected, and most people expected that knife-wielding attackers would thrust downward. But warriors knew the most lethal and effective knife attacks came from below, underhanded. He reached down and caught Taksidian's arm as it swooped down and up toward the bottom of his rib cage.

Keal yanked back on the spear, trying to get the tip of the long weapon in position to stab Taksidian. But the man's other hand seized it, keeping it extended past his body.

As furiously fast as their movements had been, they stopped just as quickly. The men stood locked in place like statues. Their faces were so close, Keal could smell Taksidian's foul breath. He felt the continued upward pressure of Taksidian's arm, but his own arm was strong and firm.

Taksidian stared unblinking into Keal's eyes. He said, "Nice."

Keal strained with effort. He said, "Where . . . are . . . the . . . boys?"

Taksidian simply grinned, making Keal's hatred glow red-hot inside his chest.

They stood in the center of the room, the closed portal door on one side, the hallway door on the other. Keal believed they could be frozen in that position forever. It made him think of the two Zax, those Dr. Seuss characters who refused to move to let each other pass while a city rose up around them.

Quick as a blink, Keal shot his knee out. Taksidian moved his leg and blocked it.

"Now what?" Taksidian said.

Keal tried twisting Taksidian's arm to aim the dagger away from him. Taksidian resisted, held firm.

The guy's stronger than he looks, Keal thought. *And he looks strong.*

Taksidian threw his head forward, targeting Keal's face. Most combatants tried to counter the move by stiffening their necks and bracing themselves for the impact. That simply gave the attacker something solid to hit. The right response was what Keal did now. He leaned away and let his head fall back. Taksidian's forehead tapped Keal's chin. It helped that Keal had expected it.

"You're good," Taksidian said.

"You're bad," Keal said. "Guess that's why we're here."

The intensity of Taksidian's eyes showed that he was calculating, calculating . . . figuring out a move that would surprise and *end* Keal.

The portal door burst open, and water sprayed in.

In the half second that Keal flinched and looked, Taksidian released the spear and punched him. Keal flew back, but refused to release Taksidian's knife hand. Taksidian elbowed Keal's nose, and that was it: Keal sailed against the wall and dropped to the floor.

Through a haze of pain and watery eyes, Keal watched Taksidian swing his dagger back, preparing to dart in for the kill.

But David propelled out of the portal, smacking into Taksidian. Water exploded from the collision like fire. The dagger flew out of Taksidian's hand and clattered to the floor beside Keal.

David landed on his feet and staggered back, shock making his eyes big and unhinging his jaw.

Taksidian spun, saw David, and registered just as much shock. He raised his foot and kicked David in the chest, sending him back into the portal. The door slammed shut.

CHAPTER

Seventeen

FRIDAY, 1:31 P.M.

Shoved backwards, David went through the shimmering portal, turning Taksidian's image into a wavering, blurry figure. David spun around, and he was in the cave. It was gone in a blink, flooded by water crashing in from all sides. He rammed into something both hard and soft, felt arms and legs tangling around him. Xander's face flashed by, and together they broke the surface of the river. Shot out of the portal like pieces of rotten food from a mouth, they flew, arms and legs pinwheeling, back toward the path. They slammed into Phemus, and all three of them hit the ground.

Phemus grunted and waved his hands around, trying to grab them, as if swatting at flies. David kicked him in the head, rolled away, and stood. Xander pushed himself out of the way of Phemus's flailing arms, scooting backward along the path.

"Xander!" David said.

His brother saw the fighting men moving in on him, a crowd of people right behind. One of the bare-chested brawlers swung a fist at him. He ducked and spun away.

"Follow me!" David yelled and leaped over the boulders into the river.

* * *

David spilled out of the portal on a wave of water. He somersaulted and coasted into the hallway door. Keal was sitting on the floor, his back against the wall, staring at him. Blood fanned out from his nostrils, coating his lips and chin.

"Are you all ri—" David started.

Xander flew in horizontally, arms stretched out over his head, like the Man of Steel coming for a visit. He appeared to stall in midflight and belly flopped to the floor. He moaned and rolled over, holding his stomach. His eyes snapped opened. "He's coming!" he said. He rose and leaped to the portal door. He swung it around, but just before it closed, water sprayed in and something crashed into the other side. The door jarred open a foot, knocking Xander off his feet. Lying on the floor, he pushed his hands against the door. "Help me!"

Keal bolted up, rammed his shoulder against the door, and leaned into it.

David jumped up and bent over his brother to help them push. His sneakers slipped on the wet floor, and he had to continually shuffle his feet to get any kind of traction.

"Aaahhh!" Xander screamed.

David realized he had planted a foot on his brother's shoulder. He slipped it off and said, "Is it Phemus?"

"Who else?" Xander said, as the brute's fat arm slipped through the opening. It punched at David, who dodged it. "Push!" Xander yelled.

But Phemus was strong and the floor was slippery and the boys were tired. The door inched open. Keal backed away, and the door opened farther.

"Keal!" David said.

Keal returned and held a dagger over Phemus's wildly moving arm. He waved the dagger, trying to get a shot.

"Do it!" David said.

Keal jabbed, pinning Phemus's hand to the door. A howl

came through the opening. The muscles in the big man's arm tightened and bulged. His fingers flexed.

"It's stuck," Keal said. He tugged on the blade, wiggled it, and yanked it out.

The arm slipped away, and the door slammed shut.

CHAPTER

eighteen

Friday, 1:45 p.m.

David leaned his shoulder into the door, giving his throbbing arm a break. All of them pushed against it, panting. As David's breath slowed, his nerves settled. He said, "Think he can come through? Will the door open for him?"

Xander moved away from the door and plopped down on the bench. "I don't know how he could," he said. "It's closed now. We're home. The portal we used in Atlantis should be gone. He only got as far as he did because he followed us through."

"Like we did with him," David said. His shoulders slumped. His whole body slumped. He stumbled to the bench and collapsed on it, resting his head on his brother's thigh.

"What happened back there?" Xander said. "You almost killed me. Twice: when *you* crashed into me and when *we* crashed into Phemus. Why'd you come back through the portal?"

"Taks—" David raised his head. "What happened to Taksidian?"

"*You* did," Keal said. "When you ran into him, he lost his dagger, and it gave me time to raise the spear. So he ran." Keal groaned, pressed his back against the portal door, and slid down to sit on the floor. He added: "Like the coward he is."

"What do you mean?" Xander said. "Taksidian was here? In the antechamber?"

"He *kicked* me back into the portal," David said, rubbing his chest. He moaned and moved his hand to his broken arm. He squeezed it, sending a shock wave into his shoulder. "It *hurts,*" he said. "I mean, it's been hurting all along, but we were too busy staying alive to think much about it."

Keal said, "I'll take a look. I think we all need some painkillers and bandages."

"Some?" David said. "This *town* doesn't have enough." He moaned and leaned his head back to the wall. "I wish Dad was here."

Keal looked at his watch. "He and Toria won't be back till

about seven, later if they stop by the hotel to see your nana on their way home."

"Can we call them?" David said. After everything they'd gone through, hearing Dad's voice would be like a glass of ice water to a man in a desert.

"They don't have a phone," Keal reminded him. "And they don't know the numbers of the new mobile phones I picked up."

They had discovered that Taksidian had bugged their phones, so Dad had gotten rid of them. David didn't like being so cut off from the rest of his family. It felt too permanent, and losing Mom was bad enough.

Xander pointed at Keal, then touched his lip. "Did Taksidian do that?"

Keal wiped his face and looked at the blood. "And this . . ." He leaned sideways and lifted his shirt. Beneath a smear of blood were four small crescent-shaped cuts.

"Ow," David said.

"With his *nails,*" Keal said, dropping his shirt. "Other side, too."

A wind blew in under the door. Keal scooted away. It swirled about the room, over the boys and Keal, looking for particles that didn't belong in the present time. The water on the floor beaded up and rolled under the door. The air filled with mist as it pulled the water from David and Xander's hair, skin, and clothes. It made David feel clean, and he was happy to be dry. He ran his fingers through his hair, amazed that the wind could be so thorough.

He said, "I always like—" He flew off the bench and smashed into the door. His arm cracked down on the floor, and he screamed. His back was pressed to the crack under the door. His skin tightened, and he could almost hear his ribs creaking under the pressure. Time was trying to pull him under the door!

"David!" Xander said, grabbing his legs. Keal got hold of his arms.

"What's going on?" David said, his voice squeaky with panic.

"Your shirt!" Xander said. "You brought it back. Take it off."

David's hands slapped at his body, but he couldn't find the belt. "I . . . I *can't!*"

Keal flashed the dagger past him, and David felt the pressure against his ribs ease. Xander ripped at the material. He forced David to bend his arm and pushed one side of the shirt over it.

David rolled away, and the tunic zipped out from under him. It wadded up in the crack, compressed, and disappeared.

He threw his good arm over his eyes. "Oh, man," he said. "When am I going to *learn*?"

The wind returned, but it wasn't the same. This one was misty and fragrant.

David sat up, pushed away from the door, and grabbed Xander's arm. "What does it want now?" he yelled. "I don't have anything else!"

The mist filled the room, swirling like a dust devil.

The mist stung David's eyes, and he squeezed them closed. It smelled clean and fresh, like soap, but it was strong and filled his nostrils and lungs. He coughed, trying to hack it out.

With a gasp, the wind vanished under the door.

David opened his eyes, wiped goop from his lids, and blinked. His eyes felt like molten balls of fire. Keal and Xander rubbed at theirs, frowning, blinking. They gazed around the room. Everything glistened—the floor, the walls, their clothes and skin.

Keal wiped his forearm and rubbed his thumb and fingertips together. "What the—?"

David saw something on the floor that must have come in with the mist. It was flat and green. Then he recognized the fragrance and laughed. "Shampoo."

CHAPTER

nineteen

FRIDAY, 1:52 P.M.

"Well," Xander said, "I guess it works in both directions." He lifted his T-shirt over his face and rubbed. "Time wants everything back where it belongs, even here."

"Except Mom," David said. He lowered his head. After everything they'd been through, he didn't feel any closer to getting her back.

"Maybe," Keal said, "it's *working* to get her back. People

are different. When the pull tried to take your nana, the door opened. That means it knows the difference between living people and . . ." He wiped his forehead. "And shampoo."

"So?" David said.

"So maybe it has to bring her back a certain way. You know, like through certain portals or combination of portals. But if she moves too far away from the right ones, it takes longer. Look at Nana and Jesse. They both got far enough away from the house that the pull couldn't get them, even though they were both in other times so long that history thinks they belong back there."

David shook his head. "It took thirty years for Nana to make it back."

"With your help," Keal reminded him. He waited until David looked at him, then said, "So that's what you do for your mom too. Help her find her way home."

"We're trying."

"Keep trying. It seems like an impossible—"

"Shhh! Shhh!" Xander said. He was scowling at the hallway door.

David's stomach tightened. He strained his ears, but heard nothing.

"What did you hear, Xander?" Keal asked.

"I just thought . . ." Xander whispered. "I said Phemus can't come through this door because we had the item that brought us here." He looked worriedly from Keal to David. "But he has a direct portal to the house. He could come through a *different* portal!"

"Into another antechamber?" David said, scrambling to his feet. He stared at the hall door, expecting it to burst open. "Would he do that?"

"He came after us, didn't he?" Xander used the bench to hoist himself up. "We're supposed to be chained up on a ship going to war. I'm sure he's not happy that we aren't."

"So, did you hear something or not?" David's pounding heart didn't *want* to know, it *needed* to know.

"I thought . . ." Xander shook his head. "I don't know. A creak, maybe."

David thought of Phemus trudging back up the hill to Taksidian's Atlantian house, where the portal was. He said, "Could he have gotten to the portal so fast?"

"If he hurried," Xander said. "Just barely."

Keal stood. He slipped Taksidian's dagger beneath his belt at the small of his back and said, "Let's get downstairs."

Xander leaned his ear to the door. He turned the handle and cracked it open and peered through.

David grabbed a handful of Xander's shirt—the brave part of his brain thinking he'd yank him back if Phemus leaped up; the little boy part simply wanting contact, as though Xander were the "blankie" David used to sleep with.

Xander pulled the door wider and poked his head out to look in both directions.

"Xan—" David said.

Xander stepped through, pulling David with him.

Keal put a reassuring hand on David's back. They walked in a line toward the landing, where a staircase led down to the second floor. David pictured their escape route: at the bottom of the stairs were two walls, one meant to be strong and secure enough to keep trespassers from other worlds from coming into the main part of their house; the other, six feet from the first, was designed to look like the other walls in the house, to keep the third floor secret.

Trouble was, Phemus had knocked down the walls. Keal had rebuilt them, but had not yet installed the doors.

Past the two walls, on the left, was their Mission Control Center—MCC—where they had planned to record their trips to other times and try to figure out what the house was all about. Nothing in there that would help them now.

A short hallway led to a right-hand corner into the second floor's main hall. From there, they could take the grand staircase to the foyer and the front door.

No problem.

Then a problem did occur to him. "What if Phemus already came through? What if he's waiting for us downstairs?"

"Shhh," Keal said, patting him.

Will this never end? David thought. The danger. The fear. The feeling in his gut as tight as a clenched fist. He wanted to feel normal again. He wanted Mom back . . . their life back.

Bam!

Their heads swung toward the sound behind them.

"That was a portal door," Xander said.

A door opened. Light poured out of an antechamber, filling the far end of the hallway.

"Go!" Keal said. But they continued to watch as Phemus stepped through and turned his face toward them.

Keal shoved David at the same time that Xander took off, yanking him forward. He stumbled, almost fell, found his feet, and ran. He followed Xander around the corner to the stairs.

Behind him Keal was saying, "Go, go, go, go, go . . ." It sounded more like a chugging train engine than a command no one needed.

CHAPTER

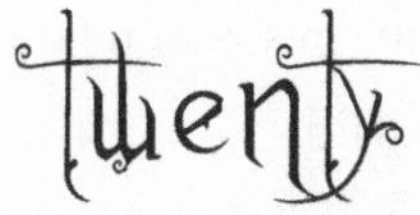

FRIDAY, 1:56 P.M.

David, Xander, and Keal pounded down the stairs and through the doorless openings in the two walls, Phemus somewhere behind them.

David and Xander were almost to the corner that would take them to the second floor's main hall when David realized Keal wasn't behind him. He braked, yanking Xander to a stop as well.

Keal was back at the second wall, struggling to get a big rectangle of wall—the one that acted as a secret door—into place over the opening.

"Keal!" Xander said. "There's no time."

"Hand me a two-by-four, those nails, and a hammer!" Keal yelled.

"Keal!" Xander repeated.

David ran to a stack of long wooden studs. He handed one to Keal, who crossed it over the door and the wall on either side.

David could hear Phemus coming down the stairs.

"Nails, nails!" Keal said.

Xander grabbed a handful and a hammer. He pounded one into the end of the stud. He put in another one, and ran around to Keal's other side.

"This is stupid," Xander said, as he pounded in another nail.

"David," Keal said. "Get another stud ready!"

David started to turn, and the door exploded out. Xander flew back and tumbled along the floor.

David yelled, stumbled back, and tripped over the stack of studs. Sitting on the floor, his legs hitched up over the wood, he saw Keal on the floor, flat on his back. The door lay over him. Only his chest, head, and arms protruded out from it.

Phemus ducked his head to fit through the opening, and stepped on top of the door.

Keal groaned and fought to get free, but he was pinned under Phemus's massive weight.

"Keal!" David and Xander yelled at the same time.

Phemus noticed their stares and looked down at Keal. Stepping forward on the door—pushing a gasp of pain from Keal—the big man stooped, reaching for Keal's head.

David snatched up a stud and thrust it into Phemus's neck. Phemus reared up, and David rammed the stud into his stomach. The big man grabbed the wood and shook it. David held on, stumbling around like a bull rider.

Xander grabbed Keal's arm and began pulling. Keal put a hand on the top edge of the door and pushed, inching his way out.

Lightning bolts shot into David's shoulder from his broken arm, but he refused to release his grip. He had to keep Phemus busy for as long as it took to free Keal. The stud slipped over his hands, pushing splinters into his flesh. Phemus swung the stud, slamming David into the wall.

"Hurry!" he yelled.

Xander dropped to the floor. He hooked his hands into Keal's armpit, planted a foot on the top of the door, and pulled. Keal slid farther out until only his legs remained pinned.

Phemus jerked David back and forth on the end of the stud. Then he yanked it toward himself, and David stumbled forward. He had no choice: he let go just before coming close enough for Phemus to grab him.

Phemus hoisted the stud and jabbed it down at Keal. Keal twisted sideways, and the stud smashed into the floor. It broke through the hardwood, penetrating it like a pick shattering through ice. Phemus raised it for another strike.

Xander pulled. Keal thrashed, and shot out from under the door. Xander rose and fell back, pulling Keal along the floor with him.

David helped them up, and together they ran around the corner into the main hallway without looking back.

"Outside!" Keal yelled.

They hit the stairs leading to the foyer, and David leaped down, touching every fourth step.

"Haven't we done this already?" Xander said, moving past David in a near-freefall down the stairs.

"He's going to keep coming," David said, arching around the door that Xander swung open.

"Let him try," Keal said. He pushed the brothers down the porch steps. "Get to the car! The car!"

At Keal's rented Charger, David looked back. Phemus was coming down the porch stairs. David jumped into the backseat as Keal dropped down behind the wheel.

"Aaah!" Keal yelled. He reached behind him, and his hand came back holding the dagger. He dropped it into a cubby in the center console and cranked the engine.

Phemus was running now, clomping through the trees toward them. Keal didn't bother turning the car around. He looked through the rear window and peeled away in reverse.

"Pull a Jim Rockford," Xander said.

"What's that?" Keal said.

"From *The Rockford Files.* Slam on your brakes and crank the wheel. You can turn the car around without slowing down."

Keal threw him a quick glance. "I'm not Jim Rockford."

At the first bend in the road, he stopped.

The three of them stared through the windshield at the dust cloud the car had made. Slowly it settled, revealing Phemus trotting toward them. He was still a good distance away.

"What was that back there?" Xander said. "Stopping to put up the door. Come on."

"I didn't want him in the house," Keal said. "When we go back, he could be hiding somewhere."

"Till Time sucks him back," David said.

Keal looked at him in the mirror and smiled. "Forgot about that," he said. He turned the wheel, put the car in drive, and drove around the bend. When David looked, Phemus was still coming.

CHAPTER

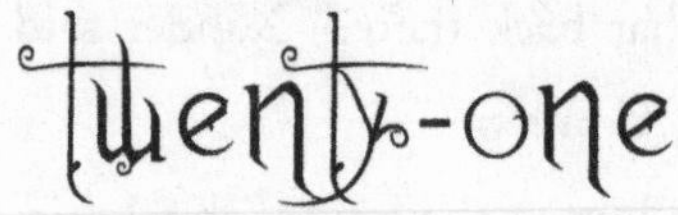

FRIDAY, 2:02 P.M.

They drove through town and out the other side. Keal followed the winding road past the turnoff to Taksidian's Pinedale house, then turned around. Cruising slowly back into town, he stopped at a gas station, where they all used the bathroom, and Keal bought a bagful of first aid supplies.

Back in the car, he looked at his watch. "Think Phemus is back in his own time now?"

Xander looked back at David, who shook his head no. "We've been able to stay in the worlds thirty, forty minutes," Xander said.

"Longer," David said, "when we went from world to world without returning to the house first."

Keal snapped his head toward him. "You *did* that?"

David had forgotten Keal didn't know. It seemed like such a long time ago when they went to the Civil War world, then went through the wrong portal to the Alps. After that, they had ended up in a torture chamber. When they finally got home, Keal had been knocked out and Phemus and Taksidian had been in the house. And then they had followed Phemus to Atlantis.

It had all started shortly after using the locker portal to get home from school during first period. *So* . . . David calculated . . . *seven-forty a.m. until now. Less than five hours!* He felt five *years* older than he did when he woke up that morning.

Xander began telling Keal about it. How David had found the Civil War doctor and somehow changed history. Keal confirmed what the boys already knew: that the war ended in 1865 and cost about 600,000 lives.

"But David remembers it differently," Xander said. "He said it ended in 1875 and over two *million* people died in it."

When Keal scowled at him, David said, "That's what I said right after the change. I don't remember that anymore."

"Like Jesse," Keal said. "He said he could remember the

old history, before he changed it, for only a little while, then it was gone."

"Right," Xander said.

Keal scratched his head. "I don't know if I'll ever get my mind around that, actually *changing* history." He looked around at the world outside the car and sighed.

David thought he was about to say something profound and wise, but what he said was, "You guys feel like ice cream? I could really use some ice cream right about now."

Xander grinned. "You sound more and more like Dad all the time."

"Hey," Keal said, "great minds think alike."

They pulled into the drive-in diner, where the Kings had stopped for treats after the first day of school. They ordered, and while waiting for the waitress to bring their food to the car, the brothers told Keal more about the worlds they'd visited.

"Atlantis!" Keal said when they reached that part. The waitress rapped on the window, and he jumped. He handed David a root beer float and Xander a chocolate cone. He licked his own cone as he listened to the rest of the boys' story.

Between sentences, they slurped and *mmm*'ed with pleasure. David didn't think anything had ever tasted so good as that float. Something about world-hopping and defying death made it the perfect reward.

When they'd finished, Keal ran his tongue over his lips and said, "But you don't think your mother's still there?"

David said, "Taksidian said the portals pull people away."

"He said he didn't know what world she went to," Xander added.

"Your nana said it was like that for her," Keal said. "She told me she sometimes woke up to find herself getting pulled into another world."

David stared into his cup—still some ice cream left, but he suddenly didn't want it. He said, "That must have been awful."

Keal nodded. "She said sometimes she'd whip through three worlds in one day, and other times she'd stay in one world for a month or longer." He looked at the brothers in turn. "Like a minnow, that's how she put it. A minnow caught in the currents of Time."

David leaned his head against the window and closed his eyes. A scene like a documentary on the Discovery Channel played out in his head: a little fish struggling against the raging waters of a river, bashing against stones, resting for a while in a still area, then zipped away again by a gush of water.

But not water. *Time.* And not a little fish. *Mom.*

"Let's go," he said. "We have to find Mom. We have to get her."

CHAPTER

twenty-two

FRIDAY, 2:50 P.M.

They sat in the idling car staring up Gabriel Road to their house.

"Well," Keal said, "what do you think?"

David looked out the side windows into the woods. He half expected Phemus and maybe a few of those other Atlantian slaves to rush out of the shadows and surround the car.

"I think it's been long enough," Xander said. "He's probably back in Atlantis by now."

Keal let the car roll closer, all the while swiveling his head around, looking.

When the car stopped in front of the house, David leaned between the front seats to squint through the trees at the house. "Door's open," he observed.

They climbed out and gathered at the front bumper.

"What now?" Xander said.

A loud *crack!* made David jump. It had come from the car. He looked to see something that looked like a bat—the animal kind—clattering against the inside of the windshield. But it didn't sound like a bat; too hard, too metallic. He realized what it was: "Taksidian's dagger!"

"I . . ." Keal said, staring in disbelief. "I left it on the center console."

"Taksidian's so mean," Xander said, "even his *dagger* wants to kill us."

"It's the pull," David said. "Wherever it came from, Time wants it back."

The dagger flipped and spun, clattering against the glass. It dropped to the dashboard, then bounced up to strike the windshield again. The glass shattered, spiderwebbing out from where the blade came through. It started bulging out, making a sound like ice breaking over a pond.

Keal grabbed Xander's and David's arms and pulled them to the side.

The dagger's handle broke through. It sailed over the hood

and fell into the dirt, then flipped up, balancing on the tip of the blade, where it spun so fast it became a black blur. It tumbled and bounced over the ground toward the house, fast as a jackrabbit. Instead of going up the porch steps and through the door, it leaped into a porch railing—going right through it in an explosion of splinters. It crashed through the window to the left of the door.

"Must be heading home," Keal said.

"Where's home?" David said.

"Wherever Taksidian comes from, probably."

"But Taksidian's been here a long time," David said. "How'd he keep it for so long? I thought Time always pulled the items back to where they belong."

"Same way he's been able to stay, I guess," Keal said. "He only stays around the house a little while, then leaves before Time realizes he's here and tries to pull him back."

"Like Jesse," David said. "He could be in the house only a little while at a time."

Keal nodded.

The three of them stood in silence, gazing at the destruction the knife had left. David turned to gape at the hole in the windshield, which had broken into tiny squares that had somehow stayed together.

"Well," Keal said, "if the dagger got pulled back, then it wasn't away from the house long enough to reset the pull. That's good to know."

"Why?" David said.

"Because when Phemus or Taksidian goes away, we know he won't be back for a while. And another thing . . ." He smiled. "There's no way Phemus is still in the house." He marched toward the front door. "Come on."

Xander looked at David, then at the hole in the windshield. He said, "This just keeps getting weirder and weirder."

CHAPTER

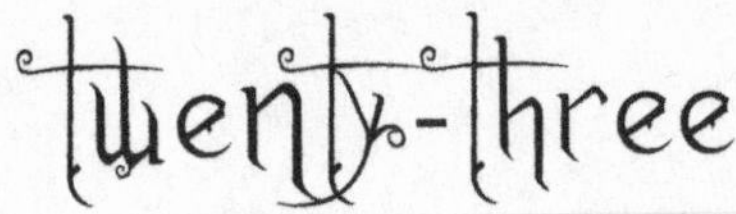

FRIDAY, 3:30 P.M.

David sat sideways on the closed lid of the toilet in the upstairs bathroom. He had his arm propped up on the counter beside the sink, and Keal was carefully unwrapping the Ace bandage Dad had wrapped around the disintegrating cast the other day.

"Ow," he groaned.

"Sorry," Keal said. "You said you think you broke it again?"

"Yeah," David said. "When I was sliding down a hill in the Alps. I shoved it into the snow."

"What'd you do that for?"

"To keep from going over a cliff."

Keal grimaced and nodded.

David smiled a little. Only in this house, only after all the crazy things they'd done, could his explanation not have sounded completely insane.

Keal poked at the arm while watching David's expression. "I'm afraid you're right," he said. "You did break it again."

"You're a nurse," David said. "Can't you fix it?"

"I can't reset it. Need a hospital for that. And a new cast."

David shook his head. "Last time we saw a doctor, he accused Dad of hurting us."

"Because of a broken arm?"

"Dad thinks Taksidian got to him," David said, feeling the heat of anger radiate in his chest. "He'd do anything to get us out of the house."

"David," Keal said, pushing his finger into a hole that went straight through the cast. "What's this?"

"That's from a Carthaginian soldier's pike. He tried to impale me," David said. "But that didn't hurt. What hurt are all the times I hit it against trees and the ground and walls and doors."

"That'll do it," Keal said. "Fresh breaks are easy to re-break or knock out of alignment."

David winced at a bolt of pain that felt like wire running up the center of his arm. He fought the urge to pull his arm away. He was trembling all over, and there was nothing he could do to stop it. A tear rolled down his cheek.

Keal gave him a sad look. "Those painkillers I gave you should have kicked in by now."

"Maybe I didn't take enough," David said.

"I can't give you any more."

"That's okay," David said. "I'll be all right after you stop messing with it." *And after I take a long, hot bath,* he thought. *Followed by, oh, eighteen hours of sleep.*

"This doesn't look good," Keal said. "You have to find a way to stop banging it, whether we get it reset and recast or not." He stopped unraveling the bandage and looked at David, a mixture of puzzlement and concern creasing his brow. His frown was deep, and all David could do was frown back. Then Keal's face softened, and his lips bent up at the corners. Soon, he was showing David a full set of teeth.

David got it: the craziness of it all. The dozen wounds he'd suffered and how he'd suffered them. No, no—*when* and *where* he'd suffered them. The Alps during Hannibal's march over them. A Civil War battlefield. A French village during World War II . . . the list went on and on. Before he realized it, he was smiling too. And laughing.

Keal added his booming laughter. Their voices bounced around the bathroom like music from a symphony orchestra.

"What's so funny?" Xander said. He'd gone to take a shower in Mom and Dad's bathroom, and now he stood in the doorway rubbing a towel over his hair, another towel tied around his waist.

"Nothing," David said. "Everything."

Xander made a face. He said, "Does this look as bad as it feels?" He turned to show them his back. A dark blue bruise ran diagonally from one shoulder blade to just above the top of the towel. The edges were red, slowly fading to yellow.

"Man!" Keal said. "Is that from Phemus?"

Xander nodded and turned around. "When he hurled the toy rifle at us in the clearing. Knocked the wind out of me."

"And you almost fell all the way to the ground," David said, remembering.

"I thought I was a goner," Xander said. "I just tried not to think about—" His eyes flashed wide, and he cried out, "*Oh!*" He was looking at David's arm.

Keal had unwrapped all but a couple of loops of Ace bandage close to the elbow. The cast itself was almost gone, crumbled away. Plaster chunks and powder were spread out on the counter around it. David's skin was mottled blue and white. Thread-thin tendrils of red networked through it, like the swirls of color through marble.

Xander said, "It looks like something from *Alien* . . . or *The Exorcist* . . . or—"

"Xander." Keal stopped him.

David moaned. Seeing it made it worse. He bit his lip.

"What's *that*?" Xander almost screamed. He pointed at a bump in David's flesh midway between wrist and elbow.

"Xander," Keal said, stern. "Go get dressed."

"No . . . just . . . what is it?"

Keal looked at David. He gently touched the bump. David yelped. He was trembling again, the laughter forgotten.

"That's your bone, David," Keal said. "It's broken, all right. And not set. We have to get you to a hospital."

"No," David said, shaking his head. He closed his eyes, squeezing out more tears.

"I'll take you someplace away from Pinedale," Keal said. "You can't go on with your arm like this."

"No," David repeated. "Look at me. I have a black eye and a bruised cheek. A bump on my head, bruised ribs, an aching foot, broken skin over my knuckles. The skin on my chest and stomach . . . I don't even know how to describe it." He looked down at himself. His entire front was scratched and road-rashed from his slide over ice down the mountain.

"I've got cuts on my shoulder and palm and probably places I don't even know about yet. If anyone saw me, especially a doctor, they'd be stupid *not* to call the cops or social services or whoever takes kids away from abusive parents."

Keal just frowned at him. "Well," he said slowly, "I could try to wrap it tightly. Can't cut off circulation, though. Didn't the hospital give you a sling?"

"Yeah," David said. "It was getting in my way. It's in the bedroom."

"I'll get it," Xander said.

"And rulers," Keal said. "You got two rulers?"

"I think Toria does." Xander darted away.

"We'll splint it," Keal said, squinting down at David's arm. "And wrap it with three or four bandages. That's the best I can do here, but it's going to hurt until you get it set."

"I can take it," David said, not sure he could.

"It can also get infected."

"I can take—"

Keal raised his palm to stop him. "You can't, David, not gangrene. You'll lose your arm. Maybe get sepsis. That's when the cells that are dying in your arm infect your whole body. Blood poisoning. You could die."

"Are you trying to scare me?"

"Yes!" Keal took a deep breath. "Look, you probably have some time. We'll wait till your dad gets back, but you know what he's going to say."

David nodded. "Hospital . . . now."

Keal reached into a bag in the sink and pulled out a new Ace bandage. He said, "I'll try to take some of the pressure off with this and the sling, and try to keep the bone from moving anymore."

Xander returned and slid two rulers onto the counter, one wood, one plastic.

"Have to do for now, I guess," Keal said.

Xander sat on the edge of the tub and dropped the sling into David's lap. He rubbed David's back. "It'll be all right, Dae," he whispered.

David forced a smile. He turned back to Keal. "Will I be able to take a bath?" He *really* wanted to take a bath.

Keal grinned. "Just try not to get it wet. I'll put plastic wrap around it, in case. Then take it off when you're done."

"I'll get it," Xander said. "But first . . ." He plugged the tub's drain, started the water, and squirted in Mr. Bubbles. He checked the water temperature, adjusted it, and headed for the door.

"Xander," David said. "Thanks."

"No problem," Xander said, a sly smile on his lips. "You can give me a foot massage later."

After he left, Keal said, "You guys are close."

"Not always," David said. "We used to play together a lot, but when he became a teenager, he . . . I don't know, became a jerk."

"Spending more time with his friends? Didn't want you around?"

"Yeah."

"That's normal," Keal said. "His interests changed. Started getting into things you weren't ready to get into. Wanting to get serious about his filmmaking, cars . . ."

"Girls."

Keal smiled. "Them too." He looped the bandage around David's arm, tugging it gently to get it tight. "So, see," he said, "something good can come out of all this horrible trouble. You and Xander are realizing how much you need each other. I bet that won't change, ever. Not even after your mom's back and you're all very far away from this house."

David thought about that. He believed it. He couldn't imagine Xander and himself *not* always covering each other's back, not after everything they'd been through together. The King Brothers, that's what people would call them. He said, "That'd be cool."

CHAPTER twenty-four

FRIDAY, 3:57 P.M.

David stepped out of the bathroom, drying himself with a towel. Every ache and pain screamed as he ran the towel over his body. Out of sight by the false walls, Keal pounded and drilled like a one-man construction crew.

David went to his bedroom for clothes. Fresh, clean clothes. He never thought he'd care so much about *clothes.*

Xander was sitting on the floor, going through a box.

Mom had been taken on their third day in the house, so they'd never had time to unpack.

"What's that?" David said.

"Junk, mostly," Xander said. "Feel better?"

"A little." He selected boxers, jeans, and a T-shirt from his dresser and pulled them on, then sat on the other side of the box from Xander. He recognized most of the items inside: soccer trophies, Matchbox cars, a pencil holder that looked like a hand with curved fingers and thumb. Xander had made it in school a few years ago. They were all things that had covered the top of their dresser, nightstands, and shelves in their room back in Pasadena.

Seeing them gave him mixed feelings. He ached for the time these things symbolized, when Mom was home and his biggest worry was whether he would do well at the next soccer game. Then again, they reminded him that the world was different from what the last week had been, different from this house. It was a nice feeling, a hopeful feeling that their lives could once again be like that.

Maybe that's why Xander was going through them.

David noticed that Xander had tied back the thin white sheers that covered their windows, and the sun was streaming in. Even the heavy woods outside couldn't stop it today. He'd never seen the room like this before. It had always seemed gloomy, like the whole house did. He tried to remember if he'd thought differently about it before Mom was taken, but he couldn't.

"You still smell like shampoo," Xander said.

"I think it's permanent. Better than whatever that stuff was that got on my tunic in Atlantis, when I was dragged through it."

Xander crinkled his nose. "That was the worst thing I ever smelled."

"I almost puked."

"The smell of puke would have been an improvement."

They laughed, and David said, "If you'd told me then, 'Someday we'll laugh about this,' I would have punched you."

"Someday?" Xander said. "That was *today*."

They smiled at each other, and Xander shook his head. He said, "Weirder and weirder."

"So," David said, "what got you looking in the box?"

"I don't know." Xander tipped the box upside down, spilling its contents between them. He picked up a rubber snake. "Remember when I scared you with this?"

"You put it between my sheets, down by my feet!" David said. "And woke me up by tickling my legs!"

"I was hiding under the bed," Xander said. "I almost broke my arm trying to reach up and get you. But it was worth it."

"I know, I know," David said. Xander had told him enough times. "I screamed like a little girl."

"That wasn't the best of it. You *kept* screaming . . . *shrieking!* In the shrieking department, you got Toria beat by a mile."

"Hey," David said, grinning, "you wake up with a snake slithering around your feet and see if *you* don't shriek."

Xander gave him a serious look. "I don't think you'd do that now."

"That was only a few months ago."

"I mean since everything that's happened," Xander said. "How could a measly little snake scare you now?"

David nodded. "After Berserkers, torturers . . . *Taksidian*? I'd pick up a real rattlesnake, toss it on the floor, and go back to sleep." He picked up a trophy. "Regional champs," he said. "Yeah, baby."

Xander pushed aside a few items and picked up a silver bracelet with thick links. "I thought I lost this." He turned it to show David an inscription on a flat arch of metal: *Danielle ♥ Xander.*

"Do you miss her?" David asked.

Xander nodded, rubbing his thumb over the inscription. "Seems like a different life."

"Yeah," David said. "You should wear it. You know, to remind you it wasn't always like this. Something to look forward to when all this ends."

"No," Xander said. He dropped it into the pile and selected something else. "This is what I want to wear." It was a strip of dark, frayed leather with fringes at either end.

"Another bracelet?" David said.

"Help me with this." He held his wrist up and David tied

it on. Xander turned it around. Burned into the leather was his name. Along its edges, a lighter shade of leather had been stitched in. "Mom made it for me."

David's heart skipped a beat. "She always makes stuff like that," he said. "Kind of hippie-ish."

Xander twisted his wrist, admiring the bracelet. "I don't know why I never wore it."

"It's like jewelry," David suggested.

"Sort of." Xander shrugged. "I guess."

"Oh . . ." David said, remembering something. He scanned the stuff on the floor, ran his fingers through it. He hopped up and ran to a stack of boxes. He looked inside the top one, moved it off, and searched the next one down. He spotted what he wanted and pulled it out. Sitting again, he slipped the necklace over his head. Tied to the center of a twisted leather cord was a thick metal cross. Along the crossbeam, engraved letters spelled out David's name.

"I remember that," Xander said. "Mom made it for you, and you refused to wear it."

"It made me feel like a priest," David said.

"Pretty cool priest."

David stared down at it. "I should have worn it," he said, a tinge of sadness slipping in. "I think I hurt her feelings."

Xander slapped David's knee. "She understood. She had fun making this stuff for us. I don't think she cared if we wore them."

"Well," David said. "I'm going to wear it now." He smiled up at Xander. "I'll have it on when we find her."

Xander raised his hand and David slapped it. Xander stared down at the bracelet, twisting his wrist back and forth. He looked at David, just gazed at him for the longest time.

"What?" David said.

"We have to find her."

David knew he meant *now*. He touched the cross pendant. Despite his exhaustion, despite his broken arm and other assorted aches, despite a morning of world hopping, he said, "Let's do it."

CHAPTER
twenty-five

Friday, 4:15 p.m.

David and Xander walked around the corner into the short second-floor hallway. Keal was on a stepladder, drilling a screw into the top of the wall at an angle. He glanced at them and said, "You boys here to help?"

Xander said, "Uh . . . no."

The way he said it made Keal stop and swivel around. "Want to go take a nap?"

That was exactly what David wanted to do, but he said, "We want to look through the portals." He rubbed the cross hanging over his chest. He noticed Xander turning the bracelet around his wrist.

"Uh-uh," Keal said, stepping off the ladder. "No way." He pulled his shoulders back as if preparing for a fight. "You've done enough for one day. You're tired and injured. Your dad's gone. Get that idea out of your heads and go to bed. I'll wake you when your dad and sister come home, if you want." He turned his back to them and climbed the ladder again, as though his words settled the issue.

"We just want to *look*," David said.

"No," Keal said without turning. He positioned a screw and lifted the electric driver.

"Keal," Xander said. "If we don't actually see her through a portal, we won't go over. Promise."

Keal lowered the tool. He turned and sighed. "What's this about?"

"We have to do something," Xander said. "It seems like we've been doing everything but looking . . . just looking. Taksidian said the portals pull at the people who don't belong in the worlds they're in. That means she may be *by* a portal. If we look through them, maybe we'll see her."

"We . . . we *miss* her," David said. His voice was weak, drowned in emotion. "Please."

Keal came off the ladder again. He set the drill down on

its top rung, then crossed his arms over his chest. "And if you don't see her?"

"We won't do anything," Xander said. "If we don't see her in two hours, we'll go take naps."

"We just have to do something," David said, repeating Xander's words.

"If you see Jesse's world?" Keal said.

"Jesse said we need to go back there," David said.

Xander grabbed his shoulder. "But we won't go over if we see it," Xander said. "This time."

Keal looked at each of them hard. He looked at his watch. "*One* hour," he said. "Come on." He stepped toward the wall's opening.

"You too?" David said, rushing up behind him.

"I'm not going to let you do this alone," Keal said. He led them through the space between the walls and through the next opening, and started up the stairs to the third floor. "If you see or hear anything unusual, yell, and we all run for the stairs, got it?"

Xander laughed. "Unusual? In this house?"

"You know what I mean."

In the third-floor hallway, Keal opened the first door. He gestured toward the antechamber with his head. "Let's go."

"What?" Xander said. "All of us?"

"Of course, Xander. Safety in numbers."

"Come on," Xander complained. "You're only giving us an

hour. Every time, we have to pick up three items to open the portal door. Then we have to look for her. I mean really look. That takes time. If we do each one together, we'll get through six or seven at the most. If we split up, we'll hit three times as many."

Keal frowned. He said, "Let's do this one together, and I'll think about splitting up."

Xander started to protest, but David stopped him. "It's better than nothing, Xander. You're wasting time."

"Go," Xander said, pushing David into the antechamber.

David scanned the items on the hooks and bench, none of which he'd seen before: a woven red shirt, a necklace of wood beads, a wooden mallet, sandals, a coin, and a roughly hewn walking stick. "Any idea what world these things belong to?"

"Could be anywhere," Xander said.

Keal leaned past them and picked up the coin. "Ancient Rome," he said, holding it up. It wasn't perfectly round. In the center was an engraving of a soldier riding in a chariot pulled by a team of horses. Under it, in a banner, was the word *Roma*.

"Not the Colosseum," Xander said. "That antechamber had a sword and shield."

"A helmet and chain mail," David added. He'd never forget Xander going over for the first time.

"Somewhere else, then," Keal said. "Rome had a vast empire that lasted centuries."

"So who's going to open the door?" David said. He wanted

to do this, to look for Mom, but Keal's attitude had spooked him. *I'm just tired,* he thought. *Not scared.*

Xander took the coin from Keal. He grabbed the necklace and mallet and stepped to the portal door.

"That didn't take so long," Keal said.

"It's not always that easy," Xander said. He opened the door. Hot wind blew in.

"Ugh," David said. "Smells like rotten eggs."

"*Burning* rotten eggs," Xander corrected.

As if to prove him right, black smoke billowed in. The portal itself appeared to be swirling smoke. It cleared, giving them a hazy, out-of-focus view of stone stairs leading down from the portal. The stairs ended at a narrow street paved with stones. It extended straight ahead of them. Single-story buildings lined the street. People, most of them dressed in tunics, ran toward them. Some darted through doorways, others reached the end of the street at the base of the stairs, turned, and disappeared out of sight.

In the far distance a mountain loomed over the town. Its top was on fire, spewing flames into the sky. A thick plume of smoke rose from it like an exploding atom bomb. A cloud of smoke rolled down the mountain toward the town, seeming to tumble.

"I think it's Pompeii," Keal said.

"That's Mount Vesuvius?" David said. "When it erupted and wiped out everything?"

"I think so," Keal said. "That smell is sulfur." He extended an arm past Xander and held his palm up to the portal. "Warm, but not hot," he said. "And I don't feel a pull, anything that would *force* you to go over."

"See?" Xander said. "We can do this alone."

"No Mom, right?" Keal said.

"I hope not," David said. How could they possibly jump into Pompeii right before it was consumed by a volcano's ashes? But then, if they saw Mom, how could they *not*? He hadn't considered that they could be faced with a choice like that. It didn't seem fair.

He imagined never coming back, and Dad, Xander, and Toria, knowing what had happened, visiting modern-day Pompeii. They would go to the museum that displayed plaster casts of Vesuvius's victims, who had been preserved in the hardened ash. They would stop at a mother embracing her son, and recognize the two of them. And they would cry.

David suddenly felt depressed. In this house such a scenario was not simply a nightmare or "the product of an overactive imagination"—as a teacher had once said about a story he'd written. It could really happen, probably *would* happen. He said, "Shut the door."

CHAPTER twenty-six

Friday, 4:22 p.m.

"I want to show you something first," Keal said, gripping Xander's shoulder to keep him in place in front of the Pompeii portal. "Listen up, guys. We're only *looking,* right? So when you open a portal door, here's what you do." He grabbed Xander's left hand and placed it on the edge of the open door, forcing his fingers to bend around it. "This is your safety grip," he said. "Even if the door swings shut, you keep holding on. Got it?"

Xander nodded.

Keal moved around to Xander's right side. Through the portal, a group of people ran toward the stairs. A churning black cloud of ashes rolled down the street and consumed them. Keal took Xander's other hand and pressed the palm firmly against the wall beside the portal. "Lock your elbow," Keal said.

Xander nodded.

Keal knelt. He took Xander's foot in his hands and brought it to the wall beside the portal, directly under Xander's hand. He angled it so the heel was on the floor and the toes bent upward on the wall.

"Okay," Keal said. "That's the stance." He rose and touched Xander's hand holding the edge of the door. He said, "One." He touched the other hand on the wall. "Two." Xander's foot. "Three. Say it."

"One . . . two . . . three," Xander said, wiggling each anchor point. His voice was crisp as a soldier's. He obviously liked Keal's militaristic approach.

"Good," Keal said. "Step back."

Xander backed away from the portal, and Keal said, "David, step up."

"I saw," David said. "One, two, three."

"Get up here."

David stepped close to the portal, trying not to see the boiling ash rushing into the buildings to find the people hiding in them. He slipped his arm out of the sling and positioned himself the way Keal had showed Xander.

"How's the arm?" Keal said.

"Feels good," David lied.

Keal turned a doubtful eye on him, and David was afraid Keal would punch his arm to see for himself just how it felt. But all Keal did was nod. He gripped David's shoulder and pulled him back away from the portal. He shut the door on Pompeii's destruction.

"So we'll split up?" Xander said.

"Here's how it's going to go," Keal said. "As you go into each antechamber, call out what the theme is."

"I can't always tell," David said.

"Guess," Keal told him. "Or say what the items are. Then, before you open the door, say, 'Opening door.' While you're at the portal, if you don't see your mother, call out, 'Nothing'—every fifteen seconds. Understand?"

The boys agreed.

"When you close the door, say, 'Door closed.' Loud enough for all of us to hear. All these things, every time. Right?"

"Right!" Xander snapped, grinning.

David's "Right" was quieter. He understood Xander's enthusiasm. Not only did he get his way, searching the portals alone, but he was doing it Dad's way as well: with caution and thoughtfulness. It was the kind of thing all of them had envisioned since setting up the MCC. The goal had always been to rescue Mom without someone else disappearing or getting seriously hurt. That meant doing it like a military operation, but their knowledge of the military came from movies like *Black Hawk Down* and *Saving Private Ryan.* Not quite the same, regardless of what Xander said. Leave it to Keal, former Army Ranger, to bring their plan together.

Even so, something bothered David. If he'd learned anything about the house, it was that nothing here was predictable. It seemed to *know* what you believed about it and then did things completely differently. Strategy and discipline were no match for chaos and confusion.

"Okay," Keal said, slapping his hands together. "You boys take the doors on this side of the hall. I'll take the other." He checked his watch. "Fifty-two minutes."

Xander dropped the coin, necklace, and mallet on the bench, and the three of them left the antechamber. Keal crossed the hall, opened the door, and stepped inside. He called, "Something to do with trees, a forest."

"If it's a jungle," David said, "watch out for tigers . . . and warriors with bows and arrows." A chill slid down his spine like a drop of ice water. "Wait a minute," he said. "Keal!"

Xander stopped at the next door on David's side of the hallway, and Keal came out of the antechamber. David said, "Other people can see the portals. It's not like we have magic eyes or something. And we can see into the antechambers from the other side."

"Yeah, but people don't always notice," Xander said. "When you thought you saw Mom in the World War II world, people were rushing by and not even noticing you. We see it because we're looking for it, and know what it looks like."

"I think it looks like heat vapors to them," David said. "Or something they don't notice unless they're looking right at it."

"Even if they can see it and us," Xander said, "so what?"

Keal answered. "So, they can send things through—at us. Remember that spear that followed you through from the Viking world?"

"It ended up in the antechamber, stuck in the hallway door," David said.

"Until it got sucked back," Xander added. "And the spear-head melted to go under the door."

"Point is," Keal said, "we can get killed just *looking* into a portal, without going through it."

"What are you saying?" Xander said, his voice rising into a whine. "We can't even look? How are we supposed to find Mom? Looking is still a lot safer than going through."

Keal rubbed his chin, thinking. He said, "Extra caution. Watch for people who see you. Shut the door if they do."

"Got it," Xander said.

Keal returned to the forest-themed antechamber. David frowned at Xander, who said, "It *is* dangerous, Dae. All of this is. But it's either face it or forget Mom."

David nodded. "You're right. I'm okay."

Xander opened the door. Before he left, David said, "Xander . . . be careful."

"You too." A few seconds later, he was inside the small room, calling out, "Uh . . . an amusement park?"

David went to the next antechamber and went in. He looked at the items and let out a long breath. He yelled, "Knives and swords . . . a bloody shirt."

CHAPTER

twenty-seven

FRIDAY, 5:08 P.M.

So far, David had seen a total of seven people in two worlds. The first four were a family enjoying a picnic in a grassy meadow. The mother wasn't Mom, but the scene had made him miss her even more. A little girl had spotted him and pointed. He shut the door before the others turned.

Next, he had witnessed a duel. Two men stood back-to-back, flintlock pistols raised in front of them. Another man started counting, and the duelists walked away from each other. At *ten* they turned. One man fired immediately, a great plume of smoke coming from his weapon and drifting off. The other duelist took his time, aiming carefully, using both hands to steady the pistol. His target didn't move, resigned to whatever happened. As David shut the door, a shot rang out.

Most of the portals opened onto pretty much nothing: an empty cobblestone street, a vast expanse of sand baking under a blinding sun, a beach, a woodsy area behind a log cabin.

He stepped into the hallway and saw Keal approaching another door. "You okay?" Keal asked.

"Not seeing very many people," David said.

"I got a few crowds," Keal said.

"You do know what she looks like, don't you?"

Keal grinned. "I've studied her pictures."

David bet he had. He suspected Keal had been trained to identify faces. Keal had never said what he'd done in the Rangers, but David imagined him as a sniper. Those guys needed to recognize a target in a split second, probably by memorizing eye shape, nose type, jaw lines. Keal could probably point out Mom in a crowd as quickly and surely as David could.

Keal raised his watch and called, "Eleven minutes!"

"Let's get two more each!" Xander yelled.

Keal winked at David. "You heard the man." He vanished into an antechamber.

David stopped at Xander's open door. His brother was standing in front of the portal, hands and foot positioned as Keal had instructed. He had a stovepipe hat balanced on top of his shaggy hair, a white scarf draped over one shoulder.

"Nothing," Xander yelled.

Listening for that word from Xander and Keal had become almost subconscious for David. He didn't realize he was doing it, but between *Opening door* and *Door closed,* if one of them missed saying *Nothing,* David noticed. At first he'd thought it was stupid; now he saw that it was a great way to keep track of each other. If one of them accidentally went over, help was no more than fifteen or twenty seconds behind.

We may get this down after all, he thought. An organized rescue party. He liked that.

He went to the next door on the left and went in. He cringed at one of the items hanging on a hook: a shrunken head. Not much bigger than an apple, the face was perfectly preserved, if a bit distorted. Eyes closed. Pursed lips. Squashed nose. Long black hair came out of the scalp and looped around the hook.

I hope that's fake, he thought, but he knew better.

The other items were a stone knife, a coil of twine, a bracelet made of unidentifiable hairy objects, and a stained blanket. Leaning against the wall, rising up from the bench, was what appeared to be a long wooden drinking straw. So he could keep his hands free to brace himself, David chose the items he could shove into his pockets: knife, twine, and hairy bracelet, which felt the way it looked, prickly and a bit oily. He said, "*Eeeww*," as Toria would say. Then: "Opening door!"

The portal swirled with greens and browns. A wet, woodsy fragrance drifted in, then the smell of burning wood. The swirling faded, first becoming mostly transparent, then disappearing altogether. The blurry landscape before him cleared, and he was looking through trees into a clearing. A half dozen men crouched around a raging fire. They were dressed in loincloths and necklaces with dangling sticklike things—*Bones?* David wondered. The bottom half of each man's face was painted bright red. They seemed only to be talking to one another, but their appearance alone scared David spitless.

He saw more of the long drinking straws. A man held one, resting it on the ground like a king with his scepter. Another was lashed to a different man's back. David suspected they were weapons, maybe bows. That made him think that these people were primitive warriors. If they were half as fierce as they looked, he felt sorry for whoever met them in battle.

Remembering the signal, he said, "Nothing." It came out barely a whisper. He didn't think sounds penetrated the portals from the antechambers. Xander had spoken to him when he'd gone into the jungle world—his first time over—but his brother's lips had moved without any words reaching David's ears. But he didn't exactly want to take a chance.

I'd rather get a berserker's attention, David thought. *Well . . . maybe.*

He turned to yell over his shoulder. "N—"

"Door closed!" Xander yelled.

David tried again: "Nothing!"

He turned back to the portal and jumped at a blur of movement directly in front of him. A warrior had leaped into view from the side, wild-eyed and screaming.

CHAPTER

twenty-eight

FRIDAY, 5:12 P.M.

The warrior's high-pitched voice reached David as if through a pillow. He glared at David as though at the most hideous thing he had ever seen. His red-painted jaw snapped shut, and opened again, drawing David's eye to a mouthful of tiny, pointed teeth.

Before David could leap away and slam the door, a hand shot through the portal and grabbed his right wrist.

"Aaaaahhhhh!" David screeched. He yanked on his arm, but the warrior's hand was like a vise. The man's skin was brown and leathery. His fingernails were black and sharp.

David's hand slipped off the wall and went into the portal, pulled in by the crazy man. The muscles in his legs strained to keep him in the antechamber. He squeezed his fingers around the edge of the door, but his broken arm throbbed and felt ready to pull apart, mid-forearm. He had no strength in that arm, and his fingers began slipping off the door.

"Heeeeelp!"

On the other side of the portal, the warrior held David's wrist in both hands, tugging. He twisted his shoulders and bounced up and down to pull David through. Beyond the man, past the trees, the other warriors had sprung up, pointing and shifting their heads to figure out what was happening. They started for him.

"David!" Xander yelled behind him. David felt his brother's arms wrap around his torso. Xander heaved back, pulling David with him. His hand returned to the antechamber, encircled by the warrior's hands.

The warrior tugged, reclaiming David's hand and wrist. Xander's arms slipped higher, over David's chest. The tug-of-war over David's upper body caused his leg to slip out from under him. It swung forward like a pendulum—right through the portal.

The warrior released his grip on David's wrist and seized hold of his ankle.

David's leg went farther into the other world, and he could no longer keep his foot pressed against the wall. His foot swiveled, then slipped off the wall and through the portal. The man grabbed that leg as well. Now he had both of David's ankles in his hands.

Both boys fell, Xander to the floor, David on top of him. David went farther into the portal. He looked down over his body and saw that everything below his waist was in the warrior's world. His blue-jeaned legs appeared a few degrees out of alignment with the rest of his body, and a little blurry, as though they were under the surface of a clear lake.

Beyond his knees and feet, the man's eyes rolled insanely. His teeth flashed as his mouth opened and closed, opened and closed, like a snapping dog's.

"I can't help you like this!" Xander yelled from under him. He shifted and pushed himself out from under David, keeping one arm over David's chest. He got to his knees at David's shoulder and grabbed David's arm—right at the break.

David let out a howl of pain.

Xander shifted his grip to David's bicep.

Something sailed over David's face and made a thunking sound in the wall behind him. He looked through the portal to see the other warriors in the forest now. One raised a wooden straw. He put one end to his mouth and pointed the other end at the brothers.

A blowgun!

"Xander!" David screamed. "They're shooting at us!"

"What?" Xander said and looked.

As if by magic, a knitting-needle-sized dart appeared in Xander's chest—up high by his shoulder. He cried out, but he did not release his hold on David's arm. He gaped at the thing protruding from his chest.

"Xander!" David said. He felt his brother's grip loosen.

"I . . . don't feel . . . so good." Xander fell forward, on top of David's arm. But he was still moving. His hand found David's chin and pushed. He was continuing his fight, trying to keep the man from taking David.

Two more warriors rushed up to the portal. Their arms came into the antechamber, grabbing for Xander. One of them got a grip on his hair and pulled. Xander slid toward the other world.

"No . . . !" David yelled.

A big foot stomped down next to him. Keal leaned over Xander, held the barrel of a pistol inches from the arm holding Xander's hair, and fired. The sound sent clattering bells through David's brain. And that was all right, for it had freed his brother. Keal pulled him into the middle of the antechamber.

The man holding David's leg pulled. He went through—

stopping only when he snagged his arm against the doorjamb. Everything below his chest was in the other world. The portal itself messed with his insides. His stomach rolled, seeming to tighten and loosen, fast as a hummingbird's heart. He gagged, feeling the contents of his stomach start to come up.

A shocking, blinding flash of pain kept him from puking. He raised his head. The man was *biting* his leg. It dawned on him: these weren't just warriors, they were *cannibals.*

Keal lowered his knee onto David's chest, pinning him down and blocking his view. He pointed the pistol.

"Keal, no!" David said, pushing the words through clenched teeth. He wanted Keal to shoot, but at the same time he *didn't* want that. David had intruded into the cannibals' world; as bad as the situation was, somehow it didn't seem fair to just *kill* them.

The gun roared again, and David thrashed his legs. Pain still shot up from the bite wound, but he was free! Keal grabbed his waistband, rose, and half pulled, half tossed David back into the antechamber.

The gun spoke again: *Bam!*

Then Keal backed away from the portal and slammed the door.

CHAPTER

twenty-nine

FRIDAY, 5:15 P.M.

David sat up and grabbed his leg. Blood had seeped through his jeans in two semicircles on either side of his shinbone. Little bite holes showed themselves like tiny mouths, opening and closing as he moved. Somehow worse—grosser—was the slime between and around the bite marks. Saliva.

Cannibals, he thought, sure he was right. He hoped he didn't get an infection. Who knew what kind of diseases those—

Then he remembered, and turned to find Xander.

His brother was lying on his stomach, his legs and arms barely moving. He was gasping for breath.

"Xander!" David yelled. "Keal, Xander's hurt, hurt bad!"

Keal knelt beside Xander and rolled him over. "Xander?" he said. He shook his shoulders.

Xander tried to lift his head. It clunked back to the floor. "Can't . . . breathe . . ."

"The dart!" David said, pointing. It had collapsed flat against Xander's chest by his fall to the floor.

Keal plucked it out and examined the tip. David could see blood, but it didn't seem to have gone in very far.

"Is it poison?" David asked.

Keal nodded. "Probably curare." He leaned over Xander and placed his palms low on his chest. He pushed down, relaxed, pushed again. Air rushed out of Xander's mouth with each push.

"Better?" Keal asked.

Xander wheezed. "Y-yeah." He gasped.

Keal continued pushing, relaxing, pushing.

David scooted along the floor to his brother's side. "Is it his heart?" he said.

"His lungs," Keal answered. "Or actually, the muscles that work the lungs. Curare is a fast-acting poison. It relaxes the muscles to the point that you can't breathe. If we don't get an antidote in him fast . . ." He closed his mouth and appeared to concentrate on working Xander's lungs for him.

"What?" David said. "What will happen if he doesn't get the antidote? Keal!"

"He'll suffocate," Keal said. "All right? He'll suffocate."

Xander gasped. His face rolled toward David. His lids were droopy, but David saw the fear in his eyes.

David reached out and squeezed his hand. "You'll be okay, Xander. We'll take care of you. Right, Keal? We can get him to the hospital in time. Tell me we can!"

"Yeah," Keal said. "We can do that." *Push, relax, push.* "We gotta move him, though, and keep helping him breathe."

"I can do it," David said. "You pull him, I'll make sure he breathes."

"Can't . . ." Xander gasped. "Can't . . . feel . . . my . . . legs . . . arms."

"The poison is paralyzing your muscles," Keal explained. "It's not permanent, Xander. Don't worry. When the poison wears off or gets neutralized by an antidote, everything will return to normal. We just have to keep you breathing in the meantime."

Xander gasped, gasped . . . helped by Keal's pushing. It was the worst thing David had ever seen. He moaned, dropped his head, and began sobbing.

"David!" Keal said. "Not now! Get ahold of yourself. Now! Xander needs you."

David's crying hitched to a jerky stop like an eighteen-wheeler slamming on its brakes. He pushed the tears away, saying, "What do I do?"

"See what I'm doing?" Keal said. "Down, up. Time it with your own breathing. Relax when you inhale, push when you exhale."

"I can do that."

"But not too hard. You'll get a feel for it when—"

Wind blew in from under the door. It swirled around them. The dart Keal had tossed aside zipped along the floor and through the gap. David spotted another dart sticking in the wall beside the hallway door—the one he had seen flash past his face. It vibrated, popped out of the wall, spun in the wind, and disappeared under the door.

He felt his pant leg flapping around. He watched the cannibal's spit come off his jeans, form into tiny beads in the air, and fly away.

Xander pulled in a breath, deep and full, like a man breaking the surface after too long underwater. He exhaled, sucked in more air.

Keal's hands were off his chest. They trembled as the big man watched Xander breathing on his own.

"What's happening?" David said.

"Look," Keal said.

The wind stopped.

Xander blinked and looked from Keal to David. He was breathing normally. He sat up and placed a palm over his chest. He inhaled deeply and let it out, almost as though he were making sure he could.

He smiled. "I feel great," he said. "I'm fine." He hopped up and held his arms out in a look-at-me posture.

They did, and David laughed. "The wind . . . *Time* . . ." David said. "It took the poison back to where it belongs, like it does everything else. It pulled it right out of your body!"

"I . . . I don't believe it," Keal stammered. "I mean, I do. I saw it with my own eyes. And of course, I know you're right, David. It's what Time does, takes back what doesn't belong here." He stopped, seeming to realize he was rambling. Then he added what David felt: "Ha!"

"Well," Xander said, sitting on the bench. "That was a little scary."

"A *little*?" David said.

"You're really fine?" Keal said. "No aftereffects? No achiness, shortness of breath?"

"Achiness, yeah," Xander said. "But nothing I didn't feel before *getting shot with a poison dart*." He said it the way he might have said, *The man jumped over the building*: it was the most amazing thing, and no one would ever believe him. He rubbed his chest where the dart had struck him. "This hurts a little," he said. "But I'm not complaining."

Keal shook his head. "What just happened is impossible in the medical world—to get every atom of poison out of your blood and muscles."

"Nothing's impossible here," David said.

"There you go," Keal said. "You remember that about rescuing your mom."

"I never thought that was impossible," David said.

"Hey," Xander said, staring down at David's leg. "What happened?"

"That cannibal guy!" David said. "He tried to eat my leg like corn on the cob!"

"Ow. You all right?"

"Hurts," David said. "I was starting to feel sorry for myself. You know, like, when am I *not* going to get hurt? Then I remembered you getting that dart in your chest and falling over. I forgot all about this little thing." He shrugged and waved a hand over his bloody pants. But it *did* throb. He wished Time could take away wounds the way it had the poison. Guess that was asking too much.

CHAPTER

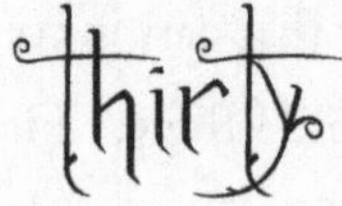

FRIDAY, 5:26 P.M.

The wind returned. It blew in under the door in a single gust and went out again, as though Time had sighed. Three objects clattered to the floor. David leaned over and picked one up. "A piece of metal. Almost flat." He handed it to Keal.

Keal smiled. "A slug . . . one of the bullets I fired at those . . . guys."

"*Cannibals,*" David said, like spitting out something disgusting.

Keal nodded. "Well, these bullets don't belong there anymore than the poison belonged here." He reached behind him and produced the pistol.

David recognized it as a semiautomatic, an army gun. He used to have a miniature one like it for his G.I. Joes. "Where'd you get that?" he said.

"One of the antechambers," Keal said. "I was looking through a portal at a modern battle—Korean War, I think—when you yelled."

"Keep it," Xander said.

"Wish I could. Soon enough, the antechamber's going to want it back. Those slugs, too, I bet. I'll put them back before they hurt someone trying to get there."

"Did you . . ." David gazed at the portal door. "Did you *kill* them?"

Keal grinned and shook his head. "David, you're the only person I know who *wouldn't* want to kill the people trying to kill him."

"Did you?"

"Not unless I scared them to death," Keal said. "I shot them in their arms. No sense killing if you don't have to." He made his facial muscles hard. "But if that hadn't worked, I would have."

David nodded.

"And for the record," Keal said, checking his watch, "time's up."

"But," Xander said, "just for today, right? We *have* to do this, look through the portals . . . for Mom."

"You're kidding," Keal said.

"Keal, we have to." Xander stood. "The only reason we're still in the house is Mom. We're here to look for her, to rescue her." He thrust a hand at the portal door. "This is how it's done. Look through or go over. If we can find her looking through, I'd rather do that. But at least *that*."

Keal dropped his head. He appeared to be examining the gun. He looked up at Xander. "I know you're right. I just don't like it." He turned to David. "What happened, son? Can we learn from this? Something we should be doing differently?"

David frowned. "I should have been paying better attention," he said. "I turned away to say *Nothing*, then . . . *bang!* That guy was all over me."

"Okay," Keal said, standing. "I'll talk to your father. Maybe we can come up with a way of making it safer." He held out his hand to help David up.

When David put his weight on the leg, it felt like the guy was still biting it, and he almost fell.

Keal grabbed him. "That bad?"

"I guess so," David said. He balanced on his good leg and gently tested the other one. The pain was less severe now that he was expecting it. "I can walk," he said, and made it to the hall door on his own.

"A broken arm and a bad leg," Xander said. "You're running out of appendages."

"Tell me about it." He opened the door and limped into the third-floor hallway. The others followed.

"Hold on," Keal said. "I gotta put this gun and these slugs in the antechamber." He walked toward the back of the hallway.

"Then what?" David said.

Keal went into the room and returned. "Then I patch up your leg, and the two of you are going to bed."

"Finally," David said. He looked at Xander, expecting a fight.

His brother said, "I'm ready."

"What about you?" David asked Keal.

"We don't need the Sleep Police today," Xander said, reminding them of when Keal sat in the hallway outside their bedroom to make sure they slept.

"I was going to work on those walls at the bottom of the stairs," Keal said, "but if you're going to be sleeping, I can find something else to do."

"Work on the wall," David said. "I could sleep through World War III."

"Me too," Xander said. "Maybe that poison did have an aftereffect. Or being crazy-scared you're going to die is exhausting. Whatever it is, I'm beat."

At the landing, David looked back at the crooked corridor. It may have looked like an old-fashioned hotel—ten doors on each side, a carpeted runner covering the hardwood floor, wainscoting and wallpaper and wall lights—but it was as far as anything could get from the normal world of hotels. *These* doors opened into all of history, every tragic event and atrocity this poor world has ever seen. He'd lost blood and tears up here, and something a million times more important . . .

"Wish we'd found Mom," he said.

Xander put his arm around David's shoulders. "Me too, Dae," he said. "Tomorrow's another day."

CHAPTER

thirty-one

Friday, 5:59 p.m.

"Keal stitched you up?" Xander said. "You mean, literally? Needle and thread through your skin?"

"Three stitches," David confirmed. They were lying on their beds, both of them staring at the ceiling, waiting for their minds to realize it was time to shut down. Xander had untied the sheers to let them fall over the windows again, but the room was still bright. But the light wouldn't keep David from sleeping. He felt like a Pony Express horse that'd just run back-to-back shifts.

Xander had gone to bed ahead of him, while Keal tended to David's gnawed-on leg.

"Let me see," Xander said, flipping his covers aside.

"I'm tired," David said. "Go to sleep."

Xander stood and pushed the covers away from David's leg. "Oh, man," he said, sitting on the edge of the bed. "That guy really bit you."

"What'd you think, that he licked me? I told you, corn on the cob."

Xander touch a stitch. David sucked in a breath and pulled his leg away.

"Sorry," Xander said. "How many teeth marks is that?"

"Eleven," David said. "Keal said only three were bad enough to need a stitch."

"And he did it himself?"

"Who else?" He could tell his exhaustion was making him grumpy. "Dad said a long time ago, parents would stitch up their kids all the time. Besides, Keal's a nurse."

"Still," Xander said. He flipped the cover back over David's leg and returned to his own bed. "Does it hurt?"

"It throbs," David said.

"You really think they were cannibals?" Xander said.

"I don't want to think about it." He already had, and imagining what would have happened to them if the cannibals had pulled him and Xander into their world had turned his stomach.

Xander was quiet for a minute. Then he said, "No school tomorrow."

David laughed. "I finally get how you feel about having to go. Finding Mom is a full-time job."

"Tell Dad."

"Yeah, right," David said. His tongue was feeling thick, his brain sluggish. He rolled onto his stomach and nestled his face into the pillow.

"I mean it," Xander said. "If we whine enough . . ."

That's all David heard. He startled awake to find himself no longer in bed. Instead he was lying on a long silver platter, surrounded by potatoes, carrots, and tiny tomatoes. The platter was at the center of a big table, around which sat cannibals. They were dressed in tuxedos and top hats, with plastic bibs tied around their necks—the kind seafood restaurants used, but instead of a picture of a lobster on them, there was a picture of David. The bottom half of their faces were painted red, and their tongues made sick, sloppy noises as they slid over their lips. Each held a fork and knife. One leaned toward him and jabbed a fork into David's leg.

That's when he startled awake for real. Sunshine still filled the room. His leg hurt, and Xander was snoring. He groaned, stuck his head under the pillow, and went back to sleep.

CHAPTER

thirty-two

Friday, 6:50 p.m.

Keal examined the two walls at the base of the third-floor stairs. He walked between them and eyed the reinforcing joists he'd mounted to the ceiling, running from one wall to the other. He slammed his shoulder into each wall. They didn't so much as creak.

He nodded with satisfaction.

He still had to install the doors. They would be the weak

points, so he intended to spend extra time on them and use industrial hardware to make sure they were as sturdy as the walls. But he wouldn't do it today, not with the boys finally getting some sleep. Didn't matter what they said. No one could sleep through pounding and drilling, especially in a house where every noise could mean approaching danger.

He walked to the doorway of the MCC and looked in. A history timeline ran the length of two walls, near the ceiling. He saw a few points the Kings could tag as places—*times*—they'd been: World War II about 1943; on the *Titanic* in 1912; the Civil War in 1862; the Roman Colosseum, circa 80; Hannibal's march over the Alps in 218 BC. He had no idea when some of their other adventures had taken place—Atlantis, the torture chamber, David's jungle jaunt, for example.

The walls were covered with white boards and corkboards and maps and movie posters—tough-guy posters like *Gladiator, 300,* and *Commando.* Keal liked it, all of it. This family of schoolkids and a principal had done an admirable job of getting ready for war. Getting ready? They'd gone to war . . . and survived.

He moved down the hall and into the second floor's main corridor. He stopped at the railing that overlooked the first-floor foyer and front door. The window next to the door was shattered. In any other house, it might have been a baseball that had crashed through it. Not in this house. No, it had been a dagger—one that seemed to have a mind of its own.

He continued down the hall. The back of a wooden chair was wedged under the linen closet's door handle, where it belonged. *Until I can put a dead bolt on the door,* he thought. So much to do.

He reached the boys' room and eased the door open. Someone was snoring. He entered and walked between the two beds. Xander, he was the snorer. The boy's mouth was wide open. His hair splayed out against the pillow like brown fire.

He turned to David, who was facedown, pillow over his head. Keal's heart ached for the child's injuries. Too much pain. It was bad enough that he'd lost his mother. To couple that grief with physical agony just seemed like . . . Keal didn't know what. Torture? Cruelty?

Keal believed everything happened for a purpose. He wondered what God had in mind for these young men. What kind of men was he forging in the fire of this house? In only a few days, Keal had already seen Xander become more compassionate, more outwardly loving and protective of his family, especially his brother.

And David—this kid had changed big-time. He was braver, more decisive. The boy had told him about the way his classmates had teased him about his name: David King . . . King David. Dae hadn't liked it, but Keal wasn't so sure the comparison was all that far off. If this house wasn't David's Goliath, then maybe Keal didn't understand the biblical story.

The first King David had become a great man, and Keal had good feelings about this one.

He shook his head. He remembered yesterday pondering how and why he had come to care so much for this family. He'd chalked it up to shared experiences and that their goodness was obvious, but he thought it might go beyond that. He didn't usually think this way, but being here felt like destiny. He was *meant* to be here. And the character of each of the Kings was what kept him here. If they weren't who they were, what they were, he wouldn't have stayed past that first night, when Jesse had brought him here. No way. Life was too short to spend it with bad people.

He managed to make it back to the door without waking the boys up. No easy task considering the obstacle course they had made in their room: boxes everywhere and a pile of stuff—trophies and knickknacks—in the middle of the floor.

He gently closed the door, and something banged overhead—upstairs, on the third floor.

Already?

He considered opening the boys' door again, rousting them and getting everybody out of the house. No, not until he knew what they were facing. Xander and David needed rest, and this house made all sorts of noises that didn't mean anything, like a giant mumbling in its sleep.

He strode to the end of the hallway and turned toward the false walls and the stairs to the third floor. As he passed the stepladder, he grabbed his hammer. He stopped, went to a box of tools and pulled out a big screwdriver. He shoved it into his back pocket. At the base of the stairs he heard another bang. He waited to see if someone appeared on the top landing. When no one did, he went up slowly, silently.

At the top step, he leaned and looked down the hallway. No one. He stepped up to the landing and stood in the entryway between it and the hall. There were no windows up here, so without the lights, it would be dark. Even with the lights, the far end of the hall was cloaked in shadows. That's how he could see the light coming from one of the last antechambers. It wasn't filling the hall—the door wasn't open—but sliding out from under the door. Something stirred shadows through the light, so it appeared to swirl and dance on the floor.

He wasn't about to march down there and open the door. Who knew what monstrosities he'd encounter? And too close for a smooth getaway. No, he could wait. This way, when he—or they—came out of the antechamber, he'd have some time to assess the danger, to figure out whether to fight or run.

But why would someone come through a portal and hang out in the antechamber? He wondered if that's the way Phemus met with Taksidian for instructions. Phemus would come over and wait for Taksidian to show up. If so, then maybe Taksidian was coming too.

Keal backed into the corner of the landing, a place where

he could see the hallway and the stairs leading to it. He tapped the hammer against his leg and willed his heart to slow.

Okay, he thought, watching the antechamber light play against the floor and carpeted runner. *Come on out, you butt-ugly ogre. Bring it on!*

CHAPTER

thirty-three

FRIDAY, 7:35 P.M.

Nothing happened. No butt-ugly ogre. No action at all, just the light—broken by moving shadows—slicing out from under the antechamber door. Then, as Keal watched, it went out. The portal door inside must have closed. He walked slowly to the antechamber and listened at the door. More nothing. Raising the hammer over his head, he pulled it open: empty.

The items inside didn't offer any clues to who had been there or why: a white medical smock, a stethoscope, other doctor-related items. He shut the door and began pacing the hallway.

What if this sort of thing was part of Taksidian's plan? Psychological warfare. Make your opponents jumpy and paranoid. It caused them to lose sleep and expend energy on false alarms. *This maybe-something's-coming-maybe-not* incident he had just experienced was not the first of its kind he'd heard about or witnessed: stomping around on the third floor while the kids were trying to sleep . . . someone in the linen closet, rattling the handle . . . using Mom's voice, recorded on Wuzzy, to lure Toria to the third floor. No wonder the family was always exhausted and nervous. They'd been terrorized—both by real threats and fake ones.

Realizing this only reinforced Keal's admiration for the Kings. *These guys are tough,* he thought. *I can learn at least as much from them as they can from me.*

He returned to the second floor, listening for any noises coming from the antechambers. Then he roamed the house, checking doors and windows. He ventured into the basement. The little room in which David had been stuck was firmly boarded up, no signs of any attempts to break through.

He was climbing the basement stairs when he heard footsteps: stomping on the front porch. He stopped to listen. The door's handle rattled and its hinges squeaked as it opened.

Tension tightened his muscles as Keal prepared to bolt up the remaining stairs.

"Anyone home?" Ed King called. "Keal! Xander! David!"

Keal relaxed.

Toria called, "Guys! We got news!"

"Down here!" Keal said. He ascended to the first floor and stepped into the hallway between the foyer and kitchen. Dad—Keal had heard Ed called that so many times, that was how he was starting to think of the man as well—was examining the broken window. Keal moved toward him.

Toria was halfway up the grand staircase. She smiled at him and opened her mouth to say something, but he held his fingers over his lips.

"Shhh." He whispered, "The boys are sleeping."

Toria's face reflected her disappointment. "But we have news," she said.

Keal cast a suspicious eye on her. "*Good* news?"

Grinning, she said, "We know where Phemus comes from."

"Uh . . ." Keal said, scrunching his face, "Atlantis?"

Toria's face dropped. "Huh? How do *you* know?"

"Your brothers," Keal said. "They went there."

Dad grabbed his arm. "What? To Atlantis? How? When? Wait, wait." He closed his eyes and pinched the bridge of his nose. "Just tell me, they're all right?"

"They're fine," Keal said.

"Does that have anything to do with Atlantis?" Dad said, pointing at the window.

"Sort of," Keal answered. "It's a long story."

"Okay," Dad said. "I want to hear everything." He stooped

to pick up two flat boxes off the floor, next to the satchel he had used to take Wuzzy to UCLA. "Picked up some pizza," he said. "How about telling us over dinner?" He headed for the dining room.

"We better eat slowly," Keal said, following the glorious aroma of baked dough, hot cheese, pepperoni, and grease.

••••••••

Toria remained disappointed that Xander and David had been to Atlantis and had found out firsthand what she and Dad had learned from a computer program.

Hoping to cheer her up, Keal said, "Hey, I got something you can play with."

She brightened. "What?"

"Hold on." He went into the kitchen and returned with the phones he'd purchased at Walmart. He handed her one. "It has games," he said. "I made sure."

"Does it have a camera?" she said.

"You bet."

She left her plate of crusts—"pizza bones," she called them—and sat in the corner to fiddle with the phone.

Keal set another phone on the table and slid it over to Dad on the other side. "Charged and ready to go."

Dad scowled at it. Keal knew he wasn't happy about his boys' putting themselves in more danger.

"What possessed them to follow Phemus?" he asked.

"They love their mom," Keal said.

"And I love my wife. But I'm not putting my head on a chopping block." He dropped a pizza bone on his plate and pushed it away.

Keal selected another piece—just one more—and bit off the tip.

"Atlantis," Dad said, "and the Civil War, the Alps, and some torture chamber?"

Keal nodded. "And that brush with the cannibals, but they didn't actually *go* there."

Dad rubbed his eyebrows. "I can't even keep it all in my head."

"Imagine how they feel. That's why I think they'll sleep till morning, if we let them."

"Of course," Dad said. "And how did you wind up with Taksidian's dagger?"

Keal told him about following the boys through the antechamber, but winding up not in Atlantis but a prehistoric cave. Then how he returned by grabbing hold of Taksidian's feet, and the fight that came afterward. He continued talking until he'd said it all.

Dad shook his head. "It never ends," he said. "Everything seems to be happening faster, getting more dangerous . . . if that's even possible."

Keal grabbed his arm. "It is possible. But you know

something? We're learning, getting smarter. We can do this. We can beat Taksidian—and this house."

"I hope you're right," Dad said, not sounding very sure. He watched Toria play with the phone. "I hope you're right."

CHAPTER

thirty-four

Saturday, 8:47 a.m.

David rolled over in bed and realized he had to go to the bathroom. He pushed the bedcovers off and blinked against the sunlight.

Sunlight? Still?

He turned to see the clock on the nightstand. Almost nine. What time did it get dark? It felt like he'd slept longer than that. Xander snorted in air and whistled it out. He had kicked off his covers and sheet, but he didn't seem to mind.

David closed his eyes again and felt himself drifting back under. He forced himself to sit and swing his legs over the edge of the bed. He didn't want the call of the bathroom to wake him in the middle of the night. That would be worse.

He stood, got a shot of pain from his leg, and sat down again. He'd forgotten about that. He rose again, careful to make his left leg carry most of his weight. He stretched. Felt pretty good, actually. Refreshed. Amazing what a couple hours of shut-eye could do. He'd feel like a new kid by morning.

He picked Xander's blanket off the floor and spread it out over him. Xander snorted again, scratched his armpit, and rolled over.

David stumbled for the door. He kicked a soccer trophy and stepped on a Matchbox car. He opened the door to the smell of bacon. Keal must have made bacon, lettuce, and tomato sandwiches for dinner. He rubbed his stomach. He was hungry, but he didn't want to eat now. Sleep first, eat later.

As he crossed the hall to the bathroom, Toria walked out of her room, heading for the grand staircase. "Hey," he said.

She stopped, then ran to him, giving him a big hug.

"When'd you get home?" he said.

"Last night, silly."

"Last night?"

"Want breakfast?" she said, stepping back from him. "I made bacon and eggs."

"Breakfast? What *time* is it?"

"Eight thirty, something like that."

"At night? Friday night?"

"Saturday morning." She laughed. "Boy, you're out of it. Keal said you went to bed at six yesterday. You slept all evening and right through the night."

He rubbed his face. "Oh, man . . ." He felt her little fist strike his stomach. "Ow, hey!"

"Keal told us you and Xander went to Atlantis! I wanted to surprise you that Phemus is from there."

"What? How do you know?"

"Wuzzy," she said, obviously proud of her teddy bear. "Dad's friend listened to Phemus's voice on Wuzzy's recorder. He put it in a computer, and the computer said it was last spoken in Atlantis. Bet you don't know what he said."

"Who, Dad's friend?"

"Phemus!"

"What? What he said to you the night he . . ." He didn't want to say *the night he took Mom*. It would bring Toria down. "The night he woke you up?"

Trying to make her voice deep, she said, "Have you come to play?"

"That's what he said? Have you come to *play*?"

"Mr. Peterson said the Atlantians liked war and they played mean games that made the kids ready to fight. He said it wasn't a place you'd ever want to go to play."

David thought about the kids beating on each other, going

for blood. They were the same kids who'd cornered him and tried to kill him. "Yeah," he said, "that's the way it is. I gotta go to the bathroom."

"Wait, wait!" She ran back to her room.

David went into the bathroom. He was shutting the door when she returned.

"David!"

"What?"

She held up a mobile phone and took his picture. She looked at the screen and laughed.

"What was that for?"

"Your *hair!*"

He shut the door on her giggles.

••••••••

David sat down on Xander's bed. He gave his brother a push. Xander groaned and rolled over, and continued snoring. David shook him.

"Whatta you want?" Xander mumbled.

"It's time to get up," he said. "It's morning."

Xander popped his head up. "It is?"

"Nine o'clock. Want to see if Dad'll let us look for Mom?"

"You want to look through the portals?" Xander blinked at him. "After what happened yesterday?"

"Like you said, that's why we're here." David shifted. "But Young Jesse's world too. I want to go if we find it."

Xander nodded. "We promised him." He dropped his head back onto his pillow and groaned again. "Okay, okay," he said. He sprang up and hopped to the floor. "Let's go."

CHAPTER

thirty-five

SATURDAY, 10:01 A.M.

In the third-floor hallway, David opened an antechamber door, peered in, and shut it again. He went to the next door. Xander was doing the same thing on the other side of the hall.

"That was pretty good," Xander said. "The way you convinced Dad not to take you right to the hospital."

"We don't need more trouble," David said.

"Yeah, but letting him poke your arm? Didn't that hurt?"

"Like he rammed a hot poker into it."

"You didn't even flinch." Xander grinned, admiration all over his face. "Just wish you could have convinced him to let us open the portal doors to look for Mom. I knew he wouldn't let us."

"Can't blame him, not after what happened yesterday. At least he said we can look for Jesse's world." David cracked open a door, saw that it didn't contain the tools that built their house, and closed it.

"But we can't look through the portals for Mom?" Xander said. "That's nuts. How are we supposed to find her?" He opened a door and closed it.

"He didn't say we couldn't ever," David said. "He just wants to be here with us."

He didn't add that he thought having Dad with them was a good idea. When Xander got it in his head to be mad at Dad, it didn't matter if Dad was as wise as King Solomon or as cool as Robert Downey Jr., Xander was going to be mad . . . until he wasn't. *Then* you could tell him something about Dad that would stick.

Dad had been pretty angry himself. All through breakfast, David and Xander endured a lecture about obedience and safety. At the end, though, Dad had hugged them and said he didn't know what he'd do if he'd lost one of his boys. As he broke from their embrace and hustled toward the kitchen, David had seen him wipe away a tear.

Another door for each of them: open and close, on to the next one.

"You know," Xander said, "there are kids my age who don't give a squirt what their parents say. They do what they want, when they want."

"Those are the kids that end up in jail, Xander." David looked into an antechamber whose items appeared to have something to do with sharks. *Yeah, I'm going there,* he thought. *When they throw my corpse in.* He shut the door. "Or in the gutter with heroin needles in their arms. Or stabbed in some bar fight. Or—"

"All right, already!" Xander said. "I hear you."

"Or marrying an emu named Daisy and having little bird-children who wind up in a bucket of KFC."

Xander looked around a door at him. *"What?"*

"Just checking."

Xander grinned. "An emu named Daisy?"

David shrugged. "A *cute* emu."

••••••••

An hour later, David headed downstairs to snag something to eat for himself and Xander. Neither boy had eaten much with Dad's lecture pounding in their ears.

Dad and Keal were working on the walls at the bottom of the third-floor stairs. Dad was steadying one of the doors while Keal drilled screws into a hinge that ran from the top of the door to the bottom. The door itself looked like it belonged on a bank vault.

"A tank's not getting through that thing," David observed.

"That's the idea," Keal said. "How's it going up there?"

"Haven't found Young Jesse's world yet."

Dad looked around. "Xander's upstairs?" He sounded worried.

"Looking for Jesse's world," David said. "He promised to come get us if he finds it."

He watched Keal for a few moments. The guy looked exhausted. He had told them he hadn't slept last night, that he couldn't without these doors being up. David said, "How you doing, Keal?"

"On my second wind, Dae," Keal said. "Thanks." He leaned into the power driver and sank a screw into the wall. "I'll feel better when these walls are finished."

"Can't Taksidian just come through the locker-to-linen closet portal?" David said.

Keal wiped sweat from his forehead with the back of his hand. "Not when I'm done with it. Until then, the chair's at least something. I think we'd hear him coming through."

"You would, anyway," David said. Keal had been bedding down in a sleeping bag in the second-floor hallway, not ten feet from the closet door. "I'm going to the kitchen. You guys want anything?"

"Coke, if you have one," Keal said. "'Preciate it."

"I'm fine," Dad said.

•••••••••

When David returned to the third floor, Xander was just closing a door and moving to the next. "What'd you get?" Xander said.

"Pop-Tarts and Cokes." David tossed his brother a packet of cinnamon Pop-Tarts and kept the strawberry for himself. He set the Cokes on a small table under a wall light that depicted a splayed-fingered hand with an eye carved into the palm.

"Why do you think Taksidian hasn't smashed these lights?" David said. "You'd think he would if they're keeping him from bringing more bad guys through, ones from other worlds."

Xander already had one of the Pop-Tarts stuffed into his mouth. "Maybe," he mumbled around the food, "he doesn't know that it's the lights keeping people out. Or he doesn't care because he's using Phemus and the other slaves from Atlantis. He doesn't need anyone else."

David took a bite and thought about it. "Or it's like Jesse said. People used to come through and cause trouble. Killing people and stuff. And he doesn't want the house getting that kind of attention . . . *any* attention."

Xander nodded. "He wants to keep them out, too."

David took a swig of Coke. "Think we'll ever know all the answers? About this house, I mean?"

"Not if I can help it," Xander said. "We won't be here long enough." He finished the second Pop-Tart, downed most the Coke, burped, and said, "Let's get to it."

They each went to a door, looked in, crossed to the next. Twenty minutes later, David opened and almost closed a door. The latch had not yet clicked when he realized what he'd seen, and he pulled it open again. Inside were Jesse's items: saw, hammer, plumb bob, planer, and tool belt. The ripped corner of a blueprint lay on the bench.

"Xander!" David yelled. "Here it is!"

CHAPTER

thirty-six

Typically, going through a portal was like waking up in a wind tunnel. It was disorienting, both physically and mentally. The first thing David noticed was the pull, as though the wind grew hands, grabbed him, and yanked. Whatever he'd seen seconds before stepping through—trees, people, a room—swirled into kaleidoscopic bits and pieces. And there was always a flash of blinding light. For these reasons, David closed his eyes at the moment of going over. But that didn't stop the feeling of being in an elevator, one that was in a plunging freefall from the highest floor and spinning and tumbling at the same time. He was sure that an X-ray would show his organs had shifted slightly out of place. The only thing that kept him from barfing every time was that it lasted only seconds; by the time the feeling in his gut reached his brain, it was over.

Then there was the touching down in the new world, as though that wind-hand had tired of him and tossed him to the ground with no concept of "smooth landing." On top of that, it seemed to have no regard for what he'd be facing on the other side: bullets, explosions, an angry mob . . . hungry tigers! The not-knowing messed with David's mind the way waking in a different place every day would: if he had to do it, he'd handle whatever he faced; but he wouldn't like it. And finally, there was the knowledge that he was leaving his home and family with no guarantee of returning. What if someone on the other side detained him? What if the antechamber items stopped showing him the way home, or—as had almost happened several times—he lost them? He'd be in the deepest cavern imaginable with a broken rope.

Despite all of this, David was determined to land—and stay—on his feet this time.

Didn't happen. As soon as his sneakered toes hit the ground, they slipped backward and he slammed down on wet grass. He was able to lift his broken arm, so it didn't hit for a change, but the air in his lungs gushed out as from popped balloons. He sucked in, getting a mouthful of dirt, pine needles, and grass.

He coughed, groaned, and rolled over—just as Xander landed in the very spot where David had been lying. His brother copied his actions exactly: his feet slipped back, and he came down hard. He lay splayed there, cheek to the ground, one eye closed, heaving for breath.

The portal hovered beyond David's sneakers, five feet off the ground. Behind a shimmering, wavy rectangle of air, the empty antechamber seemed like a perfectly good airplane from which he'd just leaped. Then the door slammed, and the portal shattered away like glass.

David turned back to Xander, who was still wheezing in the grass. "You hurt?"

"Nothing major surgery won't fix." Xander rolled over and sat up. "Glad I didn't land on these." He looked at the items in his hands: the claw hammer and planer.

David got his feet under him, rose, and helped his brother up. While Xander worked the tools into his back pockets, David slapped needles and grass off his chest and legs. He glanced at his surroundings and remembered what Xander had said when they first arrived in Pinedale: *nothing but trees.* Water dripped from tall pines and leafy oaks, sounding like the rain hadn't stopped. But the sky above them bore the blue tinge of faded jeans. In the distance, dark clouds rolled slowly away.

"Musta rained," David observed.

"You think?" Xander said. He was holding the front of his

wet T-shirt away from his body. He made a sudden worried expression and stuck his hand in the front pocket of his jeans. He pulled out the scrap of blueprint from the antechamber, sighed when he saw it wasn't wet, and pushed it back in.

"Close to the house," David said. He pointed to "Bob"—the cartoon face his family used as their special identification—carved in a tree. Jesse said he'd carved it when he was a boy, which meant the face had been in the family longer than Dad and even Grandpa Hank.

"No hammering this time," Xander said, pointing, "but I think the house is that way."

They began walking. David said, "It'll be nice to see Jesse without tubes up his nose and needles in his arm."

"He's just a kid here," Xander said. "Taksidian doesn't stab him for another eighty years."

"We gotta tell him," David said. "Maybe it won't happen if we tell him."

Xander stopped. "You think he'd remember?"

"Something like that? I would."

Xander shook his head and continued approaching a wall of bushes that David recognized: it would take them into the meadow where fourteen-year-old Jesse was carving what would become a wall light in their house in Pinedale.

"I'm not sure it'll help," Xander said. "If we tell him now, then he knew it when he came to the house the other day. It still happened."

David skipped over to him and grabbed Xander's arm before he could plunge into the thicket. "But wouldn't that be *cool*?" he said. "We go back, and there's Jesse, all better . . . never having been hurt?" He laughed at the thought.

Xander smiled back, but all he said was, "We'll see," and pushed into the bushes.

"I guess we wouldn't know that he had ever *been* stabbed either, though," David said, following in his brother's leafy wake. "It'll be a history that we changed, and we'd forget that it ever was."

On the other side, David was bummed to see that Jesse wasn't sitting on the log. He'd had it in his head that they'd come into this world at the same time they had before and everything would be the same. But that wasn't the way time travel worked. If you returned to a place, you could be there later than the previous time—which made the most sense to David—or even *earlier* than the time you were there before, which was just plain *weird*.

That got him thinking: what if they were here now earlier than the last time? Jesse wouldn't know them; he would not have met them yet in this time. But then, last time, he would have already met them. He wouldn't have been so surprised to see them then, right? Trying to figure it all out made David's head hurt.

They crossed the meadow diagonally, heading in the direction of the hammering they'd heard the first time they were here. They broke through more bushes, went over a hill, and David slapped Xander's arm.

"There it is," he whispered, as if they'd stumbled onto a sleeping beast. To David, it looked like an incomplete popsicle-stick model of their house, framed without walls.

No, not popsicle sticks, he thought. *Bones.*

He had the feeling he was seeing the skeleton of the thing that had caused so much heartache. After all, he had often thought of the house as something living. Even Jesse had said it was "hungry"—hungry for them. He half expected the towering structure to suddenly grow walls of scaly hide, spring up on dragon legs, and attack them.

"David," Xander said, and David realized he had frozen in place.

He shook off his apprehension, his "overactive imagination," and caught up with his brother. As the trees thinned, he spotted Jesse. He was sitting on the porch, elbows on his thighs, his face down in his hands.

"He doesn't look happy," Xander whispered.

David stepped on a twig, and Jesse looked up. His mouth fell open, and his eyes flashed wide. Without taking his eyes off the boys, he yelled, "Dad! Dad!"

We are *here before the last time,* David thought, figuring Jesse was reacting to seeing them as strangers.

But then he hopped off the porch and ran toward them. "David!" he yelled.

As he approached, David could tell Jesse had been crying. His eyes were puffy and bloodshot, and tears had cut clean streaks in the dirt on his cheeks. He threw his arms open and hugged David, even as he ran smack into him. David had to take backward steps to keep from falling down.

Jesse squeezed, then stepped back. He scanned David's face, his body. He reached out and touched his chest. His eyes filled again. "You're . . . you're . . ."

He turned to Xander, and a flash of anger narrowed Jesse's eyes, twisted his lips. His arm shot out, and he shoved Xander hard in the chest. He screamed, "You said he was dead!"

CHAPTER thirty-seven

"What?" Xander said. "I never said that!" He threw a confused look at David, who was too stunned to respond.

"You were just here!" Jesse yelled. "You said—" He pointed. "You washed your clothes!"

His chest rose and fell—in anger or an attempt to stop the tears, David didn't know.

"I don't know what you're doing, but it's *not funny*."

He looked at David with the saddest expression David had

ever seen, as though the idea of David dead was still on his mind.

"Jesse, I . . ." Xander said, "I would never joke about that, not after all the times he—both of us—almost *did* die. And the last time I saw you was the other day—with David."

A man brushed past Jesse—David hadn't seen him coming—and grabbed Xander's shoulder. He said, "Xander, what's going on? Why are you back?" He blinked at David. "Who are *you*?"

"Uh . . . David King, sir."

"You're . . ." The man glanced at Jesse, then back to David. "You're *David*? Xander's brother?"

"Yes, sir."

The guy looked like an old-time street boxer, tough and no-nonsense. He looked back and forth between David and Xander.

"Dad?" Jesse said. "He—"

"Sir," Xander interrupted. "I don't understand. How do you know me? Jesse said—"

The man—Jesse's dad—raised a big hand, stopping Xander. He said, "Do you remember meeting me, son? Ever?"

"No, I—"

The hand again. He turned to David. "Have you ever been seriously hurt?"

"Oh, yeah," David said, raising his bandaged arm, then pointing at the big bruise on his cheek. "And my leg—"

"I mean stabbed . . . bad, really bad?"

"Uh . . . no?" It came out as a question. David had no idea what was going on, or even what he was supposed to say.

"Dad," Jesse protested, "Xander was just here. You *saw* him. He was all covered in blood. He said it was David's. He was crying, screaming. . . ."

"That's why I believe what he said then was true." He looked Jesse square in the face. "When he was here an hour ago, his brother was dead."

"Me?" David said, weakly.

"How?" Xander said. "How can that be?"

David knew the answer: on the walk here, he had been thinking about it, how weird it was.

"When you jaunted here before," Jesse's dad said, and saw the confusion on the brothers' faces. "When you . . . came through, traveled through time from the house, you wound up here an hour ago, but you must have left your house later in your time."

"You mean in the future?" David said.

"Your future, yes. Later than when you came through just now."

"When?" Xander said. He grabbed a fistful of the man's shirtsleeve. "You said I told you David was dead. When? When will it happen?"

Jesse's dad shook his head. "There's no way to know. It could be any—" He stopped. He gripped Xander's jaw and moved his head around. "You had a bad gash on your chin. Bleeding. Probably happened at the same time as . . . *David.* Otherwise, son, you look *exactly* the same, hair and all. I'd say soon, real soon."

Jesse nodded in agreement.

Xander jerked his head away and stepped back. "No," he said. "David doesn't die. You're wrong."

Jesse's father pulled a piece of paper from his back pocket and held it out to Xander. "You wrote this while you were here."

Xander snatched it out of his hand, and David stepped over to see. The paper had been crumpled and then smoothed. Mud clung to the edges. At the top was his name, written in a shaky hand, hardly legible. Under it was a drawing: A stick figure lying on the ground. A knife protruding from its chest. Above that, a heart, the kind girls put on letters to people they love.

Extending up from the bottom right corner of the paper, obscuring the stick figure's feet, was a bloody handprint. Xander slowly put his hand over it: a perfect match.

Xander looked down at David. If Michelangelo had sculpted a face frozen in the moment of ultimate grief, it could not have been more heartrending than Xander's.

"What does it mean, Xander?" David said.

"Nothing," he said, crumpling it in his fist. He glared at Jesse's father. "We have to do something. Burn down the house."

"That's what you said before," the man said. "It won't help. You're here now. You've been using the house. You live in it. It gets built, no matter what we do today."

Xander stomped away, then came back. He laid his hand on David's shoulder. "Stay here, in Jesse's world," he said. "Don't come back."

"He can't stay," Jesse's dad said. "Time will pull him back to where—*when*—he belongs. Soon."

Xander spun on him. He raised his fist, still clutching the crumpled paper. "This isn't going to happen!" he yelled. "If you can't help, we'll do it ourselves." He grabbed David's wrist. "Come on." He started pulling him toward the woods.

"Wait," Jesse said. He walked up to David. He seemed ready to say something, then leaned in and hugged him. He pulled away and said, "I'm your . . ." He swallowed, fighting back tears. "I'm your great-great uncle, right?"

David nodded.

"So you have to obey me." He frowned, then whispered, "Stay alive."

Jesse turned to Xander. "You said Taks—" He closed his eyes, thinking. "*Taksidian* did it. He stabbed David."

"No," Xander said firmly, "he doesn't."

"When you were here," Jesse said, "you asked me why I didn't warn you." He turned sad, troubled eyes on David. "I just did."

CHAPTER

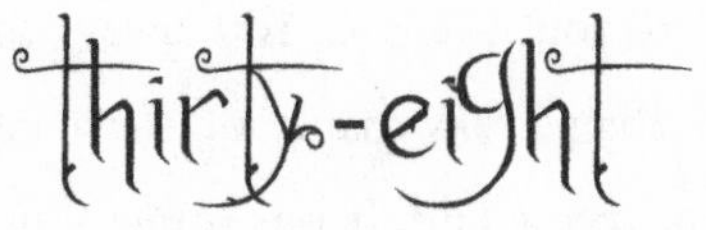

thirty-eight

"Xander, wait up!" David said.

His brother had stormed away from the partially built house and was now scrambling up a hill, kicking down clumps of pine needles and dirt.

David ran to catch him, but Xander was moving fast, and David's leg bothered him, forcing him to limp. He slipped on the wet ground. He went down onto his knees, and immediately felt water soaking into his jeans. "Xander! Please!"

His stomach hurt and his head swirled. He didn't have the energy to chase Xander down. He slumped, sitting back on his heels, and looked down at one of Xander's footprints. He'd gouged away the needles, leaving a tiny crater of dark soil. It reminded David of a grave, and he rubbed his chest over his heart. He felt it beating. If what Jesse and his dad said was true, it wouldn't continue to beat for long.

Soon, Jesse's dad had said. Death would come for David soon.

It was one thing to face danger, to know you were heading to a place where you *could* die. You always thought you'd get out alive—the chance, *any* chance of surviving was enough to make you think you would. It was something totally different to *know* you would die, to not have a chance at all.

He wanted to curl up in a ball and just let it happen. Get it over with. More than anything, and more than at any time in his life, he wanted to be in Mom's arms. He wanted her to comfort him until it was his time to go. But he couldn't even have that. He covered his face and started to cry.

A hand touched his shoulder, and he looked to see Xander kneeling beside him.

"I told you, Dae," his brother said. "It's not going to happen."

"But we know it does," David said. "You wouldn't have come back here and written that note if it doesn't." He blinked tears away and looked right into Xander's eyes. "That's my *blood* on that note. Where'd it come from, if what you said happens, doesn't?"

"I never said it happens."

"But you *will.*"

Xander rubbed David's shoulder. "Trust me, Dae. We know things that others don't. We have a heads-up. We'll think of something." He stood up. Conversation over.

David knew what he was trying to get across: it wasn't going to happen because Xander *said* it wasn't, and it was so *not* going to happen, it wasn't worth talking about.

David didn't buy it. The note. The blood. How could it not happen?

Xander stuck his hand in front of David's face, offering it to him. David gazed up at him, wanted to tell him, *No thanks, I'll just sit here until the portal drags me back to the house and my death.* But he grabbed his brother's hand and got to his feet.

Xander slapped him on the back. "Come on," he said, and headed back up the hill.

"Do you know where you're going?" David said. "Are the items pulling toward the portal?"

"Not yet, but I have to walk."

"You mean you have to get away from Jesse and his dad, get away from them saying there's nothing you can do."

Xander didn't respond; he just kept walking. They slipped a few times, but made it to the top, then started down the other side.

David saw a thick wall of bushes. He said, "I think I know where we are. We just circled around the house."

They pushed through the bushes and stepped out into the clearing. It was an almost perfect oval, about half the size of a football field. The ground here was grassy, slightly wavy, but otherwise flat. Dense trees grew around it like the walls of an amphitheater; their top branches and leaves arched in, toward the center, forming a domed roof—a *canopy*—with a wide opening in the center. Dad had shown them the true magic of the place: Here, you could *fly*. Well, sort of; what you really did was ride invisible currents of air. It amounted to the same thing.

It was here that David had first broken his arm, falling from way up when he saw Taksidian watching from the woods. And it was here that they'd gotten away from Phemus when he came after them—gotten away by riding the current up to the highest branches.

Dad had brought them here for the first time shortly after Mom had been kidnapped, because he knew they needed a break from the sadness. Something about the clearing made you happier, almost giddy. Sailing around, laughing at how the air here made your voice as squeaky as Mickey Mouse's—how could you *not* feel better?

Suddenly, David didn't want to be here. He didn't want to feel better. He didn't want to pretend he wasn't going to die soon.

"Let's go somewhere else," he said, starting back through the bushes.

Xander grabbed his arm. "Dae, wait," he said. "Just sit here with me. We don't have to do anything." He scowled at the trees beyond the bushes. "I don't want to go out there. This is the only place that's *different.* It's not gloomy. It's not like the house."

David knew what he meant. The house was big and imposing and dark—dark in every way, with an absence of light and an absence of *heart,* of good. The woods around it were the same, as though they were part of the house.

David let Xander pull him back into the clearing and sat beside him.

"When the pull starts, we'll go," Xander said.

David looked up into the opening of the canopy, where cotton balls of clouds drifted in a blue sky. Even the sky made him sad, because he wouldn't see it anymore. He thought of all the things he would never do again: score the winning goal in a soccer championship, taste a root beer float, wrestle on the floor with Dad and Xander. And all the things he had never done and never would: drive a car, kiss a girl, have a family. He had never really thought about those things, but somewhere inside he had assumed that would be his life. Of course, he wouldn't miss not doing them when he was dead, but he missed them now.

He said, "I think it would be better not knowing." He gave

Xander a crooked smile. "You know? Better not to know you're going to die."

"Stop it," Xander said. "You're not going to die." He shrugged. "Someday, sure. None of us gets out alive. But not soon. You're going to be an old man, Dae, like Jesse. You'll think the music your grandkids listen to is trash. You'll fart around them and cackle like a witch when they run away. You'll tell them stories about how you met their grandmother and bungee jumped from some crazy-high bridge and—"

"And fought Hannibal's army," David said, grinning.

"That's when they'll put you away," Xander laughed.

"I'll say, 'But it's true! Ask Uncle Xander!'" Yeah, that's what he wanted, times like that. He sighed, and Xander patted his knee.

"Wait and see," Xander said.

CHAPTER

thirty-nine

The bushes rustled a dozen yards away, and Jesse stumbled through. He brushed leaves out of his hair and said, "I thought I saw you guys come in here."

He stood, just staring at them. David knew that after the way they'd left him and his dad, the boy didn't know if they wanted him here. He patted the grass next to him.

Jesse smiled, came over, and sat. He said, "You know about this place?"

"Flying?" David said. "Yeah."

Xander leaned forward to look past David to Jesse. "What's it all about, anyway? Do you know?"

"Know what?"

"The currents. What are they?"

"You don't know?" Jesse said. "Those are the—what do you call them?—the portals."

David pulled his head back. "What?"

"Yeah, they're currents of Time, that's what Dad says. They come through this clearing, and this close to where they come together, they're strong enough to let people stand on them."

"What do you mean, they come together?" Xander said.

"The currents sort of focus into portals over there." He pointed behind them. "Back where we're building the house. That's why we're putting it there, to catch them when they form. Dad thought he could build something that forced them into one place—well, twenty places, but always the same twenty places."

"You're *catching* them in the house?" David said.

"We will," Jesse said. "Soon as it's built. Better than climbing trees to get to them."

"You *did* that?" Xander said.

"Dad did. Glad *I* won't have to. It wasn't so bad getting *to* the time openings—the portals—but coming back was a doozie. Once Dad broke his leg, falling from one."

David couldn't imagine. "But why do it at all?" he said. "Why not just leave them alone?"

Jesse looked at him as if he'd just said he was from Mars. "'Cause fixing time is what we do. It's what our family was made to do, the way the Levites in the Bible were set aside to be priests. The whole tribe. Or family."

"You said that before," David said. "Or later, I guess, when you're ninety. You told us the house was our destiny."

The boy nodded.

"It doesn't seem like a very good destiny," David said, and thought *Not for me . . . or Mom.* He forced himself to think of something else. Into his mind came the image of the twenty antechambers, the twenty portals, and something occurred to him. He said, "All the portals don't come together in a straight line, do they?"

"No," Jesse said, as if they had tried and failed. "You can force them to focus in one place, give or take a few yards. Some of them come together too far off to make a line of them. Close, though."

"So the hallway by the rooms you're building to catch them," David said. "It's going to be crooked, isn't it?"

"Like one of the currents," Jesse confirmed, moving his hand in the air like a swimming fish.

David smiled at Xander. "A reason for everything," he said.

Jesse nudged David. He nodded toward the clearing and said, "Do it."

"Nah," David said. "I don't feel like it."

Xander hopped up. "Come on, Dae. If there ever was a time we needed to have a little fun, it's now. Right?"

Jesse pushed him. "Go on."

Yeah, because you think it'll be my last time, David thought. Then: *Oh, why not? It might just be the last fun thing I get to do.* He got up and followed Xander into the middle of the clearing.

"Okay," Xander said. His voice was high, like what he might sound like if someone shrank him to the size of a grasshopper.

David laughed, and he sounded like a cartoon character.

"Remember?" Xander squeaked. He lifted his foot and felt around. He hopped up, came back down.

David out held his arms, as if for balance, and felt for a current with his foot. After about thirty seconds, he felt it: resistance, a firmer spot than the surrounding air. He lifted himself up onto it, as though ascending a giant's staircase. He wobbled, fell, and found himself sitting on air three feet off the ground. He pulled his feet under him and stood. He angled his body and leaned. He floated, then sailed across the clearing, climbing higher.

Movement in the corner of his vision caused him to look. Xander was flying beside him. They smiled at each other.

"Follow the leader?" Xander said.

"Sure."

Xander banked away and rose. David pursued him. They swirled and looped, zipping one way and then the other.

They slowed, then went so fast David had to squint and blink to see through the rushing air. They glided by Jesse, and David gestured to him. "Come on!" he said.

Jesse waved and said, "This is your time. Have fun."

David followed Xander toward the opening in the canopy. He zoomed up and up. Xander started to fall, and David felt it himself: the air resistance growing thin, disappearing. He plunged down, felt the resistance again, and arced up, tracing the path Xander had made.

Xander made a complete lap around the edge of the clearing, then cut straight toward the middle. He banked and went back toward the edge.

David heard something and looked to see Jesse running into the clearing, waving his hands.

"Xander!" the boy yelled. "Stop!"

David crashed into Xander in midair. Together, tumbling, they continued toward the trees at the edge of the clearing. Directly ahead of them, a portal shimmered. It was set between two trees and hovered twenty feet in the air. They were heading right for it.

"Stop!" David yelled.

"I can't!" Xander said.

Below, Jesse yelled, "Jump off! Jump off!"

Jump? David thought. *How do you do that?*

"Xander," David said, starting to panic, "what do we—"

They went through the portal.

CHAPTER

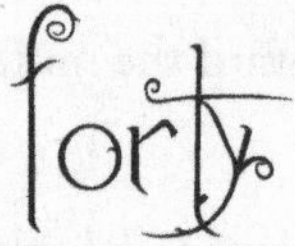

SATURDAY, 11:50 A.M.

Ed King leaned against the doorjamb of the false wall closest to the rest of the house. His arm muscles ached from hammering and lifting, and he rubbed them. He kept one ear attuned to noises up on the third floor, expecting the boys to return any moment. He hoped he wasn't being foolish letting them go over alone, but they'd come through like champs so far, despite a dozen or so close calls. And Xander was right:

the only way to do everything required to rescue their mother and make the house secure was to split up and do multiple tasks at once.

If he had his way, the most dangerous thing in their lives would be teaching Xander to drive. But life didn't let him order from a menu, and sometimes you just had to eat what it served.

In the hall, Keal grumbled. He was going through hardware bags on the floor. "I thought I got all the locks we need." He stood and stretched his back. "Wouldn't you know?"

Keal's plan involved putting locks on both sides of the two doors. That way, the family could lock themselves on either side of them, in case they were attacked from the main part of the house or from the direction of the third-floor staircase—or both at the same time. Ed checked and found no latch or lock on the backside of the door closest to the main house.

"The missing hardware is between the walls," he said. "We may never use it anyway."

Keal pinched an inch of air. "We're *this* close," he said. "Let's get it done. I'll be right back." He pulled car keys out of his pocket and disappeared around the corner, toward the front door.

"Daddy," Toria said, looking up from the small diary she occasionally wrote in. "When are the boys coming back?"

"Should be soon. Why?"

"Xander said he was going to show me how to look through the portals for Mom."

"He did?" Ed said, squatting down beside her.

She nodded. "He said you wanted all of us to do it together."

"I meant all of us staying near each other when we do it, because it's dangerous." He rubbed her head. "I didn't mean that *you'd* do it."

"But I *want* to. I can do it."

"I know you can," he said. "It's just that—"

"I'm too little?" she said. "You were younger than me when you did it, when Nana got taken. You were seven, you said so. I'm two years older than that."

He nodded. "But—" He was going to say he knew more now than he did then, but her anxiousness pushed her to cut him off again.

"Don't say"—she made her voice deep and scrunched her face, exaggerating her dad's way of talking—*"It's guys' work, sweetie. Too dangerous for young ladies."* Then back to herself: "Mom wouldn't like that."

He laughed. "You're right, she wouldn't." He sighed. If they really were going to stay together while they looked, Toria would be exposed to portals no matter how protective he was.

He and Gee had always taken a knowledge-is-power approach to raising their kids. And one good scare—one good *safe* scare, with him at her side—would probably be all Toria needed to stay well away from the portals from then on.

"Look," he said, "I'm going up there to wait for your brothers. Come with me, and I'll show you a few things."

She brightened. "Really?"

"Really." He stood and gave her a hand up.

She ran past him, through the false-wall doorways, and pounded up the stairs toward the third-floor hallway.

"Whoa, whoa!" he said, and ran after her.

CHAPTER

forty-one

They landed on spongy soil and tumbled, all arms and legs and cocking heads. David's broken arm and bitten leg flared in pain at the same time. They slid to a stop with Xander lying on top of David crossways.

David pushed at his brother. "Xander, I can't breathe."

Xander rolled off and plopped on his back next to David. "What just happened?" he groaned.

David squeezed the elbow of his broken arm, trying to pinch

the pain off before it shot up into his brain. It wasn't working. "Owww," he said. "Why did you go right into the portal?"

"I didn't have any choice," Xander said. "We must have gotten caught in its currents. They pulled us in."

David sat up and looked around at a forest. At first he thought they had passed through the portal without it taking them anywhere, and they had crashed to the ground outside the clearing. Then he noticed that *these* trees were different from *those* trees. No pines and oaks here, but trees with thick, twisted trunks and fronds the size of beach towels. The plants were massive and dense. Fuzzy vines hung and looped from the trees. He and Xander were in a tropical jungle, which got him thinking of the first time he'd gone over: warriors with bows and arrows and spears—and tigers.

Xander rolled onto his stomach and rose to his knees. "Where are we?"

"A jungle," David whispered. "Tell me the antechamber items are pulling."

Xander reached back to his rear pocket. "Uh-oh."

"What?" David said. "Don't say uh-oh."

Xander looked around. "I lost the planer." He reached around to the other side and relaxed. His hand came back with the hammer. He bounced it up and down in his hand. "Nothing yet."

David stood, hugging his arm to his chest. "What do we do?"

"Wait here?" Xander suggested, rising.

A man's voice boomed at them: "Over here!"

Both boys ducked. "Who's that?" David said.

"He's speaking English," Xander said. "Maybe it's a search party."

"Not for us. We just got here. Probably drug runners or wild animal poachers. If they find us, we're dead."

"You don't know that," Xander said.

Someone whistled, and the sound of people moving through the jungle grew louder.

"Do you want to hang around and find out?" David said, barely audible.

"Come on." Staying low, Xander ran, moving away from the voice.

Twenty feet in, another voice cried out: "Ready! Ready!"

"We're surrounded," Xander said.

Through big billowing plants and the shadows they made, David saw rays of sunlight. He pointed and headed for them. They reached an area where the foliage became nothing more than fat green plants growing low to the ground—a glade. David squatted beside a tree, and Xander knelt beside him. Across the glade, the heavy forest started again.

"We should—"

"Shhh!" Xander said.

Off to the left, on the other side of the glade, a man stepped into the sunlight. He was dressed in camouflage army fatigues, with a utility belt of pouches and gear strapped around his waist. He carried a machine gun—an M-16 like the miniature version with which David used to arm his G.I. Joes. The guy was big and bald and looked like he ate nails for breakfast. Behind him, in the darkness of the forest, the silhouettes of more men moved around.

"Oh, man," Xander said. "I bet we're in Vietnam."

"That guy looks like a U.S. soldier," David said.

"I don't think it matters," Xander said. "Those guys are in the jungle, and people are trying to kill them. They'll shoot at anything."

"I'd rather take my chances with them," David said, scanning behind them, "than whatever we might run into on our own. Come on." He stood and stepped away from the trees.

"David!" Xander said, quiet but firm. David felt him grab at his shirt. Then Xander rose up next to him.

David raised his arms and was about to yell when the soldier started shooting—*screaming* and shooting, as though he were insane.

David yelled and covered his head with his arms.

The soldier threw down his M-16, stooped, and came up with a weapon that made the back of David's neck tingle in fear. It was a massive Gatling gun. A belt of bullets hung from it like the tail of a dragon. The soldier continued screaming and let loose with the Gatling.

The jungle disintegrated. The weapon was so fierce, firing

so many bullets so fast, it cut trees in half and sent leaves and branches flying into the air.

The soldier aimed left of the boys and began panning toward them. The ripping chaos that tore apart the forest like a horizontal tornado approached them. Covering their heads, David and Xander ran the other direction through the low plants.

Behind David, Xander yelled, "Stop! Stop! We're Americans!"—over and over.

Other soldiers sprang from the trees to join the first. They started firing as well. One of their weapons made a sound like a cherry bomb in a metal trash can—*THUMP!*—and the forest behind the boys erupted in a fiery explosion.

A wave of heat washed over David. He realized he'd never make it to the trees on the far side of the glade. Even if he did, trees were no protection against the soldiers' onslaught. He stopped and tossed up his arms. He closed his eyes and opened his mouth to beg for mercy, but all that came out was a long, anguished wail: "Aaaaaaaaaaaaaah!"

He heard a similar sound coming from Xander and realized his brother had frozen in place beside him.

He opened one eye. The soldiers were simply standing and staring. Their guns were lowered, but behind David, the forest continued to disintegrate with the sound of thousands of firecrackers. David was completely baffled. The destruction must have come from somewhere else, not the soldiers. And if so, why were they just standing there?

Then a booming voice came roaring across the glade: "Cut! Cut! Cut!"

From this new spot in the glade, he could now see an opening in the forest that wasn't part of the glade. Within this opening were a dozen or more people—and two cameras. Big movie-type cameras.

The firecrackers behind David stopped.

The booming voice said, "Who are those kids? What's going on here?"

A half dozen people came running from the opening, through the glade, toward David and Xander.

David lowered his arms. He said, "Xander, what's going on?"

When his brother didn't answer, he turned to see him gaping at the soldiers.

"Xander?"

"That's . . . that's . . ."

One of the soldiers stepped forward and threw up his hand at them. He yelled, "Watt'r you dune dare? You ruin da take!"

Heavy accent. David recognized it and the man himself.

"Arnold Schwarzenegger," Xander said, hushed by awe. He looked around at the jungle, at the crew around the cameras, the people running toward them. "David, we're on a movie set. *Predator!* We're on the set of the first *Predator* movie!"

CHAPTER
forty-two

Saturday, 11:57 a.m.

Ed and Toria had looked in each antechamber until he found one whose items appeared somewhat safe—though he knew you couldn't judge the worlds by the items that led to them. He remembered when David and Xander had looked for a "safe" world for David to check out the first time. They had thought the absence of weapons—unless you counted a machete—meant it would be less dangerous than Xander's gladiator experience. But the boy had been stalked by three hungry tigers and attacked by warriors—he had come back with an arrow-nick in his shoulder.

Still, Ed wasn't about to teach Toria about looking through portals in a room full of guns, knives, grenades, or any other weapons. That would be too much like ignoring a *Beware of Dog* sign. Entering a yard without such a sign didn't mean a nasty animal *wasn't* waiting for them, but it improved the odds against it.

So now they stood in an antechamber whose theme seemed to indicate that it opened onto a circus world: floppy shoes, which Ed wore; a red clown nose, hanging around his neck; a tube of white greasepaint, stuffed in his pocket.

"Okay," he told Toria, who stood on the bench beside the closed portal door. "First, you have to brace yourself like this." He showed her the way Keal had instructed the boys to put their hands and feet. "The most important thing is to keep your eyes open for anyone on the other side who sees you. If you even think that *maybe* they do, slam the door fast. Understand?"

"Slam the door fast," she repeated. "But even if they can't see us, we can see them, right? So we can look for Mom?"

"Right," he said. "You never know where the portal will be. It could be up high, looking down, or level with everything. Sometimes there's nothing to see, just landscape. Usually it drifts around, so you can see the world from different angles. Sometimes it's blurry, and other times clear as a TV show."

"Why is it always different?"

"I don't know." He thought about it, about all the ways each portal was different. "Maybe it's like the weather . . . a lot of things deciding how it's going to be at any given time."

Toria nodded as though she understood, but he wasn't sure she did. Heck, he wasn't sure *he* did.

"Step back a little," he said as he turned the knob and pulled the door open. Daylight flooded in, the odor of car exhaust. Colors swirled, then came together into recognizable forms: a car parked at the curb of a busy city street. They were looking at its front bumper, as though from the gutter twenty feet in front of it. An expanse of sidewalk stretched from the car to a glass-fronted building with a revolving door. People walked past, heading away from Ed and Toria. Others walked toward them.

"I can see them!" Toria said. Then, quieter: "But even if Mom's in that world, we're not going to see her—a whole city of people?"

Ed nodded. "That's what I thought when I did this as a kid, looking for your nana: like throwing a dart at a map and hitting the very place she was. But my father explained that there's a connection between the portals and the time traveler. They're sort of drawn to each other. I know that's confusing . . ."

"I get it," she said. "It's like the portal is looking for her, too, and knows more about where she is than we do."

"You got your mother's smarts," he said.

A muffled sound came through the portal, like a baby crying: waaa-waaa-waaa-waaa, but too consistent to be human. A glass door beside the revolving door opened, and two clowns stumbled out onto the sidewalk. They wore white face paint and red rubber noses; one had a big painted-on frown and the other an equally ridiculous grin. Their suits were billowy fabrics whose colors and patterns hurt Toria's eyes. They tumbled over each other and rolled across the sidewalk.

She started to laugh, but then the clowns hopped up, raised their arms, and she saw pistols in their hands. They fired back into the building. The glass door shattered. Pedestrians scattered. A clown stumbled and fell again, losing a cloth bag, which opened, spilling dollar bills onto the sidewalk, into the wind. The car door opened, and the clowns jumped in. The car leaped forward, heading directly into the portal.

Ed swung the door closed. As he did, two dollar bills fluttered in on a breeze that smelled like the burning rubber of tires. He spun and slammed his back against the door, expecting the car to come crashing through. When it didn't, he let out a breath.

Toria stared at him with eyes so big they looked like cue balls dotted with blue paint.

"See?" he said. "You never know."

"They were robbing a bank!" she said. *"Clowns!"*

"I never did like clowns." He sat on the bench to catch his breath. "Too creepy."

She jumped down and pulled the big floppy shoes off his feet. She set them on the bench and sat beside him. "Hope Mom wasn't anywhere near *that,*" she said.

"Maybe she was one of the clowns," Ed said.

Toria gasped, and he grinned at her. She punched him in the arm and said, "That's not very nice to say. Mom would *never!*"

A wind blew in under the door, and the cue-ball eyes returned to her face.

He pulled her close. "That's normal," he said. "Remember? Watch . . ." He pointed at the dollar bills on the floor. They flipped into the air, swirled around the room, and whipped away under the door with the wind.

"Coooool," Toria said. She sniffed. "Even that bad smell's gone."

He pulled the rubber nose over his head, reached up behind him, and hung it from a hook. He was digging for the tube of greasepaint when she hopped up.

She spun and bounced up and down. "Let's do another one!"

CHAPTER

forty-three

The first of the movie people reached them, a squat man with a flaming red face and bulging eyes. "What have you done?" he screamed. "My pyrotechnics! My jungle destruction! It'll take days to set it up again! What have you done?" He stumbled into the jungle behind them, picking up branches and wires.

Two men with fire extinguishers rushed past and began spraying foam at the many little fires burning within the path of destruction.

A man holding a clipboard stomped up and grabbed David's shoulder hard enough to almost knock him off his feet.

Xander knocked the man's hand away. "Hey!" Xander said. "Don't touch!"

The guy turned on Xander. "Who are you?" he growled. "Where'd you come from?" He spotted the hammer and snatched it out of Xander's hand. "Are you with one of the *set crew*?" He spun around and held up the hammer. "Who do these kids belong to?" he yelled.

Xander reached up and grabbed it back.

"Gimme that!" the man said.

Xander put it behind his back.

The man jabbed a finger at Xander's face. "I *am* going to find out who you belong to! And when I do, they're not going to find a job wiping a go-fer's nose."

David laughed.

"You think that's funny?" the man said. "Wait'll I—"

A woman in her twenties, dressed for a safari, came up behind him. She touched his shoulder. "It's all right, Mark," she said. "I'll take care of this."

"All right? Do you have any idea—?"

She turned him away from the boys and gave him a little push toward the cameras. "Go," she said.

He stormed off, casting evil glances back at the boys.

David smiled at Xander. "Wipe a gopher's nose?"

"That's a guy who gets things for people," Xander said. "Go

for this, go for that. Go-fer. He meant whoever we belong to won't even get the worst job there is in the movie business."

"Good luck with that," David said. He was so relieved not to be cut in half by crazed soldiers, he didn't care how mad everyone was at them.

The woman flashed them a smile and raised her eyebrows. She was pretty, David thought, and he liked that she was actually smiling.

"Well," she said, "talk about being in the wrong place at the wrong time."

"Lady," Xander said, "you don't know the half of it."

She held out her hand. "I'm Lizzie."

Xander shook her hand. "Xander. This is my brother, David."

She shook David's hand. "How'd you get here?" she said. "Who brought you?"

"No one," David said.

"I understand," she said. "Come, let's get you off the set."

She began walking toward the cameras. The boys followed. People everywhere scowled at them.

"Great," Xander said. "I finally get on a movie—a big-budget action set—and everyone hates me."

"Would you rather we were really in Vietnam?" David said. "Getting shot at?"

"Maybe." He tapped David's arm and pointed at a man with headphones perched on his head and a camera lens hanging from a cord around his neck. He was talking to Arnold Schwarzenegger.

"That's John McTiernan," Xander said. "Great director. He did *Die Hard!* And *Last Action Hero!* And *The Hunt for Red October.*"

Lizzie smiled at him. "You must be thinking of someone else. John didn't do any of those."

"Not yet," Xander said.

"I haven't even *heard* of those movies," she said.

"Not yet."

They walked past the cameras, to the back of the clearing. Lizzie pointed to two director's chairs. "David, Xander, why don't you sit here while we figure out what to do with you?"

David started to sit, then saw the name stenciled on the canvas chair-back. He said, "Uh . . . this is Mr. Schwarzenegger's."

Lizzie leaned close and whispered, "Don't worry. He *never* sits."

As soon as she left, Xander hopped up. "Let's go."

"Where?"

"Anywhere but here. I don't want people around us, maybe *guarding* us, when the pull starts. You want them to chase us into the portal?"

"But," David said, looking past his brother at the film crew, the cameras, the lights, the actors. "This is your thing. Don't you want to look around?"

"Like they'll let me," Xander said. "They won't even—"

A hand clamped over his shoulder, and Schwarzenegger stepped up next to him. He was grinning.

"You guys causing trouble, ya?" he said.

David gaped up at him. Phemus was muscular, but this guy was totally *ripped*. It was the difference between a boulder and a granite statue. His arms were bigger than David's legs, and they seemed to ripple and flex on their own. Black and green camouflage grease was smudged over his cheeks and forehead, and his hair was cropped short, making the top of his head look as square as a castle. David remembered where he was sitting and started to hop off. Schwarzenegger stopped him with a finger to David's chest—firm as a railroad spike.

"Stay," Schwarzenegger said. "I insist." He hitched his head toward the glade. "I guess that was really, really scary."

"I almost had a heart attack," David said.

Schwarzenegger laughed. "You should have seen your faces."

David said, "Sorry about ruining your . . . thing."

The man leaned a scowling face toward David. "Don't do it again," he said and grinned.

"Yes, sir."

The whole time, Xander had been looking up at Schwarzenegger as though at a shiny new Ferrari. The actor turned a worried eye on him. "You okay, boy?"

Xander nodded. He snapped out of his daze and said, "Great director, Mr. McTiernan."

Schwarzenegger glanced back at the director. He was showing one of the other actors how to hold the Gatling gun. Schwarzenegger said, "Want to meet him?"

"Uh . . ." Xander said. "As long as he doesn't shoot me."

"He's a pussycat. Come on."

Xander looked at David, a questioning look on his face.

"Go on," David said. He watched *Da Terminator* himself take his brother through the set. They stopped at the cameras, and Schwarzenegger pointed to things while Xander nodded. Xander shook hands with the cast and crew. Schwarzenegger wrapped an arm around Xander's shoulders like they were old buddies, and David was happy for his brother.

Xander suddenly ducked out from under the massive arm, turned, and fast-walked toward David.

Schwarzenegger called to him: "Is it my deodorant?" The other actors laughed.

"Gotta go," Xander told David. "The hammer's pulling. Hard." He grabbed David's hand, and together they darted into the forest. "That was so cool," he said.

With the hammer held out in front of him, his other hand clasped around David's, Xander led them directly to a portal. It shimmered in front of a fat green-barked tree.

David stopped, pulling Xander's arm to keep him from going through. "Is it the right one?" he said. "To the antechamber?"

"I'm just following the hammer, Dae. What choice do we have?"

All the places they've been, all the places they *could* go flashed through David's head. He braced himself for whatever they'd find on the other side and said, "Let's do it."

CHAPTER

forty-four

SATURDAY, 12:10 P.M.

Toria stood in front of the portal. She was dressed in a dirty monk's robe ten sizes too big for her. The sleeves bunched like accordions around her elbows; the heavy canvas material completely covered her legs and feet and pooled against the floor. A necklace of wood beads looped over her neck, and an ornate gold ring adorned her finger.

Standing just behind Toria, Ed clutched the back of her collar and looked through the portal over her head. The image before them was of an ancient town: stone-block buildings and streets, people herding donkeys and oxen past vendors selling bread and fish, a group of boys kicking around a ball. The portal seemed to be hovering on a raised terrace. A railing crossed in front of them, with the street scene playing out below.

"Always three things?" Toria said.

"Three antechamber items unlocks the portal door," Ed confirmed.

"Any three?"

"Yes, but you should choose ones you don't have to hold," he said. "That'll keep your hands free to hold onto the door and the wall next to the opening."

She nodded.

"Where do you think this is?" she said.

"Could be anywhere," he said. "A long time ago, probably. I don't see anything modern."

"Looks like it's going to rain." In the distance, beyond the town and flat, brown hills, dark clouds rolled toward them.

A loud bang came at them from behind, through the open hallway door.

"That must be the boys," Ed said, relieved to hear it. They'd been gone way too long. He pulled her back from the portal. "Shut the door and put the stuff back," he said.

"Aww," she whined.

He turned away and darted into the hall. "Toria, please!" He ran to the antechamber that led to Young Jesse's world.

CHAPTER

forty-five

SATURDAY, 12:11 P.M.

David tumbled into Xander, catching glimpses of hooks, a bench, Dad standing in the hall doorway: they were home! *Yes!* The portal door slammed. He climbed off Xander and sat on the bench. He leaned his head against the wall and groaned.

Xander crawled up his legs, flipped around, and sat beside him.

"You okay?" Dad said. "What happened?" He checked his watch. "You've been gone almost an hour."

David looked at Xander. "Seemed longer," he said.

"You can't stay in each world that long," Dad said. "Don't—" He stopped himself, turned his head, and yelled, "Toria?"

"Yeah?" Her voice seemed far away.

"Did you shut the door?" Dad called. "Like I told you to?"

"Just a sec!"

"Now! Come here where I can see you!" He turned back to the boys. "Don't tell me you went through the wrong portal again. Did you hit another world?"

David nodded. "We met Arnold Schwarzenegger."

"On a movie set," Xander said, with a toothy grin.

"What about Jesse? Did you see him?"

Xander's smile ran away from his face. He began breathing fast.

David's eyes watered up. He had been trying to avoid thinking of Jesse's prediction—or was it Xander's prediction? That part was confusing. But they had to tell Dad, and that meant bringing it all up.

Dad stepped in, closed the hall door, and leaned against it. "What is it?"

Xander reached into his pocket and pulled out the scribbled note. He frowned at it as though it were a disgusting bug, then handed it to Dad.

Dad studied it, checked the backside, and returned to the drawing.

"That's supposed to be a drawing of David," Xander said. "Dead."

Dad shook the paper. "What is this? Who drew it?"

"I did," Xander said. "We saw Jesse's dad, and he said I'd just been there an hour earlier. He said it must be that I go over to see them soon in the future, but when I do, I'll arrive an hour before *this* time."

Dad nodded. David knew he understood the way the portals worked. He said, "And you told them what? That David was dead?"

"I said Taksidian killed him," Xander said. He was talking quietly, as though David's death was his fault.

Dad squinted at the paper. He pointed at it. "What's the heart?"

Xander offered David a weak smile. "I love my brother." He stood. "Dad, it's not going to happen. It won't, I won't let it."

Dad looked down at David, whose tears hadn't spilled out yet; they just sat there on his lids as though waiting for a starting gun. He said, "When is this supposed to happen?"

Xander shook his head. "Jesse's dad said soon, but he didn't know."

Dad knelt in front of David. He grabbed David's thighs, crushing the paper under one palm, and stared sadly into his face.

David blinked, and the tears rolled.

"Do you believe it?" Dad said.

David nodded. "How can it *not* happen?" he said. "Xander went back—or will go back. He has to. Otherwise there wouldn't be any note, right?"

Dad leaned up and pulled David's head into his chest. "We'll change it," he whispered. "Nothing's going to happen to you, Dae. I promise."

David pushed away. "Have you ever changed the future? Have you seen it happen?"

Dad's silence was worse than anything he could have said. David hung his head and sniffed. He watched tears fall on the bench between his legs.

"That doesn't mean we *can't,*" Dad said. "Look at everything that's already happened that I would have said was impossible. Going back in time in the first place. Your changing history—saving that little girl, who went on to eradicate smallpox, and getting that doctor in the Civil War and ending the war earlier. If we can do that, then we can do this. Right?" He clamped his hands on David's shoulders and gently shook him. "Right?"

"I guess," David said.

"That's right," Dad said, standing up. He turned toward the door, then to Xander, then David. It was clear to David he was thinking, not sure what to do.

David said, "Dad—?"

Dad held up his hand. "Just a sec." He turned his back on the boys and ran his fingers through his hair.

The wind, as it always did, rushed into the antechamber. It

blew through David and Xander's hair, fluttered through their clothes. Tiny particles of dirt, some pine needles and leaves came off them and swirled through the room. It snatched the paper out of Dad's hand. He tried to grab it, but it moved too fast, whipping around like a panicked bird. A pink haze drifted from it, as though it were glowing. The paper, needles, leaves, and dirt vanished in a flash under the door.

David, Xander, and Dad stared at the small pink cloud left behind. A second later, it shrank in on itself and fell to the floor. It splattered—dark red blood. *David's* blood from the note. It belonged here, in this world. They gaped down at it, and David wondered if Xander and Dad felt as he did: that it was a bad sign. Looking at it, David had the sense that his death had already happened: there was his blood to prove it.

I'm dead, he thought. I'm not even here. *Just my spirit, watching it happen all over again.*

He ran a hand over his chest, squeezed his leg. He was real, he was here—for now.

Dad spun, pointing at David. "Go grab some stuff. We're leaving."

"But, Dad," Xander said. "It can't be that simple. Something's going to happen. Taksidian will—"

"Taksidian can't do anything," Dad said. "Not if he can't find Dae, not if Dae's not here. There was blood on this note." He waved his hand at the portal door. "That means it's fresh when you go over to Jesse's world and write it. You're here, in the house, when it happens—but it's not going to happen, because David's not going to be here. Go get your stuff, David! Now!"

David stood. "But, Dad," he said, "I think Xander's right. How can it be that easy? I mean—"

"David!" Dad looked from him to Xander. "This *will* work, it will." He stepped into the hallway and turned back, his jaw firm. "What good is the present if we can't change the future?"

CHAPTER

forty-six

SATURDAY, 12:20 P.M.

Toria screamed. "Daddy! Daddy!"

They followed David to an antechamber, where Toria was standing in front of an open portal. A blanket engulfed her. She turned a beaming smile on them. Pointing into the portal, she said, "I saw her! Mommy! I saw her!"

Dad pulled her back and stepped up to the portal. "Where?"

Xander crowded up beside him, and David jumped on the

bench to lean over and look through. A crowd was moving quickly through a narrow street.

"Where, Toria?" Dad repeated.

She ducked under David's head and said, "There!" Her hand shot out, breaking through the portal.

Dad pulled it back. "Just tell me."

"Behind the crowd. Not with the others."

"That woman?" Xander said. "That's not her."

"It—" Toria stopped and looked in silence. "She was there," she said. "I saw her. Maybe she went into that building."

David stepped off the bench. He touched her hair and said, "I don't think so, Tor. That happened to me, too, remember? When I thought I saw her and jumped into that French village during World War II?"

Dad stepped back. He nudged Xander and Toria away and shut the door.

"Daddy!" she yelled.

"Even if you did see her," Dad said, "we can't do anything about it now."

"Dad!" Xander snapped. "If it was her—"

"Xander!" He gripped Xander's arm. "Your brother's in danger. You said changing the future couldn't be as easy as getting him away. Maybe it's not, because of things like this." He shook his finger at the portal door. "Maybe something's trying to keep us here . . . or we just stay, I don't know. But the only chance we have is to get out of here."

Xander's face told David that he understood and agreed, but he wasn't happy about it. David wasn't either. Everything they'd done in the past week, all the danger and brushes with death, had been for Mom. If she was this close, *this* close . . . how could they leave?

But David knew: The plan had always been to rescue Mom without someone else in the family disappearing or dying. Maybe David understood Dad better because it was he, David, who was in danger. Plus, he'd been in Toria's place—thinking he'd seen Mom—and knew how easy it was for your eyes to play tricks on you when you wanted something so badly.

"*You* go," Xander said. "Take David and Toria, and go. Let me go over and see."

"No!" David said. "We all go, or none of us do." In the back of his head, he'd been thinking, *What if I get out of harm's way, away from Taksidian's knife, only for someone else in the family to take my place? What if Time will have its blood from the King family, and it just happened to be mine in one scenario—someone else's in another?*

"David," Xander said, "if Toria *did* see Mom—"

"Then we'll find her again," Dad said. "We're getting out of here, Xander. All of us. Once we know David's safe, we'll come back."

Xander gazed at the closed portal door. He nodded. "All right. Let's go."

"But why?" Toria said. "What are you guys talking about? What's wrong with David?" She looked at him. "Dae?"

"I'll be fine," he assured her. "We have to go now. I'll explain later."

"Keal!" David called.

"He went to the store," Dad said. "We'll have to take his rental with the broken windshield. Anything that gets us far from here."

They headed for the stairs that led down to the second floor. Dad stopped. "David, get behind me. Toria, you next. Xander, bring up the rear. Keep your eyes peeled."

They stomped down the stairs. As they moved between the two false walls, Xander said, "Holy cow. Dad, you and Keal made a fortress out of these."

"It was Keal's doing," Dad said, stopping to point at padlocks inside and outside the doors. "He thought we could use this room as a panic room. You know, we can lock ourselves between the walls in an emergency, in case people are in the house and we can't get out."

Xander pointed toward some studs and planks on the far side of the room. "I thought you were done."

"Almost," Dad said, leaving the room and heading for the second floor's main hallway. "We're going to put up some shelves for food and water." He stopped in front of the master bedroom and gave David a little push toward the boys' bedroom. "Grab some clothes, just a handful. Hurry. Toria, you too. Xander, stay with Dae."

Dad's panic was infecting David. His heart raced, and his

head swiveled like a radar antenna. He looked over the railing to the front door and foyer . . . back to the other side for a quick glance into Toria's room as he strode past . . . to the hallway ahead of him. The chair was where it was supposed to be in front of the linen closet. The spare bedroom doors were closed, the way they'd left them.

Get a grip, David told himself. *Taksidian's not here. Xander's chin isn't cut. Dad's just doing what dads do: making sure his kids are safe. Oversafe.*

He went into the bedroom and pulled open his drawers. What do you take when you're running for your life? Nothing! But he grabbed a change of clothes in case they couldn't get new ones for a while.

"Grab some for me," Xander said from the door. He was standing guard there, looking in all directions as David had done.

Holding a bundle of clothes to his chest, he headed out. "Go!" he said. They went to Toria's door. She was looking under her bed.

"Toria," Xander said. "Let's go."

"I can't find Wuzzy!"

"Forget him, come on." Xander pushed David toward the stairs before seeing if she obeyed.

"Dad!" David yelled.

"Get to the car," Dad said from his room. "Lock the doors until I get there."

They went down the stairs, and David called back, "Toria's in her room!"

"Okay! Toria!"

David jumped the last three steps. Moving to the front door, he shifted the clothes to one side to free up a hand. He swung the door open, stepping through as it swung.

Directly in front of him stood Taksidian. His hair whipped around his head in a gusty breeze. Drab-green eyes locked on David. The man held up a gleaming knife.

David focused on his startled reflection in the blade. Faster than it would have taken his mouth to form the words, his brain told him it was the last time he would ever see his own face.

Taksidian said, "I want my dagger back."

CHAPTER

forty-seven

SATURDAY, 12:24 P.M.

David's reflection vanished as Taksidian moved the blade, pulling it back for a strike.

David dropped the clothes. *Move! Move!* he thought. He willed his feet to backpedal, but nothing was happening . . . *Nothing! . . . Nothing! . . . Move!*

Xander's leg shot between David and the doorframe. His foot sailed into Taksidian's stomach. David felt himself tugged backward by his shirt. He stumbled over the threshold and spilled into the foyer. On the porch, Taksidian caught himself before hitting the steps and leaped for Xander.

But Xander was already swinging the door shut. It slammed, and he flipped the dead bolt, yelling at David, "Get up, Dae! Run! Upstairs! Go!"

The door rattled under Taksidian's impact against it.

David sprang up, grabbed the newel post at the bottom of the stairs, and swung himself around it. He leaped up the stairs, Xander right behind him. "Dad!" David screamed.

"It's Taksidian!" Xander hollered. "He's at the door! It's happening!"

Dad met them at the top. "Get behind me!"

The front door burst open. Taksidian strolled in, the knife clenched in one hand. He said, "Knock, knock," as though he were bringing cookies.

"Get out of here!" Dad yelled. He took a step down.

"Dad, no!" David said, seizing his father's arm. "He's crazy."

Taksidian stopped at the base of the stairs. His eyes moved between David and Xander. "What is it with you two?" he said. "You just won't die." He showed them the big knife. "No more games." He started up the stairs.

Dad reached behind him. David thought, *A gun! Let him have a gun!*

But it was a mobile phone. Dad's thumb flipped it open as

his other hand pushed back on David's chest. David backed up into Toria. He hadn't seen her come out of her room, but of course she would have.

Dad's phone fell to the floor. It spun and went between the balustrade's railing. David heard it hit the foyer floor, and pieces danced around on the wood. As a group, they backed up to the wall. Taksidian's head rose up . . . his shoulders . . . his chest . . . six steps from the top.

"The closet," Xander said. "Dae. Come on!"

"No," he said. "There's not enough time for all of us to go through one at a time."

"Then all of us at once," Xander said. His eyes were buggy with fear.

"We can't all fit, Xander," David said. "And we don't know what will happen if we try."

"Just you then," Xander said, his voice now as shrill as a whistle.

"I'm not leaving you. Any of you." The possibility of one of them taking his place in the grave still haunted him.

"Upstairs!" Dad said. "Move it." He pushed David toward the false walls, then stepped forward to kick out at Taksidian, missing by a mile.

Taksidian paused, but only long enough to stretch his smile wider and shake his head.

David grasped his sister's hand and pulled her around the corner toward the false walls. He banged his shoulder against the doorjamb. Xander and Dad ran up behind Toria.

"He's right behind us," Dad said.

"The room," Xander said. "Between the walls. You said it was like a panic room. Let's use it."

"It's not finished," Dad said, pushing them through the room to the next door. "There's no latch on the inside, no way to keep it closed. Go!"

They went up the stairs. David looked back to see Dad shutting the door in the nearest wall. There *was* a latch and lock on this side. "Lock it, Dad!" he yelled, knowing that was Dad's plan but needing to say it anyway.

Dad got the door closed and fumbled with the mechanism, trying to get the padlock off so he could snap it shut over the hasp.

The door crashed open, Taksidian's booted foot coming through the opening and pulling back into the darkness. He stepped into view and flashed the knife at Dad, who was scrambling backwards up the stairs. Dad spun and continued up without losing a second's momentum.

David hit the landing and turned into the hallway.

A door at the end of the hall opened. Light burst from it, as bright as an explosion. David slid on the carpeted runner and sat down hard. Toria ran into him and tumbled. Xander's knee slammed into David's back, but his brother stayed up.

Phemus lurched out of the antechamber, already swinging his arms and snarling like a wild animal.

CHAPTER

forty-eight

SATURDAY, 12:33 P.M.

The big man was covered only by a pelt around his waist. His skin was hairy and dirty and scarred. He turned toward them, and his eyes flashed with excitement. His wiry beard parted as his mouth formed a reptilian smile.

How? David thought. The man's timing was scary. He remembered Keal telling them about the light shining under the antechamber door, and wondered if waiting for a signal from Taksidian was something they did—Phemus was the army in the woods anticipating just the right time to attack.

David noticed a second open antechamber door. His breathing stopped, and he waited for another Atlantian slave to come lumbering through.

Then Dad said, "Toria, you're still wearing the items from the antechamber."

David swung his head around and, sure enough, she was. How had he not noticed that bulky blanket-thing around her before? *We were a little busy,* he thought.

Dad continued: "It locked the world in place. You can open the portal door. Run, girl, run! Do it!" He lifted her off the floor and pushed her toward the antechamber, then bent to help David.

The open antechamber was halfway between them and Phemus. Toria stopped when she saw him. Xander brushed past David, picked her up, and disappeared with her into the room.

Dad lifted David to his feet. When they reached the antechamber, Phemus was close enough to think he had them. He grunted out a laugh and swung his solid hands at them.

David dived into the antechamber, rolled, and jumped up. Pain told him his broken arm had taken another bang, but he had no time for pain. The portal door stood open. Xander held Toria in his arms and leaned his shoulder against the door, making sure it didn't shut. David knew that if the door wanted to close, it would no matter what, but he understood his brother's desire to try.

"Go!" Dad yelled, pressing his back against the hall door.

Xander spun into the portal. He and Toria wavered behind it and dropped out of sight.

The hallway door thumped. Dad jerked forward. It opened a few inches and shut again.

"Dad," David said, "they'll follow us over!"

"Grab the other items, Dae. On the bench."

David snatched up a pair of sandals, a coin, and some kind of whip with strands of leather attached to a wooden handle. "Got them!"

The hallway door jarred open again, and Dad pushed it shut. He sprang forward, tackled David around the waist, and together they sailed into the portal. David's stomach lurched. Sunlight struck his eyes, and he tumbled over something hard. He felt a sharp yank on his shoulder and realized he was dangling over a stone railing. Dad was leaning over it, gripping his wrist.

Above and behind Dad, the portal shimmered. Phemus appeared in the rectangle, frowning down on them. He swiveled his head, and David thought he was looking for the antechamber items. The door swung around. Phemus saw it and got his fingers around the edge. They slipped off, and the door filled the portal. The sparkling rectangle broke apart and was gone.

David looked down. He was hanging twenty feet above a

stone-paved street. Most of the people in sight were draped in tunics. Several stared up at him. They pointed, directing others to turn and see. Directly below lay the sandals and whip he'd taken from the antechamber. An old man rushed over, picked them up, and shambled off.

"Hey!" David yelled at him.

"I got you," Dad said.

"I lost the items!"

"That's okay," Dad said. "Toria has some, enough to get us home." He pulled David up and over the railing.

Xander stepped onto the balcony through a doorway, holding Toria's hand. He looked around. "Are we safe?"

"Away from Phemus and Taksidian, if that's what you mean," David said. "As far as safe, who knows?"

"Do you think that was it, Dad, Taksidian's attack on David?" Xander said. "Is Dae safe now?"

"No," David said. "You're not cut."

Xander rubbed his chin. "Oh, yeah," he said. "Jesse's dad said I had a gash on my chin when I went back and told him about . . . about you."

"You could have gotten it afterward," Dad said. "We can't let our guard down. Not until we're positive we've changed what you said happens."

If *we changed it,* David thought, but didn't say. Instead, he looked around. "Where do you think we are?" he said.

They scanned the area from the balcony. Animals in the

streets. Trinket and food vendors. Every structure appeared to be made out of stone, wood, or dried mud. Under the baking sun, the entire scene appeared painted from only hues of tan and beige.

"I don't know," Dad said. "Looks Middle Eastern or African. Depending on *when* it is, could be anywhere."

"Rain's still coming," Toria said.

David followed her gaze. A mass of black clouds churned in the far distance. Lightning flashed inside it. Looked to him more like a storm than a simple shower. It made him uneasy.

CHAPTER forty-nine

Xander pointed his thumb at the room beyond the balcony. "It's like an apartment in there. Old-looking furniture. I mean, not old for this time, I guess. All rough wood."

"So," David said, "what do we do?"

"Wait for the pull," Dad said. "Then hope Taksidian's gone when we get home."

"Well, I hope he is there," Xander said. "I'm going to *kill* him."

"Xander," Dad said.

"I am! Like he said, he's not playing games anymore. He came right at us, and he wasn't using that knife to clean under his nails." He backhanded David's arm. "Didn't I tell you something big was coming? I knew Taksidian wasn't going to play nice for long."

David scowled. "When did he *ever* play nice? He sent the cops after us, then Phemus and his goon-friends. He stabbed Jesse and *took his finger.* He chained us up—and tried to send us to war! If that's your idea of nice, remind me never to make you mad."

"Not me," Xander said. "Taksidian, and everything he's done before was sneaky. He got Jesse when he was alone. He got us in Atlantis, where they don't care. This time, he broke into our house—right through the front door—and came after all of us, Dad too."

"I agree, Xander," Dad said. "He just laid all his cards on the table, and he's not going to stop until either he's dead . . . or we are."

"Daddy!" Toria said, grabbing his hand in both of hers. "I'm scared."

He rubbed his hand over her cheek. "It's okay, baby. We'll figure something out."

David felt as though the storm clouds had filled his head. He wished Dad *had* an answer, not that he *hoped* to find one. He was starting to feel that they were never meant to get through this, that Taksidian was always meant to win. He said, "Maybe we should have done what Grandpa Hank did and left the house."

"After Mom was taken?" Xander said, instantly angry. "Leave her, you mean?" He shoved David hard enough to knock him down.

David landed on his butt, and his head cracked against a stone railing.

Dad grabbed Xander. "Hey! Hey!"

David rubbed his head and glared up at his brother. "I want her home too!" he yelled. "As much as you do! But look at us now! You heard Dad—Taksidian's not going to stop till we're all dead. You, me, Dad . . . *Toria*!"

"You baby!" Xander said. "I ought to—"

"Stop!" Dad said. "This isn't easy on any of us. It's the stress. I'm surprised we didn't bite each other's heads off days ago. Now more than ever, we need to be a family." He cast a sad look at David. "We need to work together."

Toria dropped down beside David and helped him rub his head. She sniffed, and he realized she was crying. "It'll be all right," she whispered between sobs.

He closed his eyes and hated himself. He swallowed, blinked, found his brother's face. It wasn't fierce, as he had expected. Xander looked confused and hurt. David said, "I'm sorry. I didn't mean it. I didn't, *really*. I don't know why I said that."

"I do," Xander said. He stepped closer and held a hand out to him. David accepted it and stood, and Xander pulled him in and hugged him. He said, "I'm scared, too, Dae."

Toria stood and wrapped her arms around the two of them. Dad joined them, squeezing them all tightly together. As corny as a family hug would have seemed to David under any other circumstance, this time it seemed right. More than right: *necessary*. Dad had said it—they were a family, they needed each other. None of them would have made it this far without the others. And David knew without a doubt that they wouldn't survive another day if they didn't work as *one,* if they didn't feel like they *could* hug like this.

The sound of pounding feet in the street broke the moment. They turned to see five men coming toward them. They were dressed like—

"Roman soldiers," Dad said.

"Rome?" Xander said. "Again?"

The soldiers wore leather body armor, metal helmets, and pleated skirts. They carried swords and spears. Two brandished the same kind of whip David had carried here from the antechamber—and lost. In fact, the old man who had taken it was leading the pack of soldiers. He stumbled along, prodded by shoves and cracks of the whips. He protected his head with one arm and held the other extended in front of him. He was pointing at the Kings.

A soldier grabbed the old man and tossed him into the side of a building, then stared up at the balcony. He jabbed a sword at them and yelled, *"Vos totus vestrum! Subsisto qua vos es!"*

"Time to go," Xander said.

CHAPTER

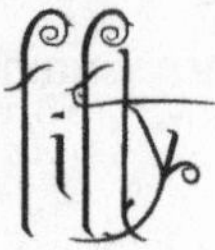

The Kings ran through into the shadowy room off the balcony. Xander led them to a wooden door and opened it. Steps descended into deeper darkness. Then a door banged open below them, and daylight splashed against the walls, broken by the shadows of moving men.

"Back in!" Xander said. He pushed them into the room and shut the door.

"Here," Dad said, running to a glassless window. He climbed through and reached back for Toria.

David climbed through, dropping onto a flat roof. Xander ran to the window and swung his leg over the sill.

David turned to see Dad kneeling at the far edge of the roof, peering over. Then he dropped onto his stomach, spun around, and slipped over the edge. David helped his brother out. When he looked again, Toria was gone.

The brothers ran to the edge. Dad and Toria were standing directly below them on another balcony. Dad reached up for David. He rolled onto his stomach and slid backward into Dad's hands. Xander dropped down beside them.

"I heard the soldiers shouting in the room," Xander reported.

"Won't take them long to figure out where we went," Dad said. He darted through a doorway, and the others followed. A man, woman, and two kids sat at a table, bowls of liquid and chunks of bread in front of each. The man bolted up, knocking his chair backward.

Dad held up his hands. "Sorry, sorry," he said.

The man yelled and pointed at a door. Dad opened it, and they piled through. A short flight of stairs led to a different street from the one they had seen.

"We'd better keep moving," David said, starting up the street away from the building whose balcony the portal had dumped them onto.

"Any pull yet?" Xander asked.

"Toria," Dad said, "let me have the robe. You keep the

necklace and ring. If you feel a tug from them, let us know."

"Looks more like a tunic than a robe," David said, once Dad had it on.

"No pull yet," Dad said, lifting the fabric and letting it drop.

"Where are we going then?" Toria said.

"Just walk," Dad said. "Moving targets are harder to hit."

The streets were narrow, more alley than avenue. They rose and fell, twisted and turned, seemingly at random. Stone bridges crossed overhead from building to building, adding to the town's cramped feeling.

They passed bakeries and butcher shops, stonecutters and woodworkers. They stopped to rest in front of a blacksmith. The man pounded on orange-glowing metal. Each strike of his hammer kicked up an explosion of sparks. He stopped, ran a forearm across his brow, and scowled at them. He said, *"Quis operor vos volo?"*

Dad shook his head. "Nothing, thanks."

The man waved his hammer at them. *"Adepto ex hic, tunc,"* he yelled. *"Vado, vos extrarius canis!"*

They hurried away. "Man, what a nice guy," Xander said.

"I think he called us dogs," Dad said. "*Canis* is Latin for dog. It's where we get our *canine.*"

"Does that mean you know where we are?" David asked.

"Somewhere in the Roman Empire, if I had to guess."

A man ran past them and turned left onto the next street. A group of soldiers on the street trotted by, followed by townsfolk—three or four at a time, then larger crowds.

"Something's happening," Xander said.

"We should head the other way then," David said, looking back past the blacksmith.

"No, we shouldn't," Dad said.

Toria squealed. "I feel it!" she said. "The ring, it's pulling my hand!"

"Let me guess," David said. "That way." He pointed to where the people were pouring by.

"Look," Dad said. The hem of the tunic was fluttering, rising up toward the next street.

"Figures," Xander said.

"Let's go," Dad said. They rounded the corner and joined the flow of human traffic. People were stepping from side streets to join the progression.

"What's happening?" Toria said.

"Guess we'll find out," Dad said. Ahead, the street rose and bent left, preventing them from seeing where the crowd was heading. But a rumble of loud voices told David they were not far away from the attraction.

He looked into a side street as they passed. More people heading their direction, and a woman writing on a wall. He walked on toward the bending street. He said, "Are you sure—"

He stopped. His heart fluttered. It felt like a bird in a cage, beating against his lungs, tickling his stomach. He began trembling.

Dad, Xander, and Toria didn't notice. They continued walking, starting up the incline toward the bend. David turned around, and on shaky legs returned to the side street. He froze at the intersection. The woman's back was to him. She wore a flowing brown tunic that might have been fashioned from a burlap sack. Something like a towel covered her head. She was using a piece of black coal or chalk to deface the wall of beige stones. But it wasn't words she was writing. It was a symbol, the top of which he recognized. She stooped to complete the image, then stepped back to assess her work: it was Bob, their family's cartoon mascot.

David tried to yell out. "Mmmm-aaaah! Mmmm-aaaah!" His mouth would not form the word he wanted.

But the woman heard him. Apparently believing she'd been caught committing a capital crime, she turned panicked eyes on him. Her expression morphed from surprise to confusion to joy. She flipped the towel off her head.

In David's eyes, everything blurred out of focus, everything except her face. Blue eyes, glimmering with wetness. That smile, connected to his heart as surely as his veins and arteries. Cheeks so smooth their touch to his own cheek never failed to calm even his worst moods. All of it framed by locks of hair the color of hay and the texture of silk.

All sound faded from his ears, leaving only his heartbeat.

"Mom!" he cried, and ran into her arms.

CHAPTER

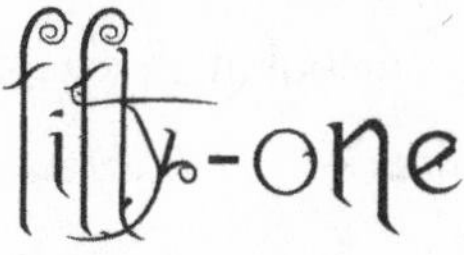

She swept him up like a warm breeze. Her arms squeezed him, her hands moved over his back, through his hair. "Dae . . . Dae . . . David, is it really you?" She pushed her face into his neck, then pulled away to look at him. She kissed his cheek, his forehead.

He pressed his lips to her skin, tasting her tears. He rubbed his face against her shoulder and pulled himself into her embrace. After finding out about his impending death, he had wanted nothing more than the comfort of his mother's arms. He had believed then that he would never have that again. But here it was, the comfort of her arms, her smell, her whispering love.

She leaned back for a longer gaze. "Look at you," she said, wiping his face. He hadn't realized he was crying. "What have you done to yourself?" she said. "Your eye! Your cheek!" She touched his bruised skin, but it didn't hurt at all.

He smiled and said, "You won't believe all we've done, looking for you."

"I know you've been looking," she said. "I saw the Bob faces. Did you see mine?"

"You . . . where?"

"Oh, my goodness," she said, brushing her hair off her wet cheeks. "Feudal Japan . . . World War I Germany . . . the *Titanic* . . ."

"Yes!" David said. "I saw it on the deck of the *Titanic*. That was really you? I wasn't sure." A tear rolled down his cheek, and he wiped it away. She pulled him into another hug, pinning his broken arm between them. *"Ow!"* he said. "Ow, ow."

She looked at his bandaged arm. "Oh, David, what happened?"

He laughed and shook his head. "It's a long story . . . a really, really long story." He noticed a nasty scratch on her temple. He touched it with feather fingers. "I'll bet you have a story too."

"All of it moving toward this moment," she said. "This very moment. How did you get here? Where are—"

She looked over his shoulder, and her lips parted. David glanced around. Dad was standing in the intersection of streets. His face bore the same angelic expression as Mom's. But he seemed afraid to move, as though doing so would shatter a hallucination, and his wife would vanish into the shadows of the street.

Toria came down the street behind him. She spotted Mom, shrieked, and ran toward them.

"Mommy! Mommy! Mommy!" They hugged and kissed and laughed. "I *knew* I saw you! I knew it!"

Xander ran up, and Mom rose off her knees to embrace him. Xander appeared to collapse into her arms. He squeezed her and didn't let go. His shoulders moved in time with his weeping. Finally, they parted. Xander wiped his face and nose. He grinned at David, then Toria. Still holding Mom with one arm, Xander reached out, got hold of David's head, and pulled him to them. Toria stepped into it.

"Two family hugs in one day," Xander said. "Wow . . . wow."

Dad approached, and the kids moved away. All three of them kept a hand on Mom, as though afraid to let her go . . . or, David thought, as though they were drawing strength from her after being drained by her absence.

Instead of the crashing, crushing reunion David, Xander,

and Toria received, Dad's was gentle as a leaf landing on grass. He kissed her, and they stepped into each other for a hug. Dad leaned back, lifting Mom off her feet. He turned, spinning her slowly around. Their eyes were closed, and matching smiles stretched across their faces. He set her down, and they kissed again. She placed her hand on his face, and they stared into each other's eyes.

Xander caught David's attention, and he rolled his eyes. But he was grinning, and David knew his brother didn't mind their parents' affection at all. It was the engine that drove the family.

Toria said, "Xander just rolled his eyes."

Dad laughed and gripped Xander's shoulder. He looked at each of his kids and nodded. His eyes were shimmering. He whispered, "Thank you."

CHAPTER

fifty-two

They hugged again, cried, sniffed, and touched one another, as though none of them could believe they were together, a complete family . . . finally. David wanted the moment to last forever. But of course it didn't, and before he was ready, life pushed its way into their happy reunion, breaking them up. It was Toria who backed away first.

"Dad," she said, staring at her beaded necklace from the antechamber. It was lifting off her chest, vibrating.

"The pull," Dad said. "It's getting stronger."

Mom wrinkled her brow. "The what?"

"It's how we get home," Dad explained. "The items show us where the portal is."

"Ah," she said. "I know about portals. Every now and then a wind comes and blows me into one."

"That's the pull," David said, though he could not imagine getting sucked into one on a regular basis. "But when it takes *you,* where do you end up—just *anywhere*?"

"I never made sense of it," she said.

"Our items want to go home, to the house. If we follow them, we end up back there."

"I wish I'd had one of those a week ago," she said.

"Oh, boy," Xander said. "I wish you had too."

David pushed his fingers into his eyes and wiped out the tears. Mom smiled at him, and he returned it. She turned and ran her hand over Toria's head. His mother amazed him. Here she was, after a week of getting tossed like a doll from one world to another, one danger to another, and at last finding her family again—and she had it together. She was cool. Crazy-happy, sure, but not the blathering glob of emotions you'd expect. Then it dawned on him: That was his mother. He knew without asking that she had *expected* to get through it, to be reunited with her loved ones. And expecting it had made her strong; having it now made her thrilled, but not terribly surprised. He hoped he could be that way someday.

A roar of voices reached them. A mob of screaming, shouting people came down the street from the bend. Had the Kings not been on this side street, they would have been swept away. The horde walked backward and sideways, their anger directed at something that had not yet come into view. Soldiers appeared, clearing a path. They pushed, kicked, and struck the people with the handles of their swords. Like slow-moving lava, the crowd flowed along the street, growing ever larger.

The object of their wrath appeared. Mom drew in a sharp breath and covered her mouth. "That poor man," she said.

"What?" David said. Then he saw. A man stumbled down the center of the street. Soldiers slapped him with whips, poked him with spears. The onlookers spat at him and stepped in to punch him. "Why are they doing that to him?" he said. His heart ached, as it had for the man on the torturer's rack. It was inhumane, cruel . . . *evil*, no matter what the man had done.

The man was beaten and bloody, barely able to carry the heavy cross on his back. Its crossbeam rose over his head, and the vertical post dragged along the stones behind him. The man tripped and fell, and the cross tipped and thudded onto the stones. Soldiers moved in to lash him.

Mom pulled Toria close and covered her eyes. "David, Xander," she said. "Don't look."

But David stepped forward. "Dad, who is he?"

"Rome conducted a lot of crucifixions," Dad said. "Could be anyone."

"But it's not!" Xander said. "Look what they've put on his head. It's a crown of thorns! Like . . . like . . . *The Passion of the Christ!*"

David's mouth dropped open. He watched as the man hefted up the cross and slipped beneath it, buckling under its weight, his back so whipped that his flesh resembled raw meat. The man gazed into the sky, his mouth gaping wide as he gasped for breath. He took a slow, agonizing step.

"Dad," David said, hurting for the man, "what did he do?"

Dad stepped beside him and held his head. "If you're brother's right, Dae, he didn't do anything."

"What are you saying?" David said. His guts—every organ—tightened. They felt heavy, like stones jammed inside a scarecrow's body. "Jesus? That's *Jesus*?"

"I . . . don't know," Dad said.

The progression flowed past. David began walking toward it.

"David!" Mom said.

He caught her eye. "I have to see," he said.

She opened her mouth, meaning—he knew—to call him back. But her lips closed and she nodded.

David ran up to the backs of people who were lurching forward to hurl rocks or sharp-sounding words. He ducked under their arms and pushed through. Someone kicked him. Someone else planted a hard fist or elbow into his back. A knee came up into his face. He touched his lip and saw blood on his fingers. He was knocked left, then right. Still he shoved through, wending his way toward the front. A protester in front of him got knocked away by a passing soldier, and the people behind him surged forward. He tumbled onto the stones. He rose to his knees at the front of the crowd.

A shadow passed over him. He squinted up as the top of the cross bobbed overhead and went by. The beaten man was steps away. David stretched his hand out to him, knowing he couldn't help, couldn't even reach, wanting to so badly.

The strands of a whip slapped down on the back of his hand. David snapped it back, saw blood in three lines, as though a tiger had swiped at him. The soldier who'd lashed him kneed him in the side of the head and continued on.

Directly in front of him, the beaten man fell to his knees, the cross pushing down on him. Blood streamed from his face. The crown of thorns, as sharp and long as nails, pierced his head in a dozen places. The man turned his head, and David stared into his eyes. Blood had filled one eye, making it dark, the other was as bloodshot as any eye could be.

The man leaned closer to David, the cross shifting, grinding into his back. Air rushed from his mouth with a groan, with blood. The tip of his tongue ran along his bottom lip. With a voice as soft and trembling as a dove's wing, he said, "David."

David's breath stuck in his chest.

A whip cracked against the man's back—against *Jesus'* back, David was sure now—and he flinched.

Blood splattered across David's face. He closed his eyes

and moaned. He felt something press against his hand, and he looked to find Jesus reaching out and touching it.

A comforting coolness, like plunging into a lake on a hot summer day, traveled up David's arm, filled his chest, head, arms, and legs. He gasped at the strangeness of it. He lifted his hand. The whip marks were gone, no sign of them at all.

When he looked again, Jesus had lifted his cross and staggered on.

CHAPTER

fifty-three

David stayed on his knees as people streamed by. They knocked into him, kicked him. He ran his fingers over the back of his hand. Smooth skin, nothing more. He pulled off the clips on the Ace bandages and unwrapped his arm. The rulers splinting his bone fell away and clattered to the stones. He peeled away the remaining wrap and saw nothing but healthy flesh: no mottled, bruised skin, no bump of bone. He squeezed it. No pain. He pushed his fingers into his cheek and dabbed under his eye. The soreness was gone.

The crowd moved on, filling some other part of the city with its hate and fear.

He rubbed his shoulder, feeling no pain where the arrow had grazed it. Then he thought of something. He shifted his leg forward and pulled up his pant leg. The teeth marks were gone, but the stitches remained, tied into healthy skin. He pushed his pant leg down.

Dad kneeled beside him and put his arm around him. "You okay?" he whispered.

David nodded. He looked at the stone-paved street where Jesus had passed, and his eyes settled on the blood. He held up his arm. "It's healed," he said.

Dad smiled, not seeming surprised. He showed David *his* hand, the one that had been struck by a padlock when the house shook them off the antechamber doors. Since then, the hand had been swollen and bruised. Now it was perfect.

"But . . . *how?*" David said.

"Like in the Bible," Mom said from his other side. Xander and Toria stood beside her. Mom knelt and touched his arm. "Jesus healed a man's son, even though the boy was in another city."

"So," David said, "all of us?"

"Look," Xander said. He lifted his hair to show the place on his forehead where the ladder had gouged it when Phemus and his friends came after him three days ago. "And . . ." He turned and hiked up the back of his T-shirt. No one would have known that minutes ago his back had been badly bruised.

David looked into his mother's eyes. "You mean, because he touched *me*, healed *me* . . . ?"

"And you love us," Mom said. She squeezed his arm. "We're family."

"Dae," Xander said, his face twisting with worry. "Your cheek."

David wiped it and looked at the blood on his palm. "Jesus' blood," he said. He stared at it a long time, then said, "With that kind of power, why did he let it happen? He was *so* beat up. It was awful." He dropped his head.

"Because he loves you," Dad said. "And this is the price he's willing to pay to make sure you know that."

Sandaled feet pounded past them. David looked to see two men, a woman, and a little girl running toward a corner, around which the crowd had disappeared with Jesus. The woman spun to stare at David. Her eyes were as wild as her hair. She seemed angry and confused. He thought she wanted to say something, some pleading question, but then she turned and rushed with the others around the corner. He supposed not everyone welcomed Jesus' punishment, but there was nothing they could do.

He said, "Why do you think we ended up *here* . . . *now*, of all places in all times?"

"The house sent you and Xander to Atlantis," Dad said. "Why *not* here? Why *not* now?"

"Mom," David said. "He knew my *name.*"

"Did you think he wouldn't?" Mom whispered.

Dad got to his feet. "The pull's getting really strong now. We'd better go."

The pull . . . the house . . . It seemed weird to David that after all this, he still had things to do. He still had to eat and sleep and breathe. He had to go to school and do the dishes. People still wanted him dead.

He looked at Dad. "What about Taksidian?"

"Let's hope he's gone when we get home," Dad said.

"And if he isn't?"

"Then we'll just have to take care of him, won't we?" Dad said.

Xander shook his head. "It's not right, what he's doing. He told me he was *king* of our house, and that's how he acts, like he can do anything and get away with it."

Dad said, "It's not over yet, son."

David looked down the street where Jesus and the mob had gone. It was empty now, nothing to mark what had happened. "My heart hurts for him," David said.

"*Heart,*" Xander repeated, pointing at David, and David saw the wheels turning behind his eyes. "I'll be right back." He ran off, heading the way they had come before finding Mom.

"Xander!" Dad called.

"Don't leave without me!"

CHAPTER

fifty-four

SATURDAY, 1:07 P.M.

Jesse bolted upright in the hospital bed. He felt fantastic. All the energy that had drained out of him with his blood was back. Even his ninety-two-year-old joints didn't ache, and he hadn't been free of that burden for ten years.

What in the world . . . ?

He felt the place just under his bottom rib where Taksidian had stabbed him. Through stiff tape and bandages, there was no pain. He pulled his gown up, worked his fingernails under the tape, and ripped the bandages away. Nothing, not even a scab or a scar.

He looked at his hand. Still missing a finger. *Oh, well.* Guess he couldn't have everything. He tore the bandages off the stub. Skin had grown over the end, as though he had been born that way.

He scratched his head. He didn't know any medicine or surgical procedure that could fix all his ailments like this.

Movement caught his eye. The covers at the end of the bed were moving. Holding his breath, he whipped them off. His feet were tapping the air, as if to some unheard tune! He wiggled his toes. He bent his knees and pulled his legs up. Eight years—that's how long it'd been since he could do that, could move his legs at all.

He looked down at the floor. What was the worst that could happen?

He ripped the IV needle out of his arm. Tore the oxygen tubes from his nose—wincing as the tape plucked whiskers out of his mustache. Stripped the heart monitor sensor and wires from his chest. An alarm sounded.

Glory be! he thought. *The sound of health and freedom!*

He sprang out of bed. His landing was anything but graceful. He stumbled forward, wobbled back, grabbed the bed to keep from spilling onto the floor. But he was standing! He tested his knees, felt his weight on his legs, and let go of the bed. He shuffled, then walked to the window. Nice, sunny day. He turned. A wave of dizziness washed over him. He took a step, clenched the bedspread, and leaned against the bed.

Here it comes, he thought. *The memories . . . the history that changed, somehow resulting in his recovery.*

But the typical flood of images, of events that had been erased, *didn't* come. Instead he became aware of something else, something even more incredible. More *miraculous.* The dizziness passed, and he raised his face toward the ceiling. "Thank you," he whispered.

A nurse ran in. She saw him, and her expression couldn't have expressed more shock if he'd been a green elephant sipping tea. "Mr. Wagner!" she said. "What are you *doing?*"

"Getting out of here, dear," he said, striding to a cabinet setup that acted as the room's closet. "Where are my clothes?"

"They . . . uh . . ." the nurse stammered. "They're gone. You have to get back to bed."

"Why? I'm fine."

"You *can't* be," she said. "You . . . you . . . I'm getting security."

"Miss!" he said, stopping her movement toward the door. He held his arms out from his sides. "Do I really *look* like I need to be in that bed?"

She stared, at a loss for words.

"I'm an old man," he said softly, going for a puppy-dog

expression he hadn't attempted in eighty years. "Give me this, at least. Please."

She thought about it, walked to the cardiac monitor, and turned off the alarm. She said, "I think I have a bedpan or two to change." She winked and walked out.

He looked into the empty closet. No matter. He reached behind him and tied his gown closed. He left the room, spotted an exit sign, and went for it.

CHAPTER

fifty-five

A few minutes after he'd left, Xander stormed up to David and the others. "I think he wants payment. He showed me some coins, but we don't have money. What can I give him?"

"Who?" Dad said.

"The blacksmith."

Dad got up. "What are you—"

"David," Xander said, "your necklace."

"Oh, the one I gave you," Mom said, touching it. "How sweet."

"Xander," David said. "It's just a cross."

"Come on," Xander said. "The guy will freak over it."

David slipped it off his head and handed it to him. Xander took off again.

"Daddy!" Toria said. Her beaded necklace was extended straight out now.

"I know," Dad said, trying to keep his tunic down. He took Toria's necklace from her and held on to it. It was perfectly stiff in his hand, looking like a thick, bumpy stick. "Let's get ready to go," he said.

They started toward the pull, keeping an eye out for Xander. As they hurried down the street, Dad told Mom about the note Xander had left—would yet leave?—in Young Jesse's world. She dropped back and put her arm around David. It felt good having her there, and he realized that as much as he had missed her when she was gone, he hadn't missed her enough. Her love was bigger than a word like *missing* could replace.

He looked up at the storm clouds, churning black masses in which bolts of lightning flashed like gunfire. They were converging on the city, rolling in from all sides.

The Kings were almost around the bend in the road when David saw Xander running for them. David called to him, and Xander waved.

"Just around the corner, I think," Dad said.

Xander caught up and David saw the piece of metal in his hand, about the size of a dinner plate. A chain hung from it.

David said, "A weapon, Xander? Really?"

He simply grinned. "We'll see."

"There it is!" Toria yelled. "The portal!"

••••••• ••

David hit the antechamber's floor and spilled onto the pile of bodies in front of him: Dad, Mom, and Toria. Xander came through the portal, landed on top, and rolled off. The portal door closed.

"Everybody off," Dad grunted.

David pushed up from Toria, grabbed her arm, and got her to her feet. He leaned past her to help Mom. He led her to the bench, encouraged her to sit, and sat beside her. He leaned his head into her shoulder and closed his eyes. For the first time in recent memory, his arm wasn't throbbing, he didn't feel like their problems would crush him, and he was happy.

"Okay," Dad said. He was holding his ear close to the hallway door. "Dae, we're getting you out of here fast. Straight for the front door. No stopping for anything, got it?"

Everyone nodded.

"Xander, you lead the way. Then Mom, Toria, Dae, and I will follow."

The wind blew in from under the door. "Oh, no!" Xander said, his eyes flashing wide. He clutched the metal he had brought from Jerusalem to his chest. "I need this!" he said.

"What—" Dad said.

"It's to protect David!"

David pulled open the door. He stuck his head out and looked around. "Get out in the hall," he said. "Go to the landing. We know it takes longer for things to get back to their worlds when they're outside the antechambers."

Xander bumped past him and stomped down the hall.

"But you know you can't keep that thing for long?" Dad yelled after him.

"Just till we get David away," Xander said.

David shook his head. "As if any weapon's going to stop Taksidian if he comes after me. Keal said he fights like he's had martial arts training."

"Well," Toria said, "he's *definitely* taken courses in how to be a mean person."

The wind billowed through their hair and clothes, plucking atoms of sand and dust off them. Mom quickly pulled off her tunic, leaving her sitting there in the nightgown she'd been wearing when Phemus kidnapped her. It was dirty and ripped, and David felt a new surge of sadness for her, thinking of what she must have gone through.

The tunic fluttered around the little room and whisked under the portal door.

David waited to feel a tingling on his face. When the wind left without scrubbing his skin, he touched his fingers to his cheek and looked at the blood on them. "Hey," he said. "It didn't take Jesus' blood. It's always taken the blood before. The Carthaginian soldier's, the Civil War guy's. It belongs back where it came from as much as dirt and clothes do."

Dad nodded, looking puzzled.

"I know," Mom said. "God lives outside of time. It's all the same to him, two thousand years ago or two thousand years from now. He's in all times *all* the time. He belongs everywhere."

"All right, enough already," David said, covering his eyes. "I'm having a hard enough time wrapping my head around time travel and changing history and meeting Jesus . . . to name just a few mind-benders."

Mom smiled and tilted her head. "I was just thinking out loud, dear."

Something occurred to David. "If you're right," he said, "if God does live outside of time, then our using the house to fix history isn't *weird* to him, right? He must see us as the same people no matter what time we're in." He shook his head. "I don't know what I'm trying to say."

Mom patted his leg. "It's nice to hear your voice, no matter what you say."

Dad stepped into the hallway. "Xander, all clear?"

"As far as I can tell," Xander called. "I don't hear anything."

"Okay, come on," Dad said, waving his arm to direct his family out of the antechamber.

David noted that the other antechamber doors were closed.

A good sign; but then again, how long would it take for Phemus or Taksidian to yank open a door and spring out? He rushed behind Mom and Toria to join Xander on the landing.

Dad peered down the stairs to the first of the false walls. "If you see anything—"

"Dad," Xander said. "We know." He pounded down the stairs, the rest of the family on his heels.

CHAPTER

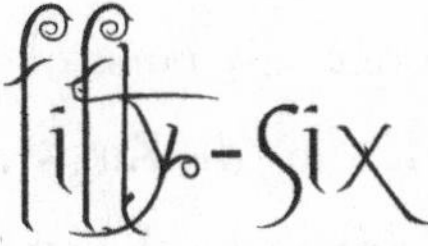

SATURDAY, 1:25 P.M.

Standing in the foyer, Taksidian heard them coming. He turned to Phemus and held his finger to his lips. He pulled the big Bowie knife from a sheath on his belt and quickly looked around for the best ambush point.

He hurried up the grand staircase, staying close to the wall and trying not to make too much noise. He stopped just before reaching the second-floor hall and pushed his back against the wall. The family was descending the third-floor steps. He suspected they would go past the walls at the bottom and come down the hallway.

A loud creaking came from below him. Phemus was putting his weight on the first step. "Shhh," Taksidian said.

He thought about how he wanted to do this. What strategy would best accomplish his goal of putting all of the Kings into shallow graves out back? Well, maybe not the little girl, he reminded himself. He owed the Atlantian royals one female. It would be too perfect if he could solve all of his nagging problems in one easy burst of activity.

The girl could be leading the Kings' charge down the stairs. *Better not use the blade right off,* he thought. *Stop them first, then cut everyone but her.* He had no doubts that he could take them out without a hitch. What were a teacher and three kids to him? He'd defeated squads of royal guards, other assassins. He was so sure of success, he allowed himself a brief thought of the trophies he'd take: a finger from one, a foot from another . . . He'd have his enemy-body-part artwork—which the boy Xander had destroyed—back together in no time.

He had not wanted it to come to this, to killing the family and making their bodies disappear. It was always better if they left on their own. With today's sophisticated crime investigations—fingerprints, DNA—it was getting more difficult to get away with nasty business. Deceit and murder were so much easier in worlds before such scientific advancements.

He shifted the knife in his hand, positioning it for a first blunt blow, then a slicing attack.

He heard their footsteps coming through the false walls.

Here we go.

They were right around the corner, running. He swung the knife—the rounded metal end of the handle first—and took the last step up onto the hall floor.

He made contact, saw instantly that he'd hit the older boy in the face. Gleaming streams of blood—Taksidian's eyes were accustomed to spotting the liquid evidence of success—flew out of the wound. The kid was going down, the others behind him crashing into him.

Taksidian pulled the knife back—*time to start slicing.*

Someone slipped around the falling boy and shot forward. *The woman! Where had* she *come from?*

In that instant of shock at seeing her, he'd given her the advantage. She slammed her two outstretched hands into his chest, and he stumbled back, down the stairs. He felt himself fall into the banister, felt it—and heard it—breaking under his weight. Then he was plunging. He landed on his back in the foyer. His head cracked down on the wood floor.

CHAPTER

fifty-seven

SATURDAY, 1:30 P.M.

David had skidded into Toria and couldn't believe his eyes. He had watched Mom lunge forward and shove Taksidian right through the stair railing. *Yeah!*

Mom's eyes caught something at the bottom of the stairs and she grimaced, wide-eyed. "The man!" she yelled. "The one who took me!"

"Phemus!" David said. "We have to go."

Dad stepped around him and picked up Toria.

David bent over Xander, who'd made a hard landing on the floor. His brother was holding his chin. When he pulled his hand away to look at it, David saw blood too.

"Dae," Xander said. "My chin! Just like Jesse's dad said. It's happening. Run, David, run!"

David staggered back and looked both directions down the hall. Where? Where? The linen closet portal to the school locker—it was the nearest exit from the house. He started for it, and Dad grabbed his arm.

"Wait," Dad said, shifting Toria in his arms. "I have an idea."

CHAPTER

fifty-eight

SATURDAY, 1:31 P.M.

Taksidian stared at the crystal chandelier above him. He raised his head and shook it to scatter the little black dots dancing in front of his eyes. Phemus leaned over him and held out a hand.

"What are you doing?" Taksidian said. "Go get them!"

Phemus turned and headed for the stairs.

Taksidian gazed at the broken banister. Spindles jutted

out, away from the stairs, like hideous dental work. He heard whispering. The Kings were still up there on the second floor. *What are they thinking?*

He reached under him, found the thing pushing into his back, and pulled it out. A broken mobile phone. He hurled it into the kitchen. He rolled over, pushed himself up, and grabbed the knife off the floor as he stood. He rushed up the stairs, catching up with Phemus at the top. Three of the family—the mom and two boys—dashed past in the hall, heading for the false walls and the third-floor stairs.

Taksidian paused to figure out what was going on: The little girl was pounding on the linen closet door, saying, "Hurry, Daddy, hurry!" It was from that direction that Mom, Xander, and David had run. They must have thought they could all get through the portal before he recovered and came for them.

But Taksidian was faster than they thought, or the portal was slower. Only the father had been able to go through. The others, apparently realizing their plan wasn't working, were now going for the antechambers on the third floor.

Taksidian slapped Phemus's arm and pointed. "Get the little girl," he said. He turned to see that the younger boy, David, had fallen at the intersection of the main hallway and the shorter one that ran toward the back of the house, ending at the false walls. His brother was helping him up, throwing frightened glances at Taksidian.

Taksidian whipped the knife back and forth in front of him. "This is too easy," he said.

Xander turned to look toward the false walls—still out of Taksidian's sight. The boy yelled, "Go, Mom, go! We're right behind you!"

Taksidian was mere feet away, thinking the little one's ear would make a fine trophy, when the brothers sprang up and darted away. He could overtake them. When they hit the stairs he'd be able to slice at their legs, which would drop them. Then he could finish the job.

The door in the first wall was wide open, so the boys were able to go through it quickly. They turned right toward the second wall's doorway.

Taksidian was right on them, stepping through the first opening as the closest boy—David—was going through the second one. Taksidian was in the space between the walls, midway between doorways, when he heard someone yell: "Now, Mom! Now!"

The door in front of him slammed shut, just as the one behind him did too, throwing him into complete darkness. He hit the door and pushed. The door wouldn't budge. He heard latches rattling from the other side—and the same sound coming from the other side of the first door as well.

He leaped to the door behind him, hoping to open it before it locked. Too late. He slammed his shoulder into it. Solid.

Hmmm, he thought. *Now what?*

CHAPTER

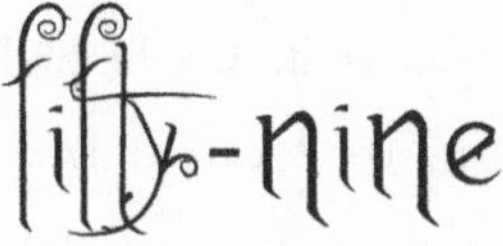

SATURDAY, 1:37 P.M.

Phemus lumbered toward Toria. She screamed and yanked open the closet door. She stepped in and pulled the door shut behind her. Phemus reached the closet and opened it. Empty. He stepped away to glance into the rooms at the end of the hall, the empty one and the boys' bedroom. He returned to the closet. Towels and sheets lay on the floor, piled up on the back wall. He leaned in to examine them.

Dad came out of the bedroom behind him and rammed

his shoulder into Phemus's backside with all of his strength. Phemus fell, grabbing at shelves to break his fall. The wood splintered and broke, spilling linens down on him.

Dad swung the door around. A protruding leg kept it from closing. Dad stomped on Phemus's foot. It disappeared through the opening, and he clicked the door closed.

He spun, put his back to the door, and slid down to sit on the floor. He felt a light breeze whooshing out from under the door, going up under his shirt, chilling his back.

He prayed that Toria had gotten out of the locker before Phemus went through to it. David had given her specific instructions for getting the locker unlatched from the inside, but she'd never gone through this portal. Probably they should have sent someone else, like David or Xander, who'd at least gone through the locker before. But Dad had wanted Toria out of the house in case something went wrong, and Xander had insisted on staying with David. Their plan had been slapped together in seconds, with no time to think it through.

He only hoped their haste didn't result in tragedy.

"Gee?" he hollered.

"We got him!" his wife called back from around the corner in the short hallway.

He leaned his head against the door and closed his eyes.

Please, Toria, he thought. *Be all right.*

••••••••

In a corridor of the Pinedale Middle and High School, Toria frantically tried to get the padlock off the locker next to the one she had just stepped out of. It had been hanging from the latch, unlocked, as Xander said it would be. He had told her that he and David had shifted the lock from the portal locker to the other one the day before, when they'd gone through to the house.

Something screamed from inside the portal-locker. She jumped and realized it was metal, stretching and pulling—Phemus was coming through!

She pulled the lock off and turned to the latch of locker 119. She tried to slip it through the latch's hole, but the locker door suddenly bulged out. She dropped the lock. She grabbed it and tried again, moving her hand with the wildly flexing door. She got the lock on and snapped it closed.

She backed away from the locker, which moaned and screeched like an angry animal. A bulge the size of a half bowling ball popped up in the locker's sloping top.

Phemus's head, she thought. The metal stopped its cries, replaced by Phemus's growls and howls. The whole row of lockers rattled and shook as he moved around inside. He started pounding, but the sound was muffled and the door wasn't moving much. She thought he had mistaken the back of the locker for the front—that, or he was too big to move around and was throwing his fists into anything he could reach.

How someone that big could fit in the locker's narrow space she didn't know. But somehow, he was in there.

She looked around. It was Saturday, so the halls were empty and the overhead lights turned off. The only light came in through a window at the end of the hall. Creepy like this, especially knowing what was in the locker, trying to get out.

She ran toward the windows and the hallway on that side of the building. That would be the way out, she thought. From her back pocket, she yanked out the mobile phone Keal had lent her and flipped it open. She punched a speed-dial button. After three rings, someone answered.

"Keal?" she said. "It's Toria!" She looked over her shoulder at the locker. It was shaking and vibrating like it was an earthquake, not a man, trapped inside. "I need a ride."

CHAPTER

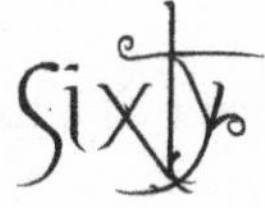

SATURDAY, 1:58 P.M.

David sat beside his brother on the steps leading up to the third-floor hallway. As they had been doing for the past twenty minutes, they gazed at the locked door in front of them, set in the false wall at the base of the stairs. Keal had installed a gate-type latch on this side of the wall. A padlock hung from a hole in the latch, keeping it from opening. David knew a latch-and-lock setup was also on the house side of the other wall, where Mom was. There was no way anyone locked between the two walls could escape . . . he hoped.

"What do you think he's doing in there?" he said.

"Thinking of a way out," Xander said. He was cupping a hand over his wounded chin.

"Think he'll find it?"

"All we have to do is keep him away from you long enough for this to heal," Xander said, moving his hand away to look at the blood. There was a lot of it. "Dad said as soon as we change one of the things Jesse's dad described, then none of it can happen."

"We have to wait for your chin to heal?" David said. "That could take days."

Something banged in the hall above them. David and Xander spun around and ran up to the landing.

"It's an antechamber door," David observed. Bright light poured out of the small room, filling the end of the hallway. "What are we going to do? We're trapped on this side of the wall."

They watched, but no one came through.

David gasped and grabbed Xander's arm. "Dad's a genius," he said.

"What?" Xander said. "How?"

"Remember how Time came to take Jesse and Nana away?"

"Yeah, yeah," Xander said. "They spent so much time in history, Time thought they belonged to it. That's why they had to leave the house and go to the motel." His head began bobbing up and down. "And it's not just people who spend too much time in history, but people *from* history, too."

"It's coming for him," David said, laughing. "*Time* is coming for Taksidian!"

"All right," Xander said, "I agree with you this time. Dad *is* a genius. We'll wait until we know the pull on Taksidian is super strong, then we'll unlock the door. He'll get sucked right in!"

A noise erupted from the wall below: *Bam! Bam! Bam!*

"What's that?" David said.

"The sound of panic," Xander said, showing David his teeth.

David smiled, but it didn't last long. He said, "What if he gets out first? Or what if he stabs me while he's getting pulled away?"

Xander nudged him. "You still think we can't change the future?"

"I don't know. You were there, you wrote that note." David swallowed, trying to ignore the lump in his throat. "It seems so . . . *sure.*"

Xander lifted the metal plate he had bought from the blacksmith. "Time for this," he said.

"What are you going to do, cut Taksidian with it? Hit him over the head?" That really wasn't such a bad idea. Time would have no problem taking him if he were unconscious.

"Ever see *A Fistful of Dollars*?"

"That old Clint Eastwood western?" David said. "Sure, but . . ."

Xander looked at him slyly. "Pull up your shirt."

CHAPTER

Sixty-one

SATURDAY, 2:12 P.M.

Mom looked at the knife blade sticking through the gap in the door. It was pushing into the back of the latch that locked Taksidian between the walls.

Bam! Bam!

"He's pounding it through," she said.

"He must have found a piece of wood in there," Dad said. "He's using it like a hammer." He rubbed her shoulder. "Don't worry, the latch is really screwed in. It can't—"

Bam!

A screw came an inch out of the wall.

Bam! Bam!

Two inches . . . and another screw joined it.

"Ed!"

Dad pushed on the latch with his hands. Taksidian's blade disappeared and came right back, slicing into Dad's fingers. He yanked his hands away. The blade quickly found the latch again and—*Bam!*—knocked the screws farther out.

Dad spun and pressed his back against the wall-like door. The pounding stopped.

Mom leaned over the lock. "It's gone," she whispered.

The blade broke through the door, an inch from Dad's head.

Mom screamed, and Dad jumped away.

Xander's voice reached them: "Mom! Mom! What's happening?"

"Stay there, Xander!" Dad yelled back.

"Yes!" Taksidian said. "Stay there, Xander. I'm taking care of everything." He laughed.

Bam!

The latch rattled, barely clinging to the wall. Mom realized that one more hit, and it would fly off. She slapped the door. "Stop it!" she yelled.

Taksidian did what she expected him to do: he plunged the knife blade through the door again—high up, near the place she'd slapped. She grabbed the tip, coming at it from the top, away from its sharp edge. She felt it slip through her fingers, and it disappeared, leaving a hole that looked like a vending machine's coin slot.

Dad ran to a pile of wood and snatched up a six-foot length of two-by-four. He returned and wedged it between the floor and the lock.

Bam!

The hasp flew off—and the door crashed open, hard enough to send the end of the two-by-four into Dad's nose. He stumbled back.

"Ed!" Mom yelled. She stepped toward him, then started to spin back toward the door. Taksidian grabbed her from behind, and she screamed, a loud, long wail of anguish.

CHAPTER

Sixty-two

Toria stretched up as high as the seat belt would let her. She and Keal had just turned onto Main Street, heading home. "Hurry," she said.

"You said Taksidian was alone?" Keal said.

"*Now* he is," Toria said. "I told you, me and Daddy got Phemus to follow me." When she had last looked, the big guy was still pounding away at the inside of the locker. It was shaking more than ever, because it had pulled out a little bit from the wall.

"But you didn't see anyone else in the house?" Keal said. "No other people like Phemus?"

Toria shook her head. "Daddy said they were going to trick Taksidian and lock him in the room between the walls."

"I hope he . . ." Keal's voice faded. He squinted out the windshield. His mouth dropped open.

Toria looked. A man was walking on the side of the road, taking big long strides, swinging his arms. He wore a hospital gown. The back of it was mostly open; it was closed in only one place, barely covering his rear end.

They cruised past, and Toria yelled, "Keal, stop! It's Jesse!"

Keal slammed on the brakes. "It can't be, sweetie," he said, turning to look. "He's in the hospital, and besides, he can't—"

The rear door opened, and Jesse's grinning face leaned in.

"—walk," Keal finished weakly.

Jesse hopped in. "Where are we going?" he said.

CHAPTER

Sixty-three

"Mom!" David yelled. He watched Xander fumbling with the padlock on their side of the wall, and crowded up behind him.

Xander pushed him back. "No, Dae!" he said. "Stay here." He got the lock off, and when he stepped back to swing the door around, David rushed through. Xander grabbed at him. "David!"

David ran between the walls and out the other side. Without

slowing, he assessed the situation: Taksidian was standing ten feet away, his back toward David. He held Mom from behind—David could see her hair and legs, how she was struggling. Dad was facing them, his legs bent, his arms held out like a wrestler facing an opponent. David could tell he was looking for an angle of attack, a way to dart in and grab Mom.

David leaped. He landed on Taksidian's back. One arm wrapped across the man's face; the other cocked back and drove a fist into Taksidian's skull. He seized a handful of hair and yanked. Taksidian's head snapped backward.

Dad rushed in. Taksidian's knife flashed out, making him jump back. Dad dropped to the floor, got a hold of Mom's ankles, and pulled her down, out of Taksidian's grasp.

Taksidian switched the blade to his left hand and raised it high. It was pointed at David. He plunged it down toward David.

Xander grabbed Taksidian's arm, halting the blade an inch from David's neck.

David angled away from it, and Taksidian's other hand reached around, pinning David's head to Taksidian's shoulder. The shoulder lowered, and David felt himself flipping up, over, and around. When he came down, he was where Mom had been: directly in front of Taksidian, his back pressed against the man.

David thrashed, but Taksidian's arm was an iron strap. It crossed like a seat belt over his shoulder, the right side of his chest, to his left hip—where the man's fingernails dug into David's flesh. David twisted and froze in pain.

David tried to control his breathing, but it was no good: He panted in time with his heart—fast, short breaths. A phrase flashed through his mind over and over again, like a shrill alarm: *This is it! This is it! This is it!* His consciousness knew too well what the "it" was: Xander's prediction . . . David's death. Would it hurt or would it be over too fast? Would he see the blood or smell it? Would his family's terrible expressions of shock and grief be the final image he sees? It didn't seem fair. With all the beautiful things in the world—flowers, clouds, babies—his last would be horrible. His eyes darted around, hoping to find something that would save him.

He craned his neck and glanced back in time to see Taksidian's elbow sail into Xander's face. His brother stumbled away, losing his grip on Taksidian's arm.

Taksidian swung around and backed into the corner formed by the two hallways. His arm was pressed so tightly over him, David's breath became fast and wheezy.

Taksidian positioned the blade a foot from David's heart, ready to plunge it in.

"Stop!" Dad yelled. He was kneeling beside Mom, who was lying on the floor. They were just inside the main hallway, between Taksidian and the grand staircase. Xander was in the shorter hall, between Taksidian and the false walls. He pressed a hand against the wall and stood. The other hand covered his chin. Blood poured out from under it.

"Let him go," Dad said, looking fierce enough to bite Taksidian's head clean off. He dragged the back of his hand across his own face, smearing the blood that was seeping out of his nostrils. "You don't have much time."

David noticed: Taksidian's overcoat was fluttering toward the false walls, the stairs to the third floor, and the portal that had opened to pull him in. The man's long, kinky hair whipped around his head, snapped straight toward the portal, then flittered around again.

"Boy," Taksidian said to Xander. "Shut that door."

"Don't, Xander!" Dad said.

Taksidian's voice boomed in David's ear: "You seem to forget who's holding all the cards!" With that, the blade flashed in front of David's face, and he felt a sharp pinch on his cheek. Taksidian was holding the tip of his knife there. David cried out before he could stop himself.

Panic rippled across Dad's face. "Wait!" Gritting his teeth, he said, "Do it, Xander."

Xander moved to the door in the false wall and swung it closed.

The pull on Taksidian settled a bit, but not much. The man moved the blade back into position over David's heart.

"Shutting the door's not going to help," Dad said, rising. He helped Mom to her feet. "You don't belong in this time.

As long as you're in this house, the pull's going to keep getting stronger."

As if to prove Dad's point, Taksidian's coat sprang out from his body. He jerked forward. He leaned back, and his boots slid across the floor a few inches. He leaned farther, pulling David back with him, and stopped moving.

"Move out of my way!" he yelled at Mom and Dad.

Dad squared his shoulders. He said, "Come over here, Xander."

Xander stooped and snatched up a two-by-four. He edged along the wall until he stood beside his parents. The three of them formed a human barricade across the hallway, blocking Taksidian's escape.

This is it! This is it!

"What are you doing?" Taksidian said. "You care so little for this one, that you defy me?" He dug his nails into David's hip, causing him to scream.

Mom cried out, "No . . . please!" She held shaking hands toward them, and David could tell she was mentally pulling the knife away from her son.

"We can't let you take him," Dad said.

"Then back away," Taksidian answered. "Clear the way to the door, and you can have this whelp."

Dad raised his arms, crossing them over Mom's and Xander's chests. Together, they backed away a step.

Taksidian pushed David forward, staying right behind

him. The knife hovered over his heart. "More," the man said. "More!" He was starting to panic.

David's family took another step back. Their bodies still blocked the path to the stairs.

"Very clever, trapping me between the walls," Taksidian said. "Holding me here long enough for Time to sniff me out. But it's not going to work. If you want this boy to see today's sunset, you'd better get out of my way." He screamed: "*Completely* out of my way! *Right now!*"

"Let him go," Dad said.

"As soon as I see a clear route to the front door, I'll release him." Taksidian paused, then added, "You have my word."

"Which means nothing," Dad said. But he nodded and dropped his arms. "Let him leave, Gee, Xander. There will be other days." He backed past the stairs. Mom went with him.

Only Xander stood between Taksidian and the front door. He held the two-by-four in both hands, crossed over his chest like a rifle. "No," Xander said. "It almost has him. We can't let him leave."

"Xander," Dad said. "Son, step back."

"Boy, if Time takes me," Taksidian said, "your brother's coming along for the ride."

Xander stood his ground.

"I do not make idle threats," Taksidian said. His hair and coat were going crazy, whipping and flapping, snapping as though caught in a hurricane. "*Look* at David!" More digging into his hip, more screams. "It will be the last time!"

Xander did, staring deep into David's eyes. He backed up to Mom and Dad.

Taksidian pushed David along in front of him. His movements were jittery and sharp. David could tell he was fighting the pull with every muscle. His knife hand shook violently, bringing the tip of the blade within an inch of David's chest. They reached the top of the stairs and stopped.

"Let him go!" Xander yelled. "Just let him go and run. Get out of here!"

"I did promise to release him, didn't I?" Taksidian said. "But I never said in what condition."

Dad's eyes sprang wide. "*Noooo!*"

Taksidian plunged the knife into David's heart.

That is, he tried to. The blade struck David's chest and bounced off. At the same time—probably planning to push his corpse into the family as he fled down the stairs—Taksidian relaxed his grip.

David rolled out of his arms and fell. He landed on his back on the floor, so close to Taksidian, one of the man's boots was between his knees.

Taksidian's shocked expression made David grin. He raised his shirt, revealing the metal plate over the left side of his chest. A chain around his neck held it in place.

"You!" Taksidian said. He bent to finish the job.

"Too late!" David said, pointing at the ceiling.

Taksidian swung his head around to see.

Directly over him, the ceiling was cracking, breaking apart. The pieces disappeared into a portal shimmering just beyond the ever-increasing hole. Taksidian turned and leaped down the stairs. But he never touched down. He floated, suspended in air. As fast as he would have gone down, he went up. He leveled into a horizontal position and smacked against the ceiling across from the hole. He was too long to go through: his head and his heels extended beyond the opening.

The knife fell out of his hand and stuck into the floor by David's thigh.

Taksidian bared his teeth at the Kings and screamed—not in fear, but in fury. His hands gripped the outside of the hole. He strained, pulling himself away from the hole.

Xander stepped beside David, directly below Taksidian. He said, "*We're* the Kings in this house, not *you,*" and he jabbed the two-by-four into Taksidian's stomach.

Taksidian *ooph'd.* His waist buckled into the hole, and his head slipped through. His body arched farther into the hole, pulled toward the portal waiting for him in the room above. His nails gouged tracks in the floor joists exposed by the ripped-out opening in the ceiling.

He yelled, "Nooooo!" and shot up into the antechamber. His voice cut off in midscream, the door up there slammed shut, and he was gone.

CHAPTER
Sixty-four

SATURDAY, 2:26 P.M.

David saw a small item fall from the opening to the floor with a soft *tink!* A fingernail, sharp and thick and tipped with blood. His blood, from his hip. The nail flipped onto its tip and spun around fast. It sailed up into the hole, leaving a drop of blood on the floor.

"Holy cow!" Xander said, gaping at the ceiling.

Dad reached down and pulled David out from under the hole. Just in time: Chunks of ceiling, joists, and flooring fell out of it and crashed down. A cloud of dust billowed up. As it cleared, it swirled around the hole like smoke.

David conked his head on the floor. He held his bloody hip and didn't care about the pain. He felt too good: They had beaten Taksidian. They had beaten the future.

"Ha!" he yelled and started to laugh. It was joyful and honest—the sound of someone whose *This is it!* didn't happen and who had a long life stretching before him like a path to a far-off horizon.

Mom, Dad, and Xander began laughing as well. They crouched around David, every one of them leaking at the eyes and stretching their smiles wide. Dad gripped David's shoulder and rubbed it.

Xander did something that at any other moment would have earned him a one-way ticket to the funny farm, but this time seemed right and totally awesome. He raised both fists high and said in a loud, deep voice, "This is Sparta!"

He flashed a toothy grin around and caught Mom's slightly unsure expression. "It's from a movie, Mom," Xander said. "Trust me."

Mom simply nodded. She lifted David's head and leaned over him, spilling tears onto his cheeks. "Dae," she said, "I was so scared."

Dad touched the metal plate. He looked at Xander and said, "*This* is what you got the plate for? You knew all along?"

Xander smiled. "When Dae said his heart hurt for Jesus, it

hit me. I didn't draw the heart on the note because I love my brother—*even though I do*," he said quickly, smiling at David. "What I meant was that Taksidian *stabs* him in the heart. And it makes sense; a guy like that, he would. That got me thinking about *A Fistful of Dollars*."

"Huh?" Dad said. "The movie?"

David laughed. "That's what *I* said."

"Clint Eastwood puts a metal plate over his heart," Xander explained, "because he knows the bad guy always shoots people in the heart. That's how Eastwood's character beats him."

Mom touched Xander's arm. "Remind me never again to complain about your movie watching." She raised her fingers to his chin. "We need to take care of that."

"A scar nobly got is honorable," Xander said. "Dad told me that." He rubbed his chin. "I don't mind having a permanent mark to remember today."

She narrowed her eyes at him. "I mind."

The plate slipped off David's chest and trembled. He unhooked it, and it zipped across the floor, looking—with its tail of a chain—like a robotic stingray. At the end of the hall, it whipped out of sight and clattered up the stairs to the antechambers above.

The front door banged open. Toria tromped in, spotted the hole, and said, "What happened?" She pounded up the stairs. "Dae, are you all right?"

"I am now," he said.

Keal rushed into the foyer. "What's going on? Everything okay? Where's Taksidian?"

"Time took him," Xander said. "He went back where he came from."

"Yah!" Toria said, clapping.

"I don't know for how long, though," Dad said.

Another voice came from the foyer: "Oh, you don't have to worry about that."

"Jesse?" David said. He rolled over to look through the railing spindles. The old man stood in the doorway, smiling up at him. "Jesse!" David scrambled to his feet and ran down the stairs. He jumped into Jesse's arms. He said, "You're better! You're . . . *walking!*"

The old man danced in place, smiling like a kid with a new pony.

At the doorway, Nana said, "Are we having a party?"

"Nana!" David said, giving her a hug.

Mom appeared at the banister. "I feel like the new kid in school," she said. "I don't know anyone."

"Jesse, Keal, Nana—we found Mom!" David said. His heart almost burst at the sound of it, so he said it again. "We found Mom!"

He took them upstairs and made the introductions. They stood in a circle on the second floor: Mom, Dad, Xander, David, Toria, Jesse, Keal, and Nana.

Jesse looked up into the hole. "Taksidian's really gone?"

Dad nodded. "Until he finds a portal back here."

"He doesn't have any antechamber items?" Jesse asked.

"No."

Jesse scratched his beard-stubbled cheek. "I met Taksidian when he first found his way to the house," he said. "He stumbled into a portal. The chances that he'll be able to find another one without an antechamber item leading him to it are . . . I don't know, one in a million?"

Dad scowled at the hole in the ceiling. He said, "I still don't like the idea that he's out there somewhere . . . *looking* for a way to get back here."

"Portals are hard to see," Xander said. "Even when you're looking for them. They're just rippling air."

"And it took Nana thirty years to find her way home," David added.

"Well," Nana said, "good riddance to bad rubbish."

"Jesse," David said, "do you think sending Taksidian away fixed the future? I mean, the destruction of Los Angeles, the end of the world?"

Jesse aimed his frown at David. "I'm afraid not, son. The damage is done. You'd have to go back and undo everything he did that led to it." He offered a knowing little smile. "That is, *if* you want to fix it."

"If we want to fix it?" David said. "How can we *not*?"

"Think about it," Jesse said, looking at each of them in turn. "It would mean staying in the house, figuring out just what parts of history he messed with, and making each one right."

"But isn't that what we're supposed to do?" David said. "You said this was our destiny."

Jesse nodded. "It's true. Fixing the messes humans made in the past has always been in our bloodline. The portals to the past have been around forever. They're a way for certain people to fix mankind's mistakes—not to make everything perfect, but to make it . . . less bad, so we don't wipe ourselves out."

"I don't understand," Mom said. "Only God has that kind of control."

"True," Jesse said. "But he gives the world doctors to repair our bodies, and . . ."

"And he gives the world *us* to repair Time," David said, getting it—at least as much as something so weird *could* be understood. "Time doctors."

"Gatekeepers," Xander said, using the word Jesse had used when they'd first met.

David said, "But why us?"

Jesse shrugged. "I know only that it *is* us. Our ancestors have always been drawn to the Time currents, like magnets to metal."

"Then," David said, "we're *supposed* to be here. We're supposed to make the present and future better by fixing the past. It's our purpose." He looked around at the others. "Right?"

Xander said, "What if we don't *want* to do that?"

"It's your choice," Jesse said. "No one can make you. But I can tell you, whenever a generation has rejected the responsibility, the world has gotten worse, darker. Think of humankind as a body, a human body. Sometimes it gets sick or injured. If we don't tend to it—stitch it up, make it right—it gets worse."

"What do you mean?" Xander said.

Jesse shrugged. "Like the future you've seen. Or as we saw when you and David caused the Civil War to end years earlier, or when he saved that little girl who grew up to eradicate smallpox: without intervention, there's a lot of death and grief that doesn't need to happen."

Overhead, something banged. David had heard the sound enough times to recognize it. "A portal door just opened," he said. "Someone's here."

CHAPTER

Sixty-five

SATURDAY, 2:49 P.M.

"Or some*thing,*" Dad said.

They were all peering up at the hole. Through it, David could see the corner of a portal door in the antechamber directly over their heads. It was closed.

"Not that portal," he said.

Another bang.

"Taksidian!" Xander said.

"No," Jesse corrected. "Can't be. Even if he could find a portal back here, it's too soon. The forces of Time—the pull—would still be holding him in his own time."

"Then who?" Dad said. "Or what?"

"Who cares?" Xander said. "Let's get out of here . . . finally." He stepped toward the grand staircase.

David grabbed his arm. "No," he said. He stooped to pick up the two-by-four Xander had brandished against Taksidian. "This is *our* house. Whoever it is, I'm going to let him know that." He shook the two-by-four. "And then I'm going to fix the future."

He looked at Dad and Mom, hoping to find in their faces the same commitment he felt, the same sense of purpose. What he saw was more like astonishment. He added, "Because that's what we're supposed to do. Who's with me? Who wants to save the world?"

Xander looked at his bloody hand. "What makes you think we can?"

"The guy who made the mess is gone," David said. "All we have to do is clean it up."

"All we have to do?" Xander laughed. He turned questioning eyes on Dad.

Dad nodded. "I believe we can. What do you think, Gee?"

Mom thought about it. "Let's see," she said. "Bake sales, Girl Scout meetings, laundry, dishes . . . or harrowing adventures through time." She smiled. "I always did want to see Genghis Khan in action."

Toria shook her head and quoted what Dad always said about Mom: "Definitely *not* a Gertrude."

"Wait a minute," Dad said. He looked at the wood in David's hand, then up at the ceiling. Something on the third floor creaked. He wrapped his arm around Mom and pulled her close. "Don't you want to . . . *rest*? Go out to dinner? Have a good night's sleep?"

"Do I *want* those things?" Mom said. "Yes . . . *yes!* I want to sip a cup of tea and watch the sunset with my family. I want to take a hot bath. I want to tuck my children into bed. And I'll do all that . . . when it's time. Right now, I want to do what we're *supposed* to do. Isn't that what we've been doing? Doesn't it feel right?" She smiled up at him.

"I'm in," Keal said. He picked up a broken piece of wood that had fallen from the ceiling.

Nana said, "I don't know if I ever want to see Genghis Khan . . . again. But I do have some skills that could come in handy, like stitching wounds, setting bones, and screaming."

"But, Mom," Dad said, "you can't stay here, not with Time still after you."

"That's okay," she said. "I saw a nice little house in town. That'll suit me just fine."

"I'm sure I can find one too," Jesse said, picking up another length of wood. "Between Nana and me, you'll practically have an encyclopedia of knowledge about history and time travel."

"Oh, yeah?" Xander said. "Then how come you didn't warn us about David's death when we first met you?"

"What?" Jesse said, looking between Xander and David. "His *death*?"

Dad gripped Xander's shoulder. "He doesn't know about it, because it never happened, and you never went back to tell him it did. You never wrote the note."

"Ooooh," Xander said, thinking it through. He gave Jesse an embarrassed smile. "Sorry."

"For what it's worth," Jesse said, "I always had a sense that you had to visit me while we were building the house. I don't know why, just a feeling."

"Your feeling saved Dae's life," Xander said. "Thank you."

"Yeah," David said. "Thank you."

"You know," Jesse said, giving Xander a sly look from the corner of his eye. "The life-saving doesn't have to stop with David's."

Xander took that in, and David could tell his brother was thinking the same thing he was: all the people—children like them, adults like Mom and Dad, Nana, Jesse, and Keal—who would live, who would be spared grief and sorrow and pain, because the Kings lived in this house. Because they did what they were meant to do.

Xander said, "Yeah . . . yeah." From the floor he selected a short board with nails sticking out of one end. "But I better get some movie ideas out of it."

The linen closet's door exploded off its hinges, and they all jumped. The school locker crashed out, falling to its side on the hallway floor. It looked like a metal coffin. The door was facing them, and David could make out the little number plate swinging back and forth by one rivet: 119. The entire locker had been beaten and battered, with dents and dings everywhere. But it had held together, and the door was still closed. A corner of the door had been bent out, exposing a triangle of blackness. A face appeared in the opening—two eyes blinking at them.

"Phemus," David said, stunned.

The big man growled. He pounded on the locker, making the metal boom like thunder.

"The pull's got him," Jesse said. "Time for him to go home too."

The locker began trembling. It flipped onto its top and tumbled end-over-end toward them.

"Look out!" Dad said. Everyone leaped out of the center of the hallway, pushing themselves against the wall or the banister overlooking the foyer.

The locker cartwheeled past them, thumping and bumping. David heard Phemus's deep-throated wail, like a frightened Incredible Hulk on a never-ending roller coaster. At the end of the hall, it turned the corner, heading for the portals. It crashed and banged against the walls, then thudded up the third-floor stairs.

David smiled and felt his heart soar at all the smiles his family and Keal returned to him. He took a deep breath and thumped the two-by-four into his palm. Turning to head for the portals, he said, "Let's do it!"

The end . . . ?

Acknowledgments

Special thanks to . . .

My son Anthony, for his countless contributions to this series, including the idea of Xander and David visiting Jesse while the dreamhouse is being built, the title of this last installment, and inspiring me to write these books.

My wife Jodi, for helping with . . . well, *everything*.

Melanie, Isabella, and Matt—for being the best children a parent can hope for.

Katrien Stanley and Emily Auday, *Frenzy*'s winners of our "Dream the Scene" contest. Katie suggested that Xander find himself on a movie set, and Emily thought the boys should portal to Atlantis.

Everyone who entered the "Dream the Scene" contest: Your creativity blows me away. I truly wish I could have used every entry—but then the Dreamhouse series would be a thousand books! Your task was difficult: not only did your idea of where to send the Kings have to be cool, but it had to fit a storyline that was only in *my* head, which added the element of chance to the contest. If I didn't use your idea, don't think it wasn't awesome or even that it wasn't the "best"; I just had to choose one that fit where I was taking the story.

My early readers, who helped me keep my eye on the ball: Nicholas and Luke Fallentine, Slade Pearce, Ben and Matthew Ford, Maddie Williams, Alec Oberndorfer, Joshua Ruark,

Alix Chandler, Deborah and Becca King, and Reid Ausband.

As always, my peerless editors: Amanda Bostic, Becky Monds, LB Norton, and Judy Gitenstein.

My publisher Allen Arnold, as well as Jennifer Deshler, Katie Bond, Kristen Vasgaard, and Susan Ellingburg for looking at these stories from a thousand angles with eyes for making every part of them better. Joel Gotler, my incomparable agent and good friend.

Authors James Rollins, Steve Berry, Douglas Preston, David Morrell, Jon Land, R. L. Stine, Matt Bronleewe, and Eric Wilson for being kind friends and exemplary colleagues. And especially Ted Dekker, on whom I can always depend for stimulating and challenging conversations; and thriller writer David Dun for suggesting the perfect location for Pinedale.

The talented Mark Lavallee, Jonathan Maiocco, Robyn Twomey, and Rebekah Ramsdell for their Dreamhouse Kings-inspired music and art, which in turn inspired *me*.

Justin S. Buus, the gifted graphic designer who created the fantastic map of Atlantis . . . well, at least the Atlantian town in which David and Xander find themselves. I would love to see Justin tackle the whole place someday. No doubt it would be awesome.

Everyone who believed in these books enough to throw their considerable talents behind them: Burke Allen, Jake Chism, Connie and Dwight Cenac, Bonnie Calhoun, Rel Mollet, Todd Michael Greene, Jeanette Clinkunbroomer, Scott Quine,

Shannon Bailey, Wayne Pinkstaff, and Paul and Jennifer Turner.

Fans like Megan McNeill, Austin Reckerd, Anna Hayes, Sara Carlton, Sarah Lezgus, Fleur Elise Wayman, Lydia and Hannah Wade, Jesse Peterson, Kendal M. Burleson, Christopher J. Millett, Jill Geren, Adam Caratenuto, Sandi Stuart, Lyndsey N. Fowks, Danny Abrahantes . . . and so many others: Thank you for your letters, e-mails, and Facebook messages; they never fail to boost my spirits.

The Dreamhouse "cast"—Dad, Mom, Xander, David, Toria, Jesse, Keal, Nana, and even Taksidian and Phemus—for taking me along on their adventures and letting me record them.

And all the readers of the Dreamhouse Kings books: Thank you for letting the Kings live!

Reading Group Guide

1. The term "character arc" refers to the changes and growth a character experiences through the course of a story. Discuss the arcs of the Dreamhouse Kings characters from their introductions to the last page of *Frenzy*. Who changed the most? In what way?
2. After all was said and done, David believed that staying in the house so they could fix the future was the right thing to do. Do you agree? Have you ever done something because it was the right thing to do, even though it was dangerous or other people thought it was foolish? What?
3. Time travel is such an odd idea—something that no one has ever done—that many people, including scientists and authors, have very differing views about it. Have you read any other books that involved time travel? How was it depicted differently than the way it worked in the Dreamhouse Kings?
4. Where *didn't* the Kings go in history that you would have liked them to go? What would have happened to them there?
5. Through the terror of losing their mother and having to face all the dangers of the worlds, the King family learned how much they love and need one another. How do you show your family that you love them? Is there anything you can do differently that would express your love even more?
6. Some of the Kings' "work" to find Mom didn't pan out; for example, Toria and Dad went to Los Angeles and discovered that Phemus was from Atlantis, but Xander and David found it out by going to Atlantis at almost the same time. The author wanted to show that not all of our efforts lead to the solutions we're looking for. Sometimes they seem wasted. Has that ever happened to you? Because we don't always know how to fix something, we have to try different

things—some of which will have great outcomes and some of which will fall flat. How do you feel about that?

7. Some of the mysteries of the house aren't explained and some problems aren't resolved. For example: *Will the Kings really fix the future? How? Is Taksidian gone forever? Why was Taksidian using slaves from Atlantis (and not from somewhere else) as helpers? Why and how are the Kings (and their forbears) responsible for fixing history?* The author had two intentions in mind for leaving these things unanswered: (1) To encourage each reader to use his or her imagination to "fill in the blanks"; and (2) to show that life's puzzles aren't always answered. Some things we learn in time . . . other things we never understand. What are your thoughts about this? Do you prefer stories that are neatly wrapped up, or ones that leave you wondering about some things?
8. In your opinion, what is the "purpose" of the house?
9. The "theme" of a story is the underlying message or messages about life the author is trying to convey. It is the lesson or moral of the story, such as Love conquers all. What do you think the theme of the Dreamhouse Kings is? (There can be more than one.)

Visit DreamhouseKings.com

The Secrets of the Dreamhouse Kings

A conversation between Jake Chism of FictionAddict.com and Robert Liparulo

SPOILER ALERT: DO NOT READ UNTIL YOU HAVE READ ALL SIX BOOKS IN THE DREAMHOUSE KINGS SERIES!

Jake Chism: First things first: They didn't fix the future! What's up with that?

Robert Liparulo: I didn't want a pat ending. Life's not like that. There's always more to do. My intention was to show that the Kings *could* fix the future. They reach a point where they're *willing* to stay and do it, which is probably the most important aspect of their being able to make the future right. But also, they've developed considerable skills and knowledge in dealing with time travel. They have the desire and the ability. And it helps that they've gotten rid of Taksidian.

JC: But did they? Is Taksidian really gone? We don't see him die, and Jesse admits there's a chance—even if it's a small one—that he could find his way back to the present, to the house.

RL: I felt that killing Taksidian was too easy, almost a cliché. Plus, it seemed to me that if the Kings killed him or somehow set it up so he died, it would almost be opposite of who they are. It would lower them to his level, and I didn't want that. Jesse tries to reassure them that the chances of Taksidian finding his way back are small, but you're right: it could happen.

JC: I love the way you used certain character traits throughout the story, such as David using his soccer skills to get away from dangers, and Xander frequently using the knowledge he gleaned from movies, which even saved David's life! But I noticed a few things that I thought would play a larger part in the story than they did. For example, Xander's moviemaking and the Mission Control Center.

RL: A few of those were intentional red herrings. I like the idea of readers trying to figure out what's going to happen and having all these things to choose from. The MCC came about because if I were in that situation, I'd want a room like that. As it turns out, events started happening so fast, they didn't get a chance to use it as much as they thought they would. Remember, Mom's gone for only a week . . . and it's one turbulent week to say the least. It's a good example of something I wanted to show: that when we're faced with a big problem to solve and we don't know the solution, we're going to do things that ultimately don't pan out. Another example is Dad and Toria going to the professor who tells them that Phemus is speaking Atlantian. They find out what Phemus said to Toria in *House of Dark Shadows;* but they really didn't have to go, because the boys follow Phemus to Atlantis anyway. It's a duplication of effort, but that's the way things happen. As the writer, of course *I* knew they didn't have to go. But there was no way *they* could have known that.

JC: I'm not sure I'm clear about why most of the portals dump those poor Kings right in the middle of chaotic, violent times. Can you elaborate?

RL: Some of that has to do with what Taksidian has been doing to cause the war that ends the human race as we know it. He's been going back in time and causing wars to happen, all eventually leading to the most devastating one, the one that happens in the near future. As a result, there are things in those wars that shouldn't have happened, that need fixing or undoing. Also, I believe that in times of great crisis, more long-lasting "accidents" happen, things that have a terrible ripple effect through the rest of history. People die, changing generations to come. These are the big things that need fixing, so that's where the portals send the Gatekeepers.

JC: So what about the linen-closet-to-school-locker and creepy basement-chamber-to-Taksidian's-pantry portals?

RL: I think of them as sort of a splattering or shrapnel from the collision of time portals at the house, almost an accidental consequence. Taksidian found the one in the basement and built his house on the other end. He used it to get into the house, until Jesse found it and blocked it off. Then Taksidian began using it to dispose of his various victims. Locker 119 just happens to catch the one from the linen closet when the school was built.

JC: Whenever an antechamber door shuts, the world on the other side changes. Why?

RL: That's an easy one: There are more errors in history that need attention than there are rooms or portals, so they have to keep shifting around so eventually they all have a chance of getting fixed. I like to think of it as all the errors of history jostling for attention, wanting to be set right.

JC: In *Frenzy,* David thinks, "The house was big and imposing and dark—dark in every way, with an absence of light and an absence of *heart,* of good." But aren't the portals—and by extension the house—from God?

RL: Yes, but just because David has an opinion, doesn't make it true. When he thinks that, he's assuming he's going to die, and up to that point, the house has caused a lot of grief for the Kings. So many times, we find ourselves in awful situations, and we don't see God's hand in it until much later. We can't always see the big picture when we're in crisis mode. By the end of *Frenzy,* David starts to understand, and he wants to stay so he can make things right, so he can fulfill his destiny.

JC: Speaking of destiny, several times in the series, the idea comes up of the King bloodline being set aside or destined to be Gatekeepers of Time. What does that mean, exactly?

RL: I think we're all given a specific gift, something we're meant to do, something we're really good at doing. It could be comforting people in need or painting beautiful works of art. For the Kings, it's being the Gatekeepers of Time. Mistakes happen that can have devastating effects for the rest of time. In the Dreamhouse Kings, God has sort of given us a way of getting a "do over." He could simply snap his fingers and change things, but we know he likes to work through his creations—*us,* the way he used Moses to free the Israelites from slavery in Egypt. Sometime in the distant past—maybe thousands of years ago—he selected this family to be the people who correct history's errors. They're especially designed to do it. David's heart for people, for example. He's wired to *want* to help people, even people he doesn't know and may never meet, and even if trying to help them means putting himself in grave danger. But like all of us, they are free to choose to do what they were designed to do . . . or not. Grandpa Hank couldn't handle it after his wife was kidnapped and he realized that his whole family was in danger. He ran. He chose to turn his back on the house, on being a Gatekeeper. During the time he wasn't there, when no one was in the house, history's mistakes weren't getting fixed, things got worse, and it allowed Taksidian to cause all sorts of trouble throughout history.

JC: So if this calling to be Gatekeepers stretches back thousands of years, how are the portals in California, which hasn't been populated for very long, relative to the rest of the world?

RL: For some reason—maybe to protect themselves—the currents of Time, which become the portals, move around. Every few hundred years or so, they drift to another part of the world, and the Gatekeepers have to find it, which they can do because they're drawn to it. Actually reaching it is another thing altogether. One of the backstories that didn't make the final cut tells how the Kings' ancestors helped fund the Lewis and Clark Expedition to the Pacific coast, and went along to reach the current location of the portals.

JC: In *House of Dark Shadows,* the real estate agent calls the house "the old Konig place." Who's Konig?

RL: It does get a little complicated, which is one reason the details didn't make it into the story. The father of Grandpa Hank (so he'd be Dad's dad's dad) was Jesse's brother, Aaron. In his late teens, Aaron decided he didn't want anything to do with the house and left, leaving Jesse as the sole Gatekeeper for decades. Aaron went into hiding and changed his surname to "Konig," which is German for King. Hoping he could convince Aaron's son, Grandpa Hank, to take up his role as Gatekeeper, Jesse added "Konig" to the deed of trust that ensured only their family line could occupy the house. Hank Konig did accept this responsibility—for a time. When he left, he changed the family name back to King, as a way of distancing himself from the house and the horrors he'd experienced there.

JC: Wait, Jesse had a brother named Aaron? Where was he in the story?

RL: One time, Young Jesse says that his brother is working on the house. The other times we don't see him I imagined he had gone through the portals, so he was in other worlds. In movie parlance, you can say he got left on the cutting room floor. His story is one I'd like to explore in future Dreamhouse stories.

JC: More Dreamhouse stories?

RL: That's the plan. I'm currently writing a non-Dreamhouse young adult trilogy that I'm really excited about. In the back of each book, we're going to include a Dreamhouse Kings short story. They'll elaborate on some things readers have asked about, such as what happened to make Jesse leave the house (hint: it coincides with Taksidian's arrival at the house from Ancient Assyria). After that series, I'd like to revisit the Kings and the dreamhouse in a new series of books. Writing their adventures is just too fun to stop doing it.

JC: That goes for reading them, too. Will we get to tag along while the Kings try to fix the future?

RL: That would be one of the storylines. I have a few in mind. I'd also like to see them visit more worlds more frequently, and interact more with the people they meet in them. I'd like to play around a bit with the complexity and paradoxes of time travel. When you fix one thing, something else goes wrong. It's like a puzzle and all the pieces have to fit just so.

Listen to part two of this interview at
FictionAddict.com/Frenzy

DOWNLOAD THE SOUNDTRACK OF THE DREAMHOUSE KINGS—FREE!

Composed and performed by Mark Lavallee, these songs truly capture the triumphs and heartaches the Kings go through. When you listen, think of the story (all the adventures and scares) and the characters, especially Xander and David (their sadness, hope and determination).

A list of the songs:

- The Kingmaker
- Brave David (I Miss Mom)
- King Xander
- The Princess of Victoria
- Taksidious
- Strong and Courageous

Plus this bonus track: "First Victim" by Jonathan Maiocco

GET THE SOUNDTRACK NOW AT DREAMHOUSEKINGS.COM

About the Author

Robert Liparulo has received rave reviews for both his adult novels (*Comes a Horseman, Germ, Deadfall,* and *Deadlock*) and the best-selling Dreamhouse Kings series for young adults. He lives in Colorado with his wife and their four children.